Boy
Meets
Girl

Books by Meg Cabot

BOY MEETS GIRL
THE BOY NEXT DOOR
SHE WENT ALL THE WAY

Young Adult Titles

THE PRINCESS DIARIES
THE PRINCESS DIARIES, VOLUME II: PRINCESS IN THE SPOTLIGHT
THE PRINCESS DIARIES, VOLUME III: PRINCESS IN LOVE
THE PRINCESS DIARIES, VOLUME IV: PRINCESS IN WAITING
THE PRINCESS DIARIES, VOLUME IV½: PROJECT PRINCESS
PRINCESS LESSONS
ALL AMERICAN GIRL
HAUNTED
NICOLA AND THE VISCOUNT
VICTORIA AND THE ROGUE

MEG CABOT

Boy Meets Girl

AVON
TRADE

An Imprint of HarperCollinsPublishers

FIRST EDITION

Design by Elizabeth M. Glover

Library of Congress Cataloging-in-Publication Data

Cabot, Meg.
    Boy meets girl / by Meg Cabot.—1st ed.
        p. cm.
    ISBN 0-06-008545-2 (acid-free paper)
    1. Personnel departments—Employees—Fiction. 2. Employees—Dismissal of—Fiction.
    3. Newspaper publishing—Fiction. 4. Actions and defenses—Fiction. 5. New York
    (N.Y.)—Fiction. I. Title.

PS3553.A278B68 2003
813'.54—dc21   2003052352

04 05 06 07 08 JTC/RRD 10 9 8 7 6 5 4 3 2 1

For Benjamin

Acknowledgments

With thanks to the many people who helped contribute to
this book (all errors are the author's own):

Beth Ader
Jennifer Brown
Elizabeth Claypoole
Carrie Feron
Michele Jaffe
Laura Langlie
Todd Sullivan
Stephanie Vullo
David Walton
Dan Wasser

THE NEW YORK JOURNAL
New York City's Leading Photo-Newspaper

Kathleen A. Mackenzie
Personnel Representative
Human Resources
The New York Journal
216 W. 57th Street
New York, NY 10019
212-555-6891

Ida D. Lopez
Craft Food Services
The New York Journal
216 W. 57th Street
New York, NY 10019

Dear Mrs. Lopez:

Last week, we met to address your continuing job-performance problems related to the ~~giving out of dissemination of~~ serving of items from the dessert cart you operate in the newspaper's senior staff dining room. These problems have persisted despite repeated counseling sessions with ~~me my boss Amy Jenkins~~ supervisors as well as staff training programs. Specifically, your refusal to ~~give disseminate~~ serve dessert to certain members of the senior staff has resulted in several written complaints from administrators at this ~~establishment paper~~ company.

Mrs. Lopez, your refusal to serve dessert to certain members of the paper's staff is disruptive to food service operations, and the explanations that you have provided for your behavior are not ~~satisfactory wholly believable inexplicable~~ acceptable. This letter is being issued as a written warning with the expectation that there will be an immediate and sustained improvement in your ~~work attitude food service dissemination~~ job performance. Failure to comply will result in further disciplinary action.

On a more personal note, Mrs. Lopez, please stop refusing to give senior staff members dessert, even if you feel, as you explained to me last week, that they don't "deserve it." Which members of the paper's staff do or do not deserve dessert is not your decision to make! And I would hate to see you asked to leave the food craft services department over something so silly! I would really miss you—and your chocolate chip cookies!

Damn it.

To do:

1. Laundry!!!!!!!!!!
2. Finish disciplinary warning letter to Ida Lopez.
3. Pick up prescriptions—Allegra, Imitrex, Levlen.
4. Get new Almay pressed powder compact.
5. Find new apartment.
6. Find new boyfriend.
7. Get better job.
8. Get married.
9. Have successful career.
10. Have children/grandchildren/big retirement party.
11. Die in sleep at age 100.
12. Pick up dry cleaning!!!!!!!!!!

Kathleen A. Mackenzie
Personnel Representative, L–Z
Human Resources
The New York Journal
216 W. 57th Street
New York, NY 10019
212-555-6891
kathleen.mackenzie@thenyjournal.com

Sleaterkinneyfan:	What are you doing?
Katydid:	WORKING. Stop IM-ing me, you know the T.O.D. doesn't like it when we IM during office hours.
Sleaterkinneyfan:	The T.O.D. can bite me. And you are not working. I can see your desk from here. You're making another one of those To Do lists, aren't you?
Katydid:	It may look like I'm making a To Do list, but really I am reflecting on the series of failures and bad judgment calls that have made up my life.
Sleaterkinneyfan:	Oh my God, you are twenty-five years old. You have not even had a life yet.
Katydid:	Then why am I in such mental and emotional anguish?
Sleaterkinneyfan:	Because you stayed up too late last night watching *Charmed* reruns. Don't try to deny it, I heard you salivating over Cole.
Katydid:	Oh my God, I'm so sorry!!!!!!!! Did I keep you and Craig awake?
Sleaterkinneyfan:	Please. Craig would sleep through a nuclear blast. And I only heard you because I got up to use the bathroom. These hormones make me have to go every five minutes.
Katydid:	I am so, so sorry. I swear I will be off your couch and out of your place just as soon as I get a line on a studio I can afford. Paula's taking me to look at one tomorrow night in Hoboken. $1100/month, third-floor walk-up.
Sleaterkinneyfan:	Would you stop? I told you, we like having you stay with us.
Katydid:	Jen, you and Craig are trying to have a BABY. You do not need an old college

Sleaterkinneyfan: roommate sacking out on your living room couch while you are trying to procreate. You did enough just getting me this job in the first place.

Sleaterkinneyfan: You more than earn your keep with all the cleaning you do. Don't think I haven't noticed. Craig even pointed out this morning that you had dusted the top of the refrigerator. Obsessive much, by the way? Who even looks at the top of the refrigerator?

Katydid: Well, Craig, OBVIOUSLY.

Sleaterkinneyfan: Whatever. You can't afford $1100/month on your salary. I know how much you make, remember?

Katydid: It's the cheapest place Paula's found me so far. That isn't on the same block as a methadone clinic.

Sleaterkinneyfan: I don't understand why YOU are the one who had to move out. Why didn't you kick HIM out?

Katydid: I can't stay in that apartment. Not with the memories of all the happy times Dale and I shared.

Sleaterkinneyfan: Oh, you mean like all those times you came home from work to find that, like, one of his bandmates had mistaken the closet for the bathroom and peed on your suede boots?

Katydid: WHY DO YOU HAVE TO BRING THAT UP AT WORK? You know it always makes me want to cry. I really loved those boots. They were perfect Coach knockoffs.

Sleaterkinneyfan: You should have thrown his stuff out onto the fire escape and changed the locks. "I don't know if I can marry you after all, I have to take things one day at a time." I

	mean, what kind of thing is that for a guy to say?????
Katydid:	Um, the kind of thing an ex-pothead who is about to land a million-dollar recording contract would say to the girl he has dated since high school. I mean, come on, Jen. Dale can get anyone now. Why would he stay with his girlfriend from high school?
Sleaterkinneyfan:	Oh my God, I swear if it weren't for the T.O.D. watching me like a hawk for any excuse to can my ass, I'd come over there and slap you. You are the best thing that ever happened to Dale, recording contract or no recording contract, and if he doesn't know it, he isn't worth it. Do you understand me, Katie? HE ISN'T WORTH IT.
Katydid:	Yes, but then what does that say about ME? I'm the one who went out with him for ten years, after all. TEN YEARS. With a guy who isn't sure now that he wants to marry me after all. I mean, what does that tell you about my ability to read people? Seriously, Jen, I probably shouldn't even be allowed to work here. How can I presume to tell my employers who they should and should not hire when I am obviously such a heinous judge of character?
Sleaterkinneyfan:	Katie, you are not a heinous judge of character. Your problem is that you—
AmyJenkinsDir:	logged on
AmyJenkinsDir:	Pardon me for interrupting, ladies, but is there or is there not a departmental ban on Instant Messaging during office hours? Ms. Sadler, please get me the blue form on the new hire in Arts. Miss Mackenzie, I need to see you in my office right away.

Sleaterkinneyfan:	logged off
Katydid:	logged off
AmyJenkinsDir:	logged off
Sleaterkinneyfan:	logged on
Katydid:	logged on
Sleaterkinneyfan:	THE TYRANNICAL OFFICE DESPOT MUST DIE
Katydid:	Her home life must be very unsatisfactory.
Sleaterkinneyfan:	logged off
Katydid:	logged off

```
┌─────────────────────────────────────┐
│      30's East Rent Stabilized        │
│      A Steal! Studio $1100. No        │
│      Fee. Call Ron 718-555-7757       │
└─────────────────────────────────────┘
```

Yo! It's Ron. Leave a message.

(Tone)

Um, hi, Ron? Hi, this is Kate, Kate
Mackenzie. I'm calling about the apartment. The rent-stabilized studio in the
East Thirties? Yeah. Please give me a call
about it. I can come to look at it any
time. Really. Like in five minutes, if you
want. Just, you know. Call me. I'll be at
212-555-6891 until five, then you can
reach me at 212-555-1324. And thanks.
Call anytime. Really.

If you sprinkle
When you tinkle
Be a sweetie,
Wipe the seatie!

This message brought to you by
The Human Resources Division of the *New York Journal*

THE NEW YORK JOURNAL
New York City's Leading Photo-Newspaper

Features Division
The New York Journal
216 W. 57th Street
New York, NY 10019

Human Resources Division
The New York Journal
216 W. 57th Street
New York, NY 10019

We, the undersigned, of the Features Department of the *New York Journal*, are hereby returning this sign, found in the restrooms on our division's floor. While we realize that this sign is the Human Resources Division's humorous way of dealing with the complaints of untidiness in the restrooms at 216 W. 57th Street, we find the sign offensive for the following reasons:

1) We in the Features Department do not "tinkle." We urinate.
2) We in the Features Department do not refer to ourselves, or anyone else, as "sweetie." (exception: Dolly Vargas has on occasion referred to people as sweeties, but not in reference to their hygienic practices)
3) We in the Features Department do not refer to toilet seats as "seaties."

A more appropriate step toward maintaining an appropriate standard of cleanliness in our restrooms might be more frequent spot checks by the custodial staff.

Please do not hang signs like these in our restrooms
EVER again.

Sincerely,

George Sanchez
Melissa Fuller-Trent
Nadine Wilcock-Salerno
Dolly Vargas

✉

To: Jen Sadler <jennifer.sadler@thenyjournal.com>
Fr: Kate Mackenzie <kathleen.mackenzie@thenyjournal.com>
Re: Amy's Toilet Signs

Oh, my God, the Features Dept. returned those signs the T.O.D. made housekeeping hang in all the toilet stalls! Too funny! Want to be there when I tell her? Amy, I mean.

Kate

✉

To: Kate Mackenzie <kathleen.mackenzie@thenyjournal.com>
Fr: Jen Sadler <jennifer.sadler@thenyjournal.com>
Re: Amy's Toilet Signs

OF COURSE I want to be there. You know how disappointed she'll be when she finds out. She says she hung signs like this all through her sorority house, and that the girls loved them. This is gonna be so good. . . .

New York Journal Employee Incident Report

Name/Title of Reporter:
Carl Hopkins, Security Officer

Date/Time of Incident:
Wednesday, 1:30 P.M.

Place of Incident:
NY Journal Senior Staff Dining Room

Persons Involved in Incident:
Stuart Hertzog, legal counsel to the *NY Journal*, 35
Ida Lopez, Craft Food Services dessert cart operator,
NY Journal, 64

Nature of Incident:
S. Hertzog asked I. Lopez for more pie.
I. Lopez said No more pie.
S. Hertzog said But I see the pie right there, give me
some.
I. Lopez said No more pie for you.
S. Hertzog said Why not?
I. Lopez said You know good and well why.
S. Hertzog summoned Security.
Security gave him pie.

Follow-up:
Incident recorded, sent to A. Jenkins in Human Resources.

To: Kate Mackenzie <kathleen.mackenzie@thenyjournal.com>
Fr: Amy Jenkins <amy.jenkins@thenyjournal.com>
Re: Ida Lopez

Kate—

Thanks for your input re: Be a Sweetie/Wipe the Seatie. However, as I'm sure you've seen by now, we have a more pressing concern than the Features Department's objections to my lavatory signs.

We've had another complaint about Ida Lopez, the dessert-cart operator in the senior-staff dining room. It appears the situation is getting worse. Today she categorically refused to give Stuart Hertzog, of Hertzog Webster and Doyle, the paper's legal counsel, a piece of key lime pie. As you know, desserts in the senior-staff dining room are supposed to be unlimited. When questioned as to her reason behind refusing pie to Mr. Hertzog, Ms. Lopez replied, "He knows good and well."

Mr. Hertzog, of course, hasn't got the slightest idea what she is talking about. He has never set eyes on the woman before today.

As Ms. Lopez is currently on disciplinary probation from her last, similar violation, I believe we can begin moving forward with termination paperwork. Therefore, please discontinue work on her disciplinary warning letter for last week's infraction and begin termination proceedings. Ms. Lopez should be informed no later than today at five o'clock that her services will no longer be required here at the *Journal*. Please see that Security escorts her to her locker and that she cleans it out thoroughly. Security is not to allow her out of their sight until her keys and employee ID have been confiscated, and she has left the building.

I have been informed by Food Craft Services management that Ida Lopez is inexplicably popular with junior members of the staff. Therefore it would be best if this case were not discussed outside the confines of the department. Please remember that personnel matters are confidential.

I will expect Ms. Lopez's termination paperwork on my desk no later than 3 P.M. today.

Amy

Amy Denise Jenkins
Director
Human Resources
The New York Journal
216 W. 57th Street
New York, NY 10019
212-555-6890
amy.jenkins@thenyjournal.com

....

✉

To: Kate Mackenzie <kathleen.mackenzie@thenyjournal.com>
Fr: Tim Grabowksi <timothy.grabowski@thenyjournal.com>
Re: Ida Lopez

Hey, Katie, Ida's one of yours, right? If so, you've got to do whatever you can to get this pie thing with Hertzog straightened out. Ida is the lifeblood of the *NY Journal*. Without her and her dessert cart, I for one will not be able to go on. And I think I speak for a lot of people here when I say if there's anybody who does not deserve pie, it is Stu Hertzog.

Counting on you, as the only human in Human Resources (not including Jen, of course) to Do the Right Thing—

T.

....

✉

To: Kate Mackenzie <kathleen.mackenzie@thenyjournal.com>
Fr: Nadine Wilcock-Salerno <nadine.salerno@thenyjournal.com>
Re: Ida Lopez

Say it isn't so! The rumor mill has it that Amy Jenkins is asking for the head of our best baker on a silver platter. DON'T GIVE IT TO HER!!!!!!!! WE NEED IDA'S CARROT CAKE! If possible, hooked into an IV and attached to my arm.

I mean it, Kate, don't let them fire her.

Nad ;-)

....

✉

To: Kate Mackenzie <kathleen.mackenzie@thenyjournal.com>
Fr: Melissa Fuller-Trent <melissa.fullertrent@trentcapital.com>
Re: Ida Lopez

Dear Kate,

I was in the senior staff room today when Ida Lopez refused to serve pie to Stuart Hertzog, the paper's legal counsel. All I can say is, Mr. Hertzog really was unforgivably rude to Mrs. Lopez, even before she refused to serve him—I mean, he acted like he had some kind of inalienable right to pie—and if you need me to make a sworn statement to that effect or anything, I would be willing to. Only please don't let them fire Mrs. Lopez . . . her chocolate chip cookies are out of this world.

Sincerely,

Mel Fuller-Trent
Features
The NY Journal

....

✉

To: Kate Mackenzie <kathleen.mackenzie@thethenyjournal.com>
Fr: George Sanchez <george.sanchez@thethenyjournal.com>
Re: Cookie Lady

Don't fire her.

I mean it. Her gingersnaps are the only thing that keep me sane around here. Besides Mountain Dew.

George Sanchez
Managing Editor
The NY Journal

✉

To: Kate Mackenzie <kathleen.mackenzie@thenyjournal.com>
Fr: Dolly Vargas <dolly.vargas@thenyjournal.com>
Re: That cafeteria lady

Darling, you simply can't let them get rid of that little dessert-cart person. Her low-fat yogurt muffins are to DIE FOR. I myself have had her cater numerous events, and have received nothing but compliments . . . her carrot cake is simply DIVINE (if not exactly easy for those of us doing the low-carb thing to resist).

And really, if you get rid of her, who are you going to get to re-place her? Good help doesn't grow on trees, you know.

XXXOOO

Dolly

P.S. Thanks for helping to bail me out of that nasty little thing with Aaron Spender. Isn't it the pits when they go all John Hinckley on you? So glad he took that job with *Newsweek*, I can't even tell you! XXOO—D

✉

To: Kate Mackenzie <kathleen.mackenzie@thenyjournal.com>
Fr: Jen Sadler <jennifer.sadler@thenyjournal.com>
Re: Dessert Cart Lady

It is all over the building that the T.O.D. is going to give the Dessert Cart Lady the heave ho for not handing over a piece of pie to Stu Hertzog at lunch today. Is this true?

J

✉

To: Jen Sadler <jennifer.sadler@thenyjournal.com>
Fr: Kate Mackenzie <kathleen.mackenzie@thenyjournal.com>
Re: Ida Lopez

It's true. The T.O.D. says *I* have got to fire her. Today. Jen, how am I supposed to fire that sweet old lady? This has to be a mistake. English isn't her first language. Maybe there was a misunderstanding. I mean, she always calls me dearie when she sees me in the hallway, and sneaks me chocolate chip cookies, even though as a new hire I am not even allowed in the senior staff dining room. Plus everyone—EVERYONE—at the paper loves her.

Everyone except Stuart Hertzog, apparently.

But he's a lawyer. *A LAWYER.* What does that tell you about his abilities as a judge of character? Hmmm?

Oh my God, I wish I had called in sick today.

Kate

✉

To: Kate Mackenzie <kathleen.mackenzie@thenyjournal.com>
Fr: Jen Sadler <jennifer.sadler@thenyjournal.com>
Re: Dessert Cart Lady

Amy is such a bitch. You know she's totally in love with Hertzog, right? Tim up in Computers says he saw them at Il Buco last Saturday, with their tongues down each other's throats. I mean, she's all but picked out the china pattern. That's the only reason she gives a crap about Ida.

I wonder if she'll change her name when the time comes. If anyone deserves to be Mrs. Stuart Hertzog, it's the T.O.D.

You know what I heard? Hertzog has a cigar-store Indian in his office. He thinks just because he's a big shot in his daddy's firm—like his father before him, and his father before him, and so on— nobody's going to say anything about how unPC it is, or the fact that he's such a pedantic phony.

Maybe that's why Ida wouldn't give him pie.

All I have to say is, that suit he had on today had to cost three grand, easy. It was Armani.

But it doesn't matter how well he dresses, he'll still always look like Barney from *The Flintstones*.

Have you tried reasoning with the T.O.D.? I realize it probably won't work, but you can be pretty persuasive, when you bat those baby-blues of yours.

J

....

✉

To: Amy Jenkins <amy.jenkins@thenyjournal.com>
Fr: Kate Mackenzie <kathleen.mackenzie@thenyjournal.com>
Re: Ida Lopez

Amy, are you really sure terminating Mrs. Lopez is the best idea? I mean, like you said, she is extremely popular with the staff. I have been inundated with e-mails from members of the staff—some of them senior members—asking that she not be let go.

It is possible that Mrs. Lopez might benefit from going through customer-service training again. Maybe if we go ahead with the written warning from last week's infraction, she'll straighten up. Like you yourself said at last month's Staff Relations Committee meeting, termination represents not just a failure on the employee's part, but a failure on the part of her supervisor, as well!

Kate

··

✉

To: Kate Mackenzie <kathleen.mackenzie@thenyjournal.com>
Fr: Amy Jenkins <amy.jenkins@thenyjournal.com>
Re: Ida Lopez

I sincerely hope you are not questioning my authority in this matter, Kathleen. As someone who has less than a year of work here at the *Journal* under her belt, I would think the last thing you would want to do is question the actions of your direct supervisor—especially while you are still on employment probation.

Ida Lopez has been a continuous problem at this company since the day she was hired. My predecessor was not successful in getting rid of her, but I will be. This time, Ida's gone too far. I want to see a complete written transcript of your interaction with her this afternoon before you leave the office for the day.

Amy Denise Jenkins
Director
Human Resources
The New York Journal
216 W. 57th Street
New York, NY 10019
212-555-6890
amy.jenkins@thenyjournal.com

This e-mail is intended only for the use of the individual to which it is addressed and may contain information that is privileged and confidential. If you are not the intended recipient, you are hereby notified that you have received this transmission in error; any review, dissemination, distribution, or copying of this transmission is prohibited. If you have received this communication in error, please notify us immediately by reply e-mail and delete this message and all of its attachments.

✉

To: Jen Sadler <jennifer.sadler@thenyjournal.com>
Fr: Kate Mackenzie <kathleen.mackenzie@thenyjournal.com>
Re: Ida Lopez

It's no good, the T.O.D. won't go for it. Oh, God, Jen. Poor Mrs. Lopez is coming down in ten minutes! What am I going to say to her? WHY did I have to be assigned the L–Zs??? WHY???

Kate

✉

To: Kate Mackenzie <kathleen.mackenzie@thenyjournal.com>
Fr: Jen Sadler <jennifer.sadler@thenyjournal.com>
Re: Dessert Cart Lady

That's it. We're going to Lupe's for mojitos after work. Damn the hormones, I need a drink.

J

Journal of Kate Mackenzie

Professor Wingblade in Soc 101 said writing down our feelings would help us organize our thoughts and enable us to approach problem-solving in a rational manner. But I don't feel very rational. What am I going to do? I can't fire Mrs. Lopez.

Okay, yeah, she did refuse service to the paper's chief legal counsel. But I've seen Stuart Hertzog in action, and the fact is, like most lawyers—the ones I've met, anyway—he's a pig. Once I had to share a cab with him to an arbitration and he yelled at the cabbie for taking Lexington Avenue instead of Park, even though the cabbie said there was construction on Park. Then when it came time to pay, Stuart wouldn't give the guy a tip and said that he can't stand immigrants because they think they know everything and that even if in the cabbie's native land he was a surgeon, like he said, that didn't mean he was qualified to navigate the streets of Manhattan in a moving vehicle, and why couldn't they all (he meant immigrants, I guess) just stay home?

I totally wanted to point out that Hertzog isn't exactly a Native-American name, which means at one point Stuart's relatives must have been new to this country as well, and who knows, maybe one of them worked as a cabbie or an omnibus driver or whatever and how would Stuart have liked it if some lawyer in a fancy suit spoke to his great-great-great-great-grandpa like that?

Only I couldn't say anything like that because Amy was there and she would have fired me. I actually don't know if you can get fired for saying something like that—right to free speech and all—but I'm sure Amy would have found a way.

I can't believe I'm the one who has to fire her. Mrs. Lopez, I mean. Why me? I've never fired anyone before. Well, okay, I fired that porter who tried to feel up that seventeen-year-old lacrosse player who was touring the paper's offices on that school field trip, but he so totally deserved it—I mean, his defense was that he couldn't help it because she looked so good in her little plaid skirt. Please! I mean, it was a pleasure to fire him.

But this! This is totally different. I love Mrs. Lopez, and really, I don't blame her a bit for what she did. I mean, they ought to fire Stuart Hertzog, is what they ought to do. I once saw him with a cigar—a CIGAR!—in the 3rd-floor hallway while he was waiting for the elevator, and when Mel Fuller from Features came by and asked him to put it out because she's pregnant, he just went, "It's not lit," which was only half true because it totally had been lit in Mr. Hargrave's office, it was still smoldering a little, even. Who does that, who smokes cigars inside a public building? And yells at poor innocent cab drivers? I mean, really.

And now Jen wants to go out for drinks and she could be pregnant RIGHT NOW, which means she'll probably have some kind of flipper baby, and it will all be my fault. Oh my God, I have got to find somewhere else to stay, I can't keep crashing on their couch. It's so nice of them, but I can tell Craig is getting sick of having to share a bathroom with not just one woman but two. I could not have timed this thing with Dale worse. I mean, Jen and Craig have been trying to have a baby since they got married, and now that Jen's on all those drugs—and really, she has to see me all day at work, and then again at home—we never get a break from each other. It's a wonder she hasn't cracked. . . .

If I could find a decent sublet I would move out in a second, but I just don't think I could handle having a roommate I don't know. I mean, that girl in the share up on East 86th—I admire people with goals and all, but shouldn't women in this day and age be striving to help improve the planet, or at least their community in some small way, instead of focusing all of their energy on finding a husband? I guess I should be more accepting of other people's dreams, but really, I don't think marrying an investment banker is going to solve all of your problems. I just don't. I mean, it might HELP, in the long run, with rent and everything, but you can't just go around life being Mrs. Investment Banker. I mean, you have to find where YOU as an individual, not Mrs. Whoever You Marry, fits into the world.

And frankly, no matter how many Upper East Side bars you hit on a

Saturday night, there is no guarantee you are going to meet someone decent in any of them. All the bridal magazines in the world aren't going to change that. I mean, you're better off volunteering somewhere. At least that way you'll be doing something to improve the earth, in addition to trolling for a man. So it won't be a COMPLETE waste of your time. . . .

Oh God, maybe I'm being stupid, maybe I should just go back to him, I mean, it isn't *that* bad, being in a relationship with someone who won't commit. I mean, lots of girls would die for a boyfriend like Dale. At least he never beat me up or cheated on me. I think he really does love me, and it IS just a stupid societal more. Marriage, I mean.

Except that I distinctly remember Professor Wingblade telling us in Soc 101 that in EVERY civilization in the world—even in places like Micronesia where for hundreds of years they had no contact whatsoever with outside cultures—there is *some* sort of ceremony where couples in love stand up before their community and pledge their devotion to each other. I mean, essentially, Dale is flying in the face of thousands of years of tradition by saying he and I don't need to do this to have a satisfying and nurturing romantic relationship. That simply isn't true.

Which is not to say that if Dale agreed to marry me today, I'd move back in with him tomorrow. I mean, I don't want him to ask me just to humor me. I want him to ask me because he honestly and truly cannot picture a future without me. . . .

Except that it seems like Dale is incapable of picturing any kind of future at all, except maybe a future where the fridge isn't fully stocked with Rolling Rock, which is why he always seems to remember to buy more. But me, I don't think he sees me in his future. . . .

And I'm not even sure I want him to anymore, because the truth is, after seeing Jen and Craig and the way they are with each other, I know what true love looks like, and it is *so* not what Dale and I have, and I think I deserve to have love like that. I think it's out there, I don't know where, but somewhere. . . .

Oh God, she's here.

Employee Interaction Transcript

Employee: Ida Lopez **Personnel Rep:** Kathleen Mackenzie
Date: Wednesday **Time:** 3:15 P.M.

KM: Um, just a second here, Mrs. Lopez. I have to turn this thing on . . . um . . . testing. . . . Testing. Oh, wait. Oops. There. I think it's on. Does that look on?

IL: The little wheels are spinning.

KM: Um, okay. Well, this is Kathleen Mackenzie, and this is . . . is an employee interaction with Ida Lopez. Mrs. Lopez, I'm required by Human Resource policy to tape this session, for both your protection as well as my own.

IL: I understand, *carina*.

KM: Okay. Well. Thank you very much for coming to see me, Mrs. Lopez. I . . . er . . . I'm afraid I—

IL: Well now, you know there's nothing I like better than a little visit with my Kate. And just look how pretty you are looking today, in that pink top.

KM: Thank you, Mrs. Lopez. I—

IL: Pretty as a movie star. Skinny as a movie star, too. Too skinny, if you ask me. I don't know about you girls today, always starving yourselves to look thinner. What's so great about being thin? You think men want to go to bed with a stick figure? What's so much fun about that? Would you want to go to bed with a stick figure? No, you wouldn't. Here, better have a cookie.

KM: Oh, thank you, but really, I shouldn't—

IL: Shouldn't what, get a little meat on those bones?

KM: No, I mean, I shouldn't . . . Mrs. Lopez, you know these desserts are supposed to be for senior staff members only. . . .

IL: I don't see why, if I made them, I cannot decide who

deserves one of my famous chocolate chip cookies, and who does not. And you deserve a cookie. Here.

KM: But Mrs. Lopez—

IL: Look, it is your favorite. No nuts. Of course, most people like them with nuts. I recommend the pecans. Come on. Take a bite.

KM: Mrs. Lopez, really, I—

IL: One little bite never hurt anybody. And it's not like that good-looking boyfriend of yours will care if you gain a little weight. That one I saw with you in the lobby after last year's Christmas party. Sorry, *holiday* party. He seemed like a man who appreciates a woman with a little meat on their bones.

KM: Oh, well, actually, he and I sort of—

IL: Oh no! You broke up?

KM: Well, yes, a little while ago. I mean . . . we didn't break up, exactly—Oh my God, Mrs. Lopez. This is the best chocolate chip cookie I ever had.

IL: You know the secret, of course?

KM: Hmmm, wait, let me guess. You melt the butter before putting it in?

IL: No, *carina*. Well, I do let it sit to room temperature. But I meant the secret to getting a man to commit.

KM: No, what is it?

IL: Find the right man. Yours—the one I saw you with— he's not right for you. I knew it the minute I saw him. He'll never appreciate you. He's too wrapped up in himself. I could tell, because of the way he kept talking about that band of his. He made it sound like his band meant more to him than you do!

KM: (*Choking sound*) Excuse me.

IL: Oh, here, better have some milk to wash that down. No, don't go on about how fattening it is. It's good for you. Helps build strong bones. There. So simple, you really could make them at home. Here, let me write the recipe down for you.

KM: Oh, Mrs. Lopez! Your secret recipe? You can't—

IL: Of course I can. Now, in a large mixing bowl, beat two sticks of unsalted butter until smooth. Then add one cup of packed brown sugar, a quarter cup of granulated sugar, one large egg, and two and a half teaspoons of vanilla extract. Beat this until very well blended. Then gently beat in half—just half—of a mixture of one and three quarter cups, plus seven tablespoons—this is important—of all-purpose flour, three quarters of a teaspoon of baking powder, one third teaspoon of baking soda, a generous quarter teaspoon of salt—

KM: Mrs. Lopez, really, this isn't—

IL: Then stir in the remaining flour mixture—but don't overmix it. Then stir in the chocolate chips and pecans. Drop the cookies by teaspoonfuls—about two inches apart—on greased baking sheets, then bake for eight to ten minutes. Remember to let the pans stand for about a minute after you take them from the oven. You don't want them to lose their shape. Then use a spatula—you have a spatula, don't you, Kate?—and put the cookies on a wire rack to cool. See? Easy! Now. Hadn't you better get on with it?

KM: What? Oh. Yes. Mrs. Lopez. The reason I've asked you here today has to do with the incident that occurred this afternoon in the senior staff dining room—

IL: Yes, of course. Señor Hertzog.

KM: Yes, exactly. Mrs. Lopez, you know you and I have met before over a similar—

IL: Yes, I remember. I wouldn't give any of my peach cobbler to that man from the Mayor's Office. Oh, your boss was very put out with me that time. That . . . What's her name again? Oh, yes, Jenkins. Amy Jenkins. You know, talking about food issues? That one has some big ones. I've seen your boss down three of my chocolate cheesecake muffins, then head straight to the ladies' room—

KM: *Okay*, Mrs. Lopez, that's great, but that's not why we're here today. We're here today to talk about Mr. Hertzog—

IL: Of course. I wouldn't let him have any of my key lime pie.

KM: But see, Mrs. Lopez, that's just it. You can't, you know, just make arbitrary decisions about who does and who does not get pie in the senior-staff dining room. You have to give pie to anyone who asks for a slice.

IL: Well, I know I'm supposed to. But you've had my desserts, *carina*. You know they are specially prepared— lovingly prepared, even—for very special people. I don't feel I should have to share them with just any-one.

KM: But see, actually, Mrs. Lopez, you do. Because if you don't, we get complaints, and then you know I have to ask you to come down here and—

IL: Oh, I know, *carina*. I'm not blaming you.

KM: And you know, it would be one thing if you owned your own bakeshop or restaurant, and you refused to serve law—I mean, people like Stuart Hertzog. But you're employed by the *New York Journal*, and the paper can't have you refusing to serve—

IL: Their lead counsel. I understand, dear. I really do. And you warned me about it before. And so now I suppose that boss of yours wants you to fire me.

KM: Mrs. Lopez, you know I—

IL: It's all right, Kate. No need to get upset. She likes Señor Hertzog. I know that.

KM: If there was anything I could—I mean, was Mr. Hertzog mean to you? Did he say something rude to you? Be-cause if I could just give Amy—I mean, my superiors— a reason why you might have refused to serve Mr. Hertzog—

IL: Oh, he knows.

KM: Well, that's just it. I mean, he says he doesn't know.

IL: Oh no. He knows.

KM: Well, maybe if you could tell me—

IL: Oh, I couldn't do that! Now, you must have Security escort me out.

KM: I'm so sorry, Mrs. Lopez. But, yes, I'm going to have to—

IL: It's all right. One of them will be the Hopkins boy. He loves my cranberry scones. I'll have to check to make sure I—Oh, yes, here's one. It was so nice visiting with you, *carina*. Let's see, you're friends with that nice Señora Sadler. Here, be sure to give her this. My gingersnaps are her favorites, and I know that, with the baby shots and all, she's very sad. But tell her she shouldn't worry. She'll have a nice baby girl by the end of next year.

KM: Mrs. Lopez—

IL: Oh, don't cry, *carina!* I'm sure you're not supposed to cry when you fire someone. Here, we'll turn this off, so we don't get you into—

✉

To: Kate Mackenzie <kathleen.mackenzie@thenyjournal.com>
Fr: Amy Jenkins <amy.jenkins@thenyjournal.com>
Re: Ida Lopez

Please see me first thing tomorrow morning concerning the recording of your interview with Ida Lopez, which I've just finished listening to.

Amy Denise Jenkins
Director
Human Resources
The New York Journal
216 W. 57th Street
New York, NY 10019
212-555-6890
amy.jenkins@thenyjournal.com

This e-mail is intended only for the use of the individual to which it is addressed and may contain information that is privileged and confidential. If you are not the intended recipient, you are hereby notified that you have received this transmission in error; any review, dissemination, distribution, or copying of this transmission is prohibited. If you have received this communication in error, please notify us immediately by reply e-mail and delete this message and all of its attachments.

LUPE'S Mexican Canteena

Appetizers:

Soup of the Day $3.75

Oh my God, I am so fired. I can't believe how fired I am.
Why did I have to start crying during the

Guacamole $3.75

interview? Why didn't I think to turn the tape off before I
started bawling my head off?

Sweet Plantains $2.75

Why can't I be like the T.O.D.? SHE would never cry while
firing someone. But I don't WANT to be

Yucca Fries $2.75

like the T.O.D. I hate her. I should just quit. Now I have to
find a new job on top of a new apt. and

Nachos with Cheese $3.95

boyfriend. WHY IS EVERYTHING BAD HAPPENING TO
ME ALL AT ONCE???? And why

Nachos with Jalapeños $4.95

can I never find my journal when I need it? Which begs the
question, where is it? What if

Nachos with Beef $5.95

Amy or one of the housekeeping staff finds it? And reads it?
Then I will be fired for sure. And

Nachos Grandes $6.95

where the hell is Jen? She said to meet at Lupe's after work,
and so I'm here but she's not, and now I

Salsa Cruda $1.50

am sitting here by myself pretending to be jotting important business notes on this menu so that creepy

Quesadillas $3.50

guy in the corner won't come over here and start talking to me. Must try to appear like imp. business

Quesadilla Grandes $6.95

woman with no time for casual flirtation in Mexican restaurant. Oh my God, what if Jen doesn't come

Mini-Quesadilla Grandes $5.95

and I end up having to eat here by myself and that guy comes over and tries to join me and it turns out

House Salad $3.95

he's the vestibule rapist and he follows me back to Jen's building and pulls a knife on me? Thank

Mexican Salad $5.95

God I took that self-defense class through the Staff Resource Program. Won't he be surprised when

Mexican Grilled Chicken Salad $8.25

I break his nasal cartilage with an upthrust heel of the hand and send it back into his brain stem, instantly

Mexican Bean Salad $6.95

paralyzing him? Although on the whole I would much rather just meet Jen for drinks like we planned.

Sides:

Oh, God, I need a beer. Poor Mrs. Lopez! I guess she is looking for a job now, too. Only she has

Chips   **$1.00**

a lot more chance than I do of getting something decent. Those cookies were delicious, anybody

Spanish rice   **$1.75**

would hire her in a minute, whereas I am totally useless. I can only type 35 words per minute and God

Jalapeños   **$1.00**

knows I can't supervise, my people skills are for shit, I can't even get a decent boyfriend let alone tell

Sour cream   **$1.00**

people how to do their jobs. It is such a joke, the paper hiring me, it is just a wonder I have even

Chopped onion   **$1.00**

lasted this long, at this point I should just—Oh, there's Jen, THANK GOD!!!!!!!!!!!!!!!!!!!!!!

Dear Kate,

Sorry to leave a note taped up to the door like this (hi, Jen, hi, Craig), but it's not like you've really given me much of an alternative. I mean, if you'd stop screening your calls at work and on your cell and pick up once in a while, I wouldn't have to pull this stalkery crap. I've seriously got to talk to you, I'm going crazy here. You won't return my messages, and every time I try to reach you at Jen's, she says you're out. I know you're not out, I know you're probably sitting right there on the couch right now watching freaking Charmed, or whatever.

Anyway, about that whole One Day at a Time thing. Look, maybe we WILL be together forever. Or maybe we won't. I mean, I'm not omission. I can't see into the future. I don't know what's going to happen.

Why can't things go back to being the way they were, you know? How come all of a sudden we have to put, like, these labels on things? I mean, like why is it so important to you that I say I'll love you forever? Why can't I just say I love you, like, for now? Why isn't that enough, all of a sudden? It was enough for the past ten years.

Katie, COME HOME. I miss you. The guys miss you, too.

Love,
Dale

P.S. I could really use your advice. The studio's being really assholish, they're trying to make us change our name from I'm Not Making Any More Sandwiches to just Sandwich. What kind of name is that for a band? Who's gonna buy a record from a band called Sandwich?

Hi, you've reached Kate and Dale. We can't come to the phone right now, so at the tone, please leave a message, and we'll get back to you. Thanks!

(Tone)

Dale, you have got to change that message. I don't live there anymore, remember? Anyway, about your note . . . Oh my God, I don't even know why I called. Just forget it, okay? Nothing's changed, I just—Oh, never mind.

(Click)

Hi, you've reached Kate and Dale. We can't come to the phone right now, so at the tone, please leave a message, and we'll get back to you. Thanks!

(Tone)

Oh my God, you have got to change that message. It's Jen, by the way. You remember me, right? Your ex-girlfriend's best friend? The word is *omniscient*, buddy, not *omission*. Got it? Good. Oh, also, don't come around here anymore. You just make Kate sad. And no, I'm not drunk right now, but am totally hopped up on hormones, so you'd better be scared, because I swear to God, if I catch you around here again, I'll—

(Click)

(Tone)

Hi, you've reached Kate and Dale. We can't come to the phone right now, so at the tone, please leave a message, and we'll get back to you. Thanks!

(Tone)

Stupid machine cut me off. I really mean it. Remember that time in college when I threatened to kick the ass of that friend of yours who brought the smack to the house party Kate and I had? Remember? I didn't care that he had a gun, I wasn't scared of him. Well, that's what I'm going to do to you, too, bud, if you keep on. . . . What do you mean hang up the phone? No, I will not hang up the phone, Craig, I happen to be helping Kate. She had a very bad day and I am just—no, I am not making things worse, I'm helping. I happen to be a trained human resources representative, and I'm—don't you—Give me that!

(Click)

Hi, you've reached Kate and Dale. We can't come to the phone right now, so at the tone, please leave a message, and we'll get back to you. Thanks!

(Tone)

Dude, it's Craig. Sorry about that. Jen and Kate went out for mojitos, and Jen just had one, but she's wasted. You know, she's on all those fertility drugs, so she gets really drunk on just like one drink. So, sorry, man. I took the phone away from her and hid it in the closet. She should be all right in the morning. I hope.

(*Click*)

To do:

1. Quit job (unless fired; if fired, see #2).
2. Start packing up belongings.
3. ASPIRIN????? Maybe in bottom drawer.
4. Find new job.
5. Find new apartment.
6. Find new boyfriend.
7. Oh, God, I don't know, my head is throbbing. . . .
   Did I call Dale last night? God, I hope not.
8. Pick up dry cleaning!!!!!!!!!!

Kathleen A. Mackenzie
Personnel Representative, L-Z
Human Resources
The New York Journal
216 W. 57th Street
New York, NY 10019
212-555-6891
kathleen.mackenzie@thenyjournal.com

Yo. It's Ron. Leave a message.

(Tone)

Hi, Ron? It's Kate. Kate Mackenzie, I left a message yesterday? About the studio in the East Thirties? Well, I never heard from you. Does that mean the studio's taken already? Well, even if it is, can you call me back? Because I saw your ad for the place in Chelsea. The one that's eleven ninety-five? Could you call me about that one? Because I'm really interested. Again, it's 212-555-6891 until five, then you can reach me at 212-555-1324. And thanks. Thanks a lot. Call anytime.

Sleaterkinneyfan:	Does your head hurt as much as mine does?
Katydid:	More. You only had one drink, remember? I had seven. Do you think I'm fired?
Sleaterkinneyfan:	For coming in with a hangover? Whatever. They'd have to fire the whole department. Especially the day after the Christmas party.
Katydid:	No, for crying while I fired Mrs. Lopez.
Sleaterkinneyfan:	Oh, please. This is Human Resources. They never fire anybody in this department. Maybe if you stripped off your blouse and started singing "Everybody Wang Chung Tonight" in the mailroom.
Katydid:	The T.O.D. wants me in her office at ten. I will bet you anything it's to give me a verbal warning.
Sleaterkinneyfan:	Would you stop? They are not going to fire you. If anybody's getting fired, it's the T.O.D. Did you see all the senior staff members standing around outside the dining room this morning, looking (ineffectually) for Mrs. L's dessert cart? There are going to be some phone calls today, believe me, when word gets up to the VPs that there aren't going to be any more chocolate cheesecake muffins.
Katydid:	They'll just find some other outside vendor.
Sleaterkinneyfan:	Yeah, but no one's muffins can match Mrs. L's.
Katydid:	True. Jen, I think I have to quit.
Sleaterkinneyfan:	WHAT?????????????????
Katydid:	Seriously. I mean, how can I stand by and let them do that to poor Mrs. Lopez? I mean, it isn't right. She's a sixty-four-year-old woman.

Sleaterkinneyfan: A sixty-four-year-old woman who wouldn't give pie to the head of personnel's boyfriend, who also happens to be one of the most powerful lawyers in the city, and this company's chief legal counsel. Kate, you had no choice. Mrs. Lopez brought it on herself. You'd warned her before. It isn't like she wasn't aware of the consequences.

Katydid: Yeah, but maybe I wasn't stern enough with her. Maybe she didn't take me seriously. Nobody does, you know. Takes me seriously. I mean, why should they? I'm just like this IDIOT from Kentucky who dated the same guy all through high school and college. Why did I even major in Psych in college? I mean, seriously. I am the worst judge of character of ALL TIME.

Sleaterkinneyfan: Because you suck at everything else, remember? Besides, weren't we going to help people?

Katydid: WHO ARE WE HELPING?

Sleaterkinneyfan: Come on. You know you've helped a lot of people. What about that girl you hired for the Art Department last month? The one who was so happy when she found out she got the job, she cried and sent you flowers?

Katydid: So I had one good day. But come on, Jen. We're not exactly Making a Difference. Like we planned. I mean, remember when we were going to open Jen and Kate's Free Therapy Clinic?

Sleaterkinneyfan: Yes, but that was before we moved to Manhattan and had to dedicate half of our salaries to rent.

Katydid: Maybe we should have stayed in Kentucky.

Sleaterkinneyfan: So we could be spending our weekends

	eating pork tenderloin at the NASCAR races? No thank you.
Katydid:	I happen to like pork tenderloin. Um . . . Speaking of Kentucky, do you remember if I called Dale last night? I have this dim memory that I did.
Sleaterkinneyfan:	So what if you did? I mean, the goober asked you to, remember? In that stupid note. Seriously, there is something wrong with him. Who leaves NOTES on people's DOORS in New York City? And what was that slur against *Charmed*? *Charmed* happens to be a very good show.
Katydid:	I know! Witches! Helping people!
Sleaterkinneyfan:	Totally helping people. And killing demons at the same time. In halter tops.
Katydid:	I wasn't mean to him, was I? When I called him back?
Sleaterkinneyfan:	Oh, would you get over it? Who takes relationships one day at a time? I mean after TEN YEARS, three of which you lived together, for crying out loud.
Katydid:	WHY DID I STAY WITH HIM FOR SO LONG????? I'm such a loser.
Sleaterkinneyfan:	You are not a loser. You know who's a loser? The T.O.D. Did you see what she has on?
Katydid:	Oh my God, I know. The same thing she was wearing yesterday.
Sleaterkinneyfan:	The T.O.D. got some! Did you see that hickey on her neck? She tried to hide it with concealer, but it is SO OBVIOUS. Why didn't she go home to change before coming in this morning? That is so . . . gross. It's like she WANTS us to know. Like she's rubbing it in.

Katydid:	It's working. I can't believe the T.O.D. is having sex and I'm not.
Sleaterkinneyfan:	And you so know who she's doing it WITH. Mr. No Pie For You himself. Oh my God, wait. . . . Did you see that?
Katydid:	See what?
Sleaterkinneyfan:	When she waved her hand just now, talking to Steph at the reception desk. Is that a DIAMOND ON HER LEFT RING FINGER????
Katydid:	ohmygod
Sleaterkinneyfan:	That is the hugest rock I have ever seen. It's the size of my belly button!!!!!!!!!!!!!!
Katydid:	She's engaged. I can't believe it. The T.O.D. is engaged.
Sleaterkinneyfan:	MRS. STUART HERTZOG!!!!!!!!!!!!!!!!!
Katydid:	I can't believe someone asked the T.O.D. to marry him. I can't even get a guy to agree to admit he might still be going out with me this summer, let alone FOR THE REST OF HIS LIFE.
Sleaterkinneyfan:	*I* can't believe she hasn't come over here to throw it up in our faces. I mean, that has to be three carats, at least. Although compared to my paltry .5, anything would look big.
Katydid:	Hey! Craig spent what he could afford. It wasn't easy, picking out a ring on a computer programmer's salary. A computer programmer's *starting* salary.
Sleaterkinneyfan:	Cool it! I wouldn't trade my .5 for that barnacle creeping all the way up her knuckle for all the money in the world. I'm just saying— hey, who's that guy in the suit heading for the T.O.D.'s office?
Katydid:	Her wedding planner? Geez, she works fast.
Sleaterkinneyfan:	Is that a SUMMONS he's holding?

Katydid:	Oh, God, I hope so. I hope it turns out the T.O.D. is being sued for incompetence.
Sleaterkinneyfan:	Um, you don't think it's the pre-nup, do you?
Katydid:	Oh my God, Stuart Hertzog would SO make his potential bride sign a pre-nup! What is she doing now, can you see? Is she crying? If she's crying, it's definitely the pre-nup.
Sleaterkinneyfan:	I can't tell if she's crying or not. She's still reading it. Okay, he's leaving the T.O.D's office. Maybe I can . . . Hey, why is he walking over toward YOU?
Katydid:	Oh, n—

Hertzog Webber and Doyle
ATTORNEYS AT LAW
444 Madison Avenue, Suite 1505
New York, NY 10022
212-555-7900

Kathleen A. Mackenzie
Personnel Representative, Human Resources
The New York Journal
216 W. 57th Street
New York, NY 10019

Dear Ms. Mackenzie,

Pursuant to Article 29, page 31 of the Collective Bargaining Agreement between the *New York Journal* and the United Staff Association of NYJ, Local 6884, former employee Ida Lopez has chosen to file a grievance concerning the termination of her employment at the *New York Journal*.

You are hereby notified of pending arbitration—in which your employer, as well as you personally, are named as defendants for breach of contract—and during which my firm will be representing you. Please notify my assistant as soon as possible of your availability for a pretrial discovery conference.

Sincerely,
Mitchell Hertzog

ak/MH

To: Jen Sadler <jennifer.sadler@thenyjournal.com>
Fr: Kate Mackenzie <kathleen.mackenzie@thenyjournal.com>
Re: OH MY GOD

Mrs. Lopez is suing me! ME!!!!!!!!!! After everything I tried to do for her!!!!!

Which, considering she did lose her job, isn't all that much, I guess. But still. I mean, I TRIED. I warned her plenty of times of what might happen if she didn't stop refusing to let people have pie.

And now she's suing me! Can she even have a legal leg to stand on? Did I do something wrong? Oh my God, what if I did something wrong? Then *I'll* be fired too!

Oh my God, this is so like an episode of *Charmed*: Whatever you put out into the world comes back to you, times three, good or bad. I fired Mrs. Lopez, and now I'm going to have THREE TIMES the bad luck as I did before.

As if I didn't already have the worst luck of any girl on the eastern seaboard.

And who the hell is Mitchell Hertzog? I thought the T.O.D.'s boyfriend's name was STUART!!!!!!!!

Kate

✉

To: Kate Mackenzie <kathleen.mackenzie@thenyjournal.com>
Fr: Amy Jenkins <amy.jenkins@thenyjournal.com>
Re: (None)

See me at once.

Amy Denise Jenkins
Director
Human Resources
The New York Journal
216 W. 57th Street
New York, NY 10019
212-555-6890
amy.jenkins@thenyjournal.com

This e-mail is intended only for the use of the individual to which it is addressed and may contain information that is privileged and confidential. If you are not the intended recipient, you are hereby notified that you have received this transmission in error; any review, dissemination, distribution, or copying of this transmission is prohibited. If you have received this communication in error, please notify us immediately by reply e-mail and delete this message and all of its attachments.

✉

To: Jen Sadler <jennifer.sadler@thenyjournal.com>
Fr: Kate Mackenzie <kathleen.mackenzie@thenyjournal.com>
Re: OH MY GOD

The T.O.D. wants to see me at once!!!!!!
Which means I have to have done something wrong!!!!!!!!
HELP!!!!!!!!!!!!!!!!!!!!!!

Kate

✉

To: Stuart Hertzog <stuart.hertzog@hwd.com>
Fr: Amy Jenkins <amy.jenkins@thenyjournal.com>
Re: Mitchell Hertzog

Stuart, I have just received a letter from someone whom I can only presume is a family member of yours.

If this is a joke, I have to say it is in highly questionable taste.

If it is not a joke, might I ask why, considering the fact that I had Ida Lopez's employment terminated at your request, someone *else* from your law office will be representing me and my employer when we go to court against this woman for breach of contract?

I swore I wasn't going to bring my personal feelings into this, but I can't help it. After what happened between us last night, Stuart—how *could* you let something so important be handled by some underling . . . even if he IS a relative of yours?

Amy

Amy Denise Jenkins
Director
Human Resources
The New York Journal
216 W. 57th Street
New York, NY 10019
212-555-6890
amy.jenkins@thenyjournal.com

This e-mail is intended only for the use of the individual to which it is addressed and may contain information that is privileged and confidential. If you are not the intended recipient, you are hereby notified that you have received this transmission in error; any review, dissemi-

. . . .

✉

To: Amy Jenkins <amy.jenkins@thenyjournal.com>
Fr: Stuart Hertzog <stuart.hertzog@hwd.com>
Re: Mitchell Hertzog

Amy, darling, I'm so sorry. Mitch was supposed to wait until I'd had a chance to call you this morning before sending that letter.

The fact of the matter is, sweetheart, I can't represent you or the paper, due to the fact that I am so personally involved in the case. However, Mitch—my younger brother—is an excellent lawyer, one of the best we've got, and will do just as good a job as I would myself, I swear.

On a personal note, how could you entertain the idea, even for a moment, that after what happened between us last night, I would ever do anything that might hurt you or your career? When I woke up this morning and gazed down upon your sleeping face, it was as if I was gazing at the face of an angel, and all I could wonder was, what did I ever do to deserve such good fortune? Amy, you are my everything.

I promise you, you're in the best of hands.

Yours, now more than ever,
Stuart

Stuart Hertzog, Senior Partner
Hertzog Webber and Doyle, Attorneys at Law
444 Madison Avenue, Suite 1505
New York, NY 10022
212-555-7900

To: Mitchell Hertzog <mitchell.hertzog@hwd.com>
Fr: Stuart Hertzog <stuart.hertzog@hwd.com>
Re: Ida Lopez

Mitch, you asshole. What do you think you're doing? I told you not to messenger those letters to the *Journal* until I'd had a chance to call Amy. Have you been drinking, or are you just criminally stupid? Or do you just not care?

I'm warning you right now: Fuck up this case and you're a dead man.

Stuart Hertzog, Senior Partner
Hertzog Webber and Doyle, Attorneys at Law
444 Madison Avenue, Suite 1505
New York, NY 10022
212-555-7900

✉

To: Stuart Hertzog <stuart.hertzog@hwd.com>
Fr: Mitchell Hertzog <mitchell.hertzog@hwd.com>
Re: Ida Lopez

Stuie! Nice to hear from you. Isn't it funny how two people can work down the hall from each other—can come, in fact, from the same gene pool—and yet manage to go weeks without exchanging a single pleasantry?

In reply to your e-mail, I am neither drunk nor, to the best of my knowledge, criminally stupid. It's true I don't care, though. Does that bother you? Sorry. But when a little old lady takes on a titan of publishing like Peter Hargrave, aka owner of New York's leading photo-newspaper, in a breach of contract suit, it's kind of hard for me to root for the home team, if you know what I mean.

Mitch

P.S. Where were you last night? I called during the Michigan game, but got no answer. I know you never go anywhere except out for drinks with Webber and Doyle, and they're in Scottsdale with Dad for the golf tourney. Could you, perhaps, have Hooked Up? With *AMY*?

....

✉

To: Mitchell Hertzog <mitchell.hertzog@hwd.com>
Fr: Stuart Hertzog <stuart.hertzog@hwd.com>
Re: Ida Lopez

I don't know what Dad was thinking, asking you to join the firm. You're as big a slacker now as you were when we were kids.

And as for my hooking up, that is none of your business.

Stuart Hertzog, Senior Partner
Hertzog Webber and Doyle, Attorneys at Law
444 Madison Avenue, Suite 1505
New York, NY 10022
212-555-7900

....

✉

To: Stuart Hertzog <stuart.hertzog@hwd.com>
Fr: Mitchell Hertzog <mitchell.hertzog@hwd.com>
Re: Ida Lopez

As for Dad hiring me, you'll remember that it was right after his heart attack. Clearly he wasn't in his right mind. I warned him then, but he wouldn't listen.

So. The hookup. It *is* that chick from the *Journal,* isn't it?

Stuie, Stuie, Stuie. Have you learned nothing under my tutelage? I thought I told you to stay away from personnel rep types. They're all psychiatrist wannabes. You really want to get your head shrunk at the same time you're getting your, um, ego stroked? Not a good idea.

Hey. Balucchi's for lunch?

Mitch

....

✉

To: Mitchell Hertzog <mitchell.hertzog@hwd.com>
Fr: Stuart Hertzog <stuart.hertzog@hwd.com>
Re: Ida Lopez

You leave my ego out of this, you son of a bitch. Mom's right: You have no sense of family loyalty. Oh, sure, you took the job when Dad had his triple bypass. But the old guy's doing fine now. So what are you still doing here?

And don't try to give me that shit about Dad wanting you around. I bet you haven't talked to Dad in weeks, just like the rest of us.

Why don't you go back to defending crackheads and the other lowlifes you seem to enjoy hanging around with so much?

And Amy Jenkins happens to be my fiancée—a word I'm aware you wouldn't understand, because you've never gone out with a woman longer than a single basketball season. I would thank you not to screw up this ridiculous lawsuit against her and her employer—

who also happens to be one of our biggest clients, if you'll trouble yourself to recall.

And I wouldn't go to the *corner* with you, let alone to some chintzy chain ethnic eatery. What the hell is wrong with you? You're a partner now, you can afford to eat lunch in places that don't offer a $6.95 all-you-can-eat special, you know. Oh, but wait, I'm sorry, you're probably saving your money to give away to some bleeding heart Save-the-Crackhead Fund.

Stuart Hertzog, Senior Partner
Hertzog Webber and Doyle, Attorneys at Law
444 Madison Avenue, Suite 1505
New York, NY 10022
212-555-7900

....

✉

To: Stuart Hertzog <stuart.hertzog@hwd.com>
Fr: Mitchell Hertzog <mitchell.hertzog@hwd.com>
Re: Ida Lopez

Touchy touchy touchy! Fiancée, huh? So you're finally taking the plunge, huh? That's quite an accomplishment, Stuie. You're aware that if you go through with it, you might actually have to start sharing your stuff with her? You know, like the remote control, and the SUV, and your wine-of-the-month-club membership, and all of that.

Admit it, you're just mad because I made Law Review and you didn't. Come on, Stuie. You're the one who got into Yale, while I had to make do with a state education.

Congrats on the whole wedding thing. I'm sure you two will be happy. And I didn't mean it about the bulimia thing. Much.

Mitch

P.S. Have you told Mom yet? I wouldn't know, see, on account of how Mom's still not speaking to me over the whole Janice thing. So if you're hoping to make her regret ever giving birth to me by telling her all the mean things I said about your girlfriend, too bad.

She already does.

Hate me, I mean.

....

✉

To: Mitchell Hertzog <mitchell.hertzog@hwd.com>
Fr: Stuart Hertzog <stuart.hertzog@hwd.com>
Re: Ida Lopez

Your congratulations are accepted.

P.S. Stop calling me Stuie!

Stuart Hertzog, Senior Partner
Hertzog Webber and Doyle, Attorneys at Law
444 Madison Avenue, Suite 1505
New York, NY 10022
212-555-7900

....

✉

To: Stacy Trent <IH8BARNEY@freemail.com>
Fr: Mitchell Hertzog <mitchell.hertzog@hwd.com>
Re: You'll never believe this one:

Stuie's getting married.

Mitch

P.S. No, this is not a joke.

To: Amy Jenkins <amy.jenkins@thenyjournal.com>
Fr: Stuart Hertzog <stuart.hertzog@hwd.com>
Re: Mitchell Hertzog

Don't worry, Amy. It's all taken care of. I spoke to my brother, and he's offered us his congratulations. Everything is going to be fine. Mitch just has some issues, because I'm the oldest and—frankly—the best liked by our parents of the four of us kids. That kind of thing can eat away at a person—well, you know that, being in the field you're in. My sisters—well, my sister Stacy, anyway—have handled it better than Mitch. He has never really lived up to his potential—he has a 165 IQ, but he got lousy grades in school, and didn't even bother to apply to any good colleges. In fact, he took a year off between high school and college and just roamed aimlessly around the globe, managing to spend his entire two-hundred-thousand-dollar share of the inheritance from our grandfather. I have a feeling he gave most of it away to the Dalai Lama, or some other loser.

He finally ended up at Michigan State and fell in with a bad crowd—you know the sorts I mean: writers . . . artists . . . democrats. He didn't even join a fraternity. I was as surprised as anybody when he decided to go to law school instead of joining the Peace Corps or becoming a mime or something.

Of course, when he graduated, Dad offered him a job with the firm—familial loyalty, and all of that. But would you believe Mitch had the nerve to turn it down? The guy spent four years working as a public defender (!) before finally agreeing to come work for Dad—but not until the old guy was on his deathbed . . . or thought he was, anyway, since he's apparently doing fine now, given that he never seems to come in off the links.

Anyway, I can't say spending all that time with murderers and drug addicts did Mitch's disposition any good.

But he's a damned good lawyer. So you can quit worrying and meet me for lunch at Lespinasse, as we planned. I can't wait to gaze into those sparkling eyes of yours over a glass of Cristal . . . I hope they're still shining as brightly as that diamond on your finger. . . .

Yours, as ever,
Stuart

Stuart Hertzog, Senior Partner
Hertzog Webber and Doyle, Attorneys at Law
444 Madison Avenue, Suite 1505
New York, NY 10022
212-555-7900

....

✉

To: Stuart Hertzog <stuart.hertzog@hwd.com>
Fr: Amy Jenkins <amy.jenkins@thenyjournal.com>
Re: Mitchell Hertzog

Oh, Stuart, that's so sweet! I knew you'd take care of it. Thank you so much!

And don't worry about that stuff with your brother. We all have family members we'd prefer to have little to do with. I myself have both a sister and a brother I'm not exactly looking forward to introducing to you. And my parents—well, I won't get into that.

But there are some family members of mine I'm dying for you to get to know—my Pi Delt sisters! I just know you're going to love them—they're really a swell group of gals. A bunch of us are meeting at the Monkey Bar after work . . . PLEASE say you'll stop by so I can show you off to them. I can't wait for you to meet them!

Looking forward to our lunch . . . and to proving to you that my eyes are still shining just as brightly as they were last night. . . .

Amy

Amy Denise Jenkins
Director
Human Resources
The New York Journal
216 W. 57th Street
New York, NY 10019
212-555-6890
amy.jenkins@thenyjournal.com

Mrs. Stuart Hertzog

Mrs. S. A. Hertzog

Mrs. Amy Denise Hertzog

Jenkins-Hertzog

Mrs. Jenkins-Hertzog

Mrs. Amy Jenkins-Hertzog

Mrs. A. D. Jenkins-Hertzog

Stuart, Amy, Heath, and Annabelle Hertzog

Heath Hertzog

no

Connor Hertzog

Annabelle Hertzog

Connor Jenkins-Hertzog

Annabelle Jenkins-Hertzog

Mr. and Mrs. Stuart Jenkins-Hertzog

Amy Denise Jenkins
Director
Human Resources
The New York Journal
216 W. 57th Street
New York, NY 10019
212-555-6890
amy.jenkins@nyjournal.com

To: Kate Mackenzie <kathleen.mackenzie@thenyjournal.com>
Fr: Jen Sadler <jennifer.sadler@thenyjournal.com>
Re: OH MY GOD

SO⁇⁇⁇⁇⁇⁇⁇⁇ WHAT HAPPENED⁇⁇⁇⁇⁇⁇

J

✉

To: Jen Sadler <jennifer.sadler@thenyjournal.com>
Fr: Kate Mackenzie <kathleen.mackenzie@thenyjournal.com>
Re: OH MY GOD

I don't know. It's the weirdest thing. I went into the T.O.D.'s office, and she was . . . doodling. And humming. Doodling and humming, almost like . . .

Like a human being!

She seemed surprised to see me—like she'd forgotten about the whole thing. I asked her about the letter, and she just went, "Oh, that's Stuart's brother. He'll be representing the paper in the arbitration." Then she SHOWED ME HER RING!

I'm not kidding. She went, "I thought I should tell you before you heard it through the departmental grapevine . . . Stuart Hertzog and I are engaged."

Then she waved that massive rock—you were right, it IS three carats, she told me—under my nose and went, "Oh, Kate! I'm so happy!" in this very weird voice. Almost like she knows she SHOULD be happy, so she's determined to ACT happy. You know what I mean?

I didn't know what to do—genuflect and kiss the stupid thing, or just say congratulations—so I just said congratulations and got the hell out of there.

Oh my God, I still feel unclean. I think I'll need a bacon cheeseburger for lunch before I feel like myself again.

Kate

Sleaterkinneyfan:	Okay, now THAT is weird.
Katydid:	Are you crazy? Quit I.M.-ing me, she's gonna catch us.
Sleaterkinneyfan:	Hello, you said she was doodling. And HUMMING. Doodling, humming, newly engaged bosses do not pay attention when their employees are I.M.-ing. So did you ask if she's taking his name?
Katydid:	No, of course not.
Sleaterkinneyfan:	She will. I can't WAIT to address my first employee action form to Amy Hertzog. Oh my God, it is going to be great. OH MY GOD, IF THEY HAVE KIDS, THEY'LL BE HERTZOGS TOO!!!!!!!!!
Katydid:	You so know if she has a boy she'll name it Connor. It's like the number-one most popular name for boys right now, and God knows, Amy has to do whatever's popular.
Sleaterkinneyfan:	Totally. And if it's a girl, it will be Annabelle. ANNABELLE HERTZOG!!!
Katydid:	Stop it. The guy can't help what his last name is.
Sleaterkinneyfan:	Um, hello, he so can. You think my last name is really Sadler? No, it was Sadlinsokov, until my ancestors got to Ellis Island and wisely shortened it.
Katydid:	I think Sadlinsokov sounds nice. It has character.
Sleaterkinneyfan:	So . . . admit it. Things are getting good around here. You don't want to quit anymore, do you?
Katydid:	For what they made me do to Mrs. Lopez? Yes, I do.
Sleaterkinneyfan:	Oh, right. And miss out on all this fun? I know—after lunch, let's ask the T.O.D. if

	that's a hickey on her neck. 10 to 1 she'll say it's a bruise from the gym.
Katydid:	You're on. But YOU ask. I did it last time.
Sleaterkinneyfan:	Deal. Winner buys the bacon cheeseburgers.
Katydid:	Oh, all right.
Sleaterkinneyfan:	logged off
Katydid:	logged off

Hi, you've reached the desk of Kathleen Mackenzie. I'm sorry I'm not able to take your call. I'm either on the other line, or away from my desk at the moment. At the tone, please leave a message, and I'll get back to you as soon as I can. Thank you!

(Tone)

Katie, it's me. Dale. Listen. I got your message. Katie, I know we can work things out, if you'll just give me another chance. I mean, I'm not saying I can change or anything, but I promise—I mean, it isn't like there's another girl, or anything. I mean, well, you know, there's lots of girls, we're a pretty popular band. There are girls around all the time. But there's no special girl. I mean, more special than you. Aw, come on, Katie. You know I'm doing the best I can. But I'm just not the standing-up-in-church-in-a-tux-in-front-of-everyone-and-declaring-my-eternal-love-for-a-woman kind of guy. And you know it! I mean, is that the kind of guy you fell in love with back in Kentucky? Was it? No, it wasn't. So cut me a little slack, will ya? And come home. I really miss you. Also, I can't find my Clash T-shirt. Did you take it to the laundry-by-the-pound place? Because it's like—

(Click)

Hi, you've reached the desk of Kathleen
Mackenzie. I'm sorry I'm not able to
take your call. I'm either on the other
line, or away from my desk at the moment. At the tone, please leave a message, and I'll get back to you as soon as I
can. Thank you!

(Tone)

Kate, hi, it's Dolly. Listen, sweetie,
there's been some sort of misunderstanding. Well, not a misunderstanding,
exactly. It's just that the new fax boy . . .
Well, he and I ended up in what I believe is called a *contretemps* . . . at least in
Bazaar it is . . . and I'm afraid he might
have gotten the wrong idea. And the
truth is, darling, I honestly thought he
was interested, but apparently, he plays
for the other team—I can't imagine
what happened, I used to be so good at
telling them apart. Anyway, I think he's
going to file some sort of a . . . What's it
called again, Nadine? Oh, yes, sexual harassment suit against me. But honestly,
darling, my hand just slipped. . . . Oh
well, anyway. Call me. Maybe we can do
lunch tomorrow, and talk. Ciao!

(Click)

Hi, you've reached the desk of Kathleen
Mackenzie. I'm sorry I'm not able to
take your call. I'm either on the other
line, or away from my desk at the mo-

ment. At the tone, please leave a message, and I'll get back to you as soon as I can. Thank you!

(Tone)

Okay, I found the shirt. It turns out Scroggs was using it to keep his cymbals from getting scratched. Anyway. The thing is, Kate . . . Okay. Here's the thing. I really do love you. You know? And this is a really bad time for you to have, you know, moved out. Because like, we've got to make all these decisions . . . me and the band . . . and like, I'm not used to making decisions without you around to like, talk them through. Like I told you, they want to change our name to Sandwich? Well, also, they want Scroggs to shave his head. But I'm like—you know, a bald drummer, that is just derivative. But then these suits, you know, they were all, derivative of what, but like, I didn't know. I could've really used your help there, you know? Yeah, whatever, I KNOW, I HEAR YOU GUYS, I'LL BE THERE IN A SECOND. . . . So. Whatever, Kate. If you could just, you know, call me. But not tonight, because we've got a gig. But like tomorrow. No, tomorrow's no good either. Well, I'll call you. I'll—I SAID IN A MINUTE! I really love you, Kate. Stop being such a—

(Click)

Hi, you've reached the desk of Kathleen Mackenzie. I'm sorry I'm not able to take your call. I'm either on the other line, or away from my desk at the moment. At the tone, please leave a message, and I'll get back to you as soon as I can. Thank you!

(Tone)

Katie, honey? Hi, it's Mom. Charlie and I have been trying to reach you, but it seems like you and Dale are never home anymore—everything is all right between you two, isn't it?—Well, of course it is, I'm just being silly, I suppose. Anyway, I just thought I'd try you at work. I wanted to let you know we're in Taos. That's right, New Mexico! Oh, it's just stunning here, sweetie. The view from the lot they assigned us is spectacular—this really *is* the way to see our country, just like the dealer said. Well, love you, and you have my cell phone number if you need to reach me. Love you!

(Click)

Hi, you've reached the desk of Kathleen Mackenzie. I'm sorry I'm not able to take your call. I'm either on the other line, or away from my desk at the moment. At the tone, please leave a message, and I'll get back to you as soon as I can. Thank you!

(Tone)

Hello, Ms. Mackenzie? This is Anne Kelly, Mitchell Hertzog's assistant. Mr. Hertzog asked me to call you to try to set up a conference for pretrial discovery concerning you and an employee I believe your company terminated yesterday—Ida Lopez? Anyway, if you could call me back at your convenience so we could set up that appointment, I'd appreciate it. The number is 212-555-7900. Thank you so much.

(Click)

To: Mitchell Hertzog <mitchell.hertzog@hwd.com>
Fr: Stacy Trent <IH8BARNEY@Freemail.com>
Re: You'll never believe this one:

> Stuie's getting married.

You lie.

What even makes you think I'm going to fall for this? I'm no naive housewife, you know. I mean, I am a housewife, but I'm not naive. I happen to be a good five years your senior, on top of which, we actually do get sarcasm out here now in Greenwich. I know it's hard to believe, but it turns out sarcasm—and irony, even—have been imported to Connecticut from the city for years.

So quit lying like a rug and tell me why you didn't call Mom for her birthday. Is it still the Janice thing? Mitch, you have got to let Janice fight her own battles. She's not just our kid sister anymore, she's over eighteen, and legally an adult.

Which, if you think about it, is something I should be telling Mom and not you, but whatever, I already told Mom, to no perceptible effect.

Oh, God, I'm as bad as you.

But at least I'm not spreading unfounded rumors about our esteemed eldest sibling. Haven't I warned you about this before, Mitch? Use your impressive cerebral powers for good and not evil. Stuart is so beneath your intellectual capabilities. Making fun of him is like shooting fish in a barrel, it just isn't worthy of your prodigious talents.

Now Mom, on the other hand . . .

Just kidding.

Hey, are you coming out this weekend, or what? The kids were asking. And Jason's been dying to show you this new putter he got.
Or something golf related, anyway.

Stacy

....

✉

To: Stacy Trent <IH8BARNEY@Freemail.com>
Fr: Mitchell Hertzog <mitchell.hertzog@hwd.com>
Re: You hurt me
Attachment: ✉ Ida Lopez

Seriously, how can you imagine, even for a minute, that I would
joke about something as deadly serious as the impending nuptials
of our esteemed elder brother? I have it in writing from the Stu
Meister himself (see attached e-mail, plus quote from it below):

> Amy Jenkins happens to be my fiancée—a word I'm aware you
> wouldn't understand, because you've never gone out with a
> woman
> longer than a single basketball season.

See. I told you so. You know I could never make up anything that
sounded half that smug. *He's getting married.* To that harpy from
the personnel office at the *Journal.* Remember, the one he
brought to your place for Thanksgiving dinner last year? Who
went jogging after we finished, while the rest of us sat in cata-
tonic stupors?

Yeah. *That* one. He's marrying *her.*

Personally, I think there should be a law against strenuous exercise
after a large holiday meal. But then, I would never agree to marry
a blowhard like Stuie, so maybe it's just me.

And you don't need me coming out there to visit all the time. You have your ever-escalating horde of in-laws to keep my nieces and nephew entertained.

Much love,
Mitch

....

✉

To: Mitchell Hertzog <mitchell.hertzog@hwd.com>
Fr: Stacy Trent <IH8BARNEY@Freemail.com>
Re: I am in shock

I can't believe it. Stuart's getting married. He's actually going to share his much-vaulted millions with someone other than his dry cleaner and doorman. How can this be? Has there been a rift in the space-time continuum?

Of course, the fact that he's marrying someone so heinous explains a lot. Did you know I actually overheard Amy Jenkins telling Mom that she thinks it's a travesty that Martin Luther King's birthday was made into a national holiday?

Mom, of course, agreed with her.

Have I mentioned that Jason asked me not to invite Stuart back for Thanksgiving next year? This is apparently on account of the half-hour lecture Stu gave him on the difference between a multepuciano and lungarotti. Jason's actual words were that if he'd had to hear a second more about it, he'd have lunged at Stu's rotti.

Which I thought rather witty myself. You know, for Jason.

Speaking of Jason, you're right: I do love my in-laws dearly. The Trents cannot be rivaled for pure Kennedy-esque familial catfights.

But for self-delusional psychodrama, no one can hold a candle to the Hertzogs. And that's why it bothers me when you don't come around more. It's no fun laughing at Mom, Dad, and Stuart all by myself.

Oh, wait, I have an idea. Why don't YOU get married? To someone fun. Then she and I can dish the dirt on Mom and Dad when you're too busy to join me.

Just a suggestion.

Stace

....

⊠

To: Stacy Trent <IH8BARNEY@Freemail.com>
Fr: Mitchell Hertzog <mitchell.hertzog@hwd.com>
Re: Nice try . . .

. . . but law is definitely not the field to go into if you're looking to meet a nice girl. So far the only women I've met since graduation are other lawyers . . . and of course the hookers I was defending.

No offense to any female lawyers you might have in your acquaintance, but I kind of preferred the hookers. I mean, at least they didn't care what kind of shoes I had on.

Mitch

Katydid: What do I do???? There's a message on my phone from Mitchell Hertzog's assistant! She wants me to call to schedule an appointment for pretrial discovery! About Mrs. Lopez!!!!!!

Sleaterkinneyfan: So? Schedule an appointment.

Katydid: But . . . I'm on Mrs. Lopez's side.

Sleaterkinneyfan: Better not let the T.O.D. catch you saying that.

Katydid: No worries. She's not even here. She went to go meet the Stepford Wives at the Monkey Bar. I overheard her on the phone with one of them.

Sleaterkinneyfan: Oh, you mean her sorority sisters. That's right, they meet the first Thursday of every month. I can't understand how they can bear to tear themselves away from *Friends*. Isn't Jennifer Aniston like the sorority girl icon of all time, or something?

Katydid: Hey. I like Jennifer Aniston.

Sleaterkinneyfan: Whatever. Better make the appointment. And leave the T.O.D. a message to let her know you did it. Then let's get out of here. There's a sale at Nine West.

Katydid: But isn't my cooperating with the paper's soulless corporate lawyers tantamount to supporting the dismissal of Mrs. Lopez, an act which grates against every fiber of my being?

Sleaterkinneyfan: You already lost your apartment. You want to be out of a job too?

Katydid: Roger. Over and out.

Amy, just to let you know, I got a message from Mitchell Hertzog's assistant, asking me to call to schedule an appointment to give a deposition concerning Ida Lopez's grievance suit.

So I went ahead and scheduled an appointment for tomorrow morning at nine . . . which of course means I probably won't be in to the office until after eleven or so.

I hope this is okay.

Kate

Kathleen A. MacKenzie
Personnel Representative, L-Z
Human Resources
The New York Journal
216 W. 57th Street
New York, NY 10019
212-555-6891
kathleen.mackenzie@nyjournal.com

To: Paula Reznik

Paula, I waited for you for half

```
     CVS Pharmacy
```

an hour, then I finally gave up

```
      Thank you for
       shopping at CVS
```

and left. You must have gotten

```
   Imitrex        $10.00
```

held up. I tried your cell and

```
   Levlin-21      $10.00
```

got no answer. Hope you find

```
   Allegra        $10.00
```

this note. I was really looking

```
   Total:         $30.00
```

forward to seeing this apart-

```
   Paid:          $40.00
```

ment, too. Call me tomorrow

```
   Change:        S10.00
```

so we can reschedule.

Thanks! Kate

P.S. Sorry, this was the only

paper I could find.

Salamander Slim's
The East Village's Number-1 Destination
for Live Music, All the Time

TONIGHT'S BAND:

I'm Not Making Any More Sandwiches

FEATURING:

Dale Carter: Guitar, Vocals
Jake Hartnett: Guitar, Vocals
Marty Hicks: Bass
Scroggs: Drums, Vocals

I'm Not Making Any More Sandwiches™ appears
courtesy of Liberation Music Records

PLAYLIST:

Kate and Me   Random Acts of Kate
In the Bedroom with Kate   I Love U, Kate, for Now
Kate, Y Did U Leave Me   Chasing Kate
Come Back, Kate   Ice Weasels Gnaw My Brain

All songs, lyrics by Dale Carter &
I'm Not Making Any More Sandwiches™

Y Won't U B With Me, Kate?

Oh, Kate, Y won't U B with me?
Kate, Don't U know what U mean to me?
I look at the dirty dishes piling up in the sink
and all I can think
is Kate
U kept the place so clean
Kate, I treated U like a queen

Oh, Kate, U mean the world to me
Kate, Come home to me

Oh, Kate, Y can't it B
Like it used to B
Because this world ain't meant for lovers
No, this world ain't meant for U and me
Because the bureaucrats in Washington, they'll set off
    the bombs, so what's the point, Kate?
We're all just going to die, anyway.
So, Kate, Y won't U B with me?

—Dale Carter, All Rights Reserved

Journal of Kate Mackenzie

Dale shoved another one of his songs about me under the door. This one was written on the back of a playlist. Craig found it when he got home today from the office. Seriously, what am I going to do about him? Dale, not Craig. I think eight songs about me is a little much (could "Ice Weasels Gnaw My Brain" be about me, too? No, surely not. I mean, what do I have to do with ice weasels? What ARE ice weasels? Are they real? Are there really weasels that live on ice? What do they eat?).

Oh God, I have got to get some sleep, I can't be groggy in the morning, I've to go get deposed by Stuart Hertzog's brother. What am I even going to say to him? What if I accidentally let slip that I don't think Mrs. Lopez should have been fired in the first place, and he tells the T.O.D. what I said? You so know he will, he's Stuart Hertzog's BROTHER. Stuart I'm-engaged-to-the-T.O.D. Hertzog. Plus he's a lawyer. Lawyer + Stuart Hertzog's brother = mean, evil person with no conscience or soul. He'll tell Stuart, and Stuart'll tell Amy, and then I'll get fired. I'll get fired just like Mrs. Lopez got fired. Only I don't belong to a union, so I won't even have anyone to defend me. I'll just become a statistic, another member of Manhattan's homeless, jobless community.

Oh my God, I hate my life. Something has GOT to give. It's just GOT to.

Appearances:
Kathleen Mackenzie (KM)
Mitchell Hertzog (MH)
Recorded by Anne Kelly (AK) for later comparison with
  stenographer's transcript
Miriam Lowe, Shorthand Reporter and Notary Public within
  and for the State of New York

AK: Good morning, Ms. Mackenzie, thank you so much for
  coming. Please have a seat. May I get you a cup of cof-
  fee, tea, soda—whatever you prefer?
KM: Coffee would be good, thanks.
AK: Fine. Mr. Hertzog should be joining us in a second. I'll
  just be a moment while I get your coffee. Do you take
  cream or sugar?
KM: Yes, both, thank you.
  (Sound of door closing)
  (Sound of door opening)
MH: Oh, sorry, wrong room.
KM: No problem.
  (Sound of door closing)
  (Sound of door opening)
MH: Wait a minute. You're Katherine Mackenzie?
KM: Kathleen. Kate, actually.

MH: Oh, Kathleen. Sorry. I didn't . . . I expected someone . . .

KM: Yes?

MH: Never mind. Nice to meet you. I'm Mitch Hertzog.

KM: *You're* Mitchell Hertzog?

MH: Last time I checked. Why?

KM: I . . . Nothing. I just—you're not—

MH: I think it's safe to say neither of us is what the other expected.

KM: It's just that . . . Well, you don't look anything like your brother.

MH: Thank God. Sorry. It's the tie, isn't it?

KM: I'm sorry? Oh, the tie. Is that . . . Rocky and Bullwinkle?

MH: 'Fraid so. Gift from my nieces.

KM: It's . . . colorful.

MH: I know it throws people when we turn out to have a sense of humor.

KM: We?

MH: Lawyers. Oh, I see Anne's got the recorder going already. Where'd she go?

KM: To get coffee.

MH: Great. And here's the stenographer. So I guess we can start—

KM: Shouldn't Mrs. Lopez be here? And her lawyer?

MH: This is just a pretrial conference, not a deposition. I've found it's good to get all the facts straight before moving on to any formal proceedings. Less surprises that way. That okay with you?

KM: Sure. I guess.

MH: Great. Like I said, I'm Mitchell Hertzog, and I'm representing the *New York Journal* against Ida Lopez, for whom I understand you were . . .
    (Sound of papers shuffling)

MH (con't) . . . a personnel rep?

KM: That's right. Not for very long. I mean, I just started working at the *Journal*.

MH: Is that right? When did you start working there?

KM: Last fall. I was a social worker, with the city, before.

MH: Really? But—excuse me for pointing it out—you obviously aren't from around here—

KM: Oh, no. My accent, you mean? I'm from Kentucky, actually. I just moved here, you know, after I got my degree. Social work.

MH: I see. And if social work's your thing, New York City's the place to be?

KM: Well, yes. That, and my boyfriend—ex-boyfriend—well, he's a musician—

MH: Say no more. Did it work out better for him than it did for you?

KM: I beg your pardon?

MH: The social work thing. I mean, you're not doing it anymore.

KM: Oh. No. I took the job with the *Journal* because, you know, working for the city . . . it was kind of depressing.

MH: Sure.

KM: All these people, they don't have anything, or any way, really, to make things better. And there were these programs, you know, to help them, but—I don't know—it didn't quite work out the way I thought it would. I mean, a lot of the programs got eliminated because the city ran out of money, or sometimes my clients didn't qualify for them for whatever reason . . . and it just seemed like no matter how hard I tried, you know, things never got better, and there was really nothing I could do about it, and I took the job because I thought I could help make a difference. Only it turned out, I couldn't. So I was going home every night and crying into my chicken in garlic sauce, and finally, it just seemed healthier to quit.

MH: Chicken. In garlic sauce.

KM: That sounded stupid, didn't it?

MH: Absolutely not.

KM: No. It did. You're just being nice.

MH: I'm not. I swear I'm not. I'm not nice.
    (Sound of door opening)
    Oh, look. Here's Anne with the coffee.

AK: Here you go.

MH: Cream or sugar, Ms.—

KM: Kate. Both, thanks. I . . . oops.

MH: Sorry about that.

KM: No, it was my fault—

MH: Here you go. Now, uh, where were we? Oh, yes. So you quit social work. . . .

KM: Oh, right. Well, my friend Jen got a job there right out of college, and when a position came up in her department, she recommended me. And I've been there ever since. I mean, it isn't my dream job, or anything. We're not really helping anybody. Well, maybe occasionally. But at least, you know, I don't go home anymore and—

MH: Cry into your chicken with garlic sauce.

KM: Exactly.

MH: Right. So I take it you inherited Ida from your predecessor?

KM: Yes, I did. From Amy Jenkins. She's my supervisor now. Ida's file is, like, three inches thick.

MH: So it would be safe to say that Ida was considered a troublemaker before you even got there.

KM: Not a troublemaker, no. Not everything in Mrs. Lopez's file is bad. There are letters in there from administrators saying how much they like her. She's really—*was* really—very popular—

MH: But not with everyone, clearly.

KM: No. Not with everyone. But the people who didn't like her were people who, you know, nobody else really liked. Mostly just people like Stuart Hertz—

MH: Go on.

KM: Um. No. Sorry. That's it. That's all I had to say.

MH: You were saying something about Stuart Hertzog.

KM: No, I wasn't.

MH: Yes, you were.

KM: No, I wasn't. I really wasn't.

MH: Kate, this is being recorded, remember? I can just play the tape back if you want. Also, Miriam's taking it down. Miriam, could you read back to me Kate's last—

KM: Well, I was just saying. You know. How everybody at the paper really, really likes Mr. Hertzog. He's very, very popular.

MH: Kate. This is Stuart you're talking about. No one likes Stuart. But what specific problem did Ida have with him?

KM: She won't tell me. When Mrs. Lopez didn't consider somebody worthy of her desserts, that was it. They just . . . you know. They were cut off.

MH: And my brother being cut off was what? The last straw?

KM: Well, she'd had a number of verbal warnings, and we'd sent her to, you know, customer service training. Several times. But I guess it never really took. But sometimes it takes more than just a couple of training sessions. Some people just need more time than others. It isn't right to expect every single employee to be exactly the same. I mean, would you want people to expect you to be exactly the same as every other lawyer in the world, Mr. Hertzog?

MH: Mitch. You can call me Mitch. And, uh, it seems to me like some people already do.

KM: Which is not to say that I don't completely understand why Mrs. Lopez did what she did, because you know, sometimes you give and you give and you give, and people, they just take, and take, and take, and you start feeling like you're never going to get anything back, and you wait and wait for something, anything, any kind of acknowledgment, even the tiniest crumb, like, "Yeah, okay, I do want to be with you forever and not just, you know, till someone better comes along, and yeah, I'm an ex-pothead and I can only take it one day at a time, but you, I know I want you in my future." Only it never comes. And the next thing you know, you're looking at hellholes in Hoboken for eleven hundred a month and landlords named Ron won't return your calls . . . er. I mean. What I mean is . . .

MH: I think I get what you mean.

KM: What I meant was, you know. Pie.

MH: Exactly. Pie.

KM: Yes. Mrs. Lopez, she's human. And you know, clearly, she'd like people to show some appreciation for her hard work. But if people just, you know, take her pie and don't even say, "Hey, nice pie," they just scarf it down or whatever—

MH: I could see how that would get to be annoying. I mean, if you're constantly providing . . . pie. And getting no positive feedback—

KM: Right! And what about your future? I mean, how do you know people are still going to want your pie in the future? Supposing they become a famous rock star or something. People are going to be offering them pie all over the place. If they haven't promised only to eat your pie, well, where does that leave you?

MH: With perfectly justifiable insecurities over your own self-worth.

KM: Absolutely! See what I mean? I mean, it's no wonder she cracked. Mrs. Lopez, I mean.

MH: Right. Mrs. Lopez.

KM: So you see what I mean, then? It's wrong to fire somebody because they had one bad day. And without even any warning. I mean, yes, she was on probation, but I think she still should have gotten a written warning first. Just to let her know. And then if she messed up again, we could have fired her. But to just fire her like that, for not giving someone pie . . .

MH: Oh. Yes. Now I see what you mean. So there was no written warning?

KM: No. Just the verbal. Not that I think the *Journal* was wrong to fire Mrs. Lopez. I mean, I would never say that. I love working at the *Journal*. I would never say anything to make the *Journal* look bad.

MH: Don't look so panicked, Kate. Nothing you say here is going to get back to your employer.

KM: Yeah, but, I mean, the T.O.D.—I mean, Amy. She's your brother's fiancée.

MH: She's not here.

KM: But . . . Never mind.

MH: What you're saying is that in your opinion, the firing of Ida Lopez wasn't justified.

KM: That's not what I said. That's not what I said at all. Is that what I said?

MH: You said—excuse me, Miriam—It's wrong to fire somebody because they had one bad day.

KM: Well, it is. And okay, Mrs. Lopez had a bunch of bad days. But only because bad people—

MH: Like my brother.

KM: Oh my gosh. Is that the time? Really? Because I have to go.

MH: Go?

KM: Yes. I have to meet my broker.

MH: Your broker?

KM: My real-estate broker. See, I'm looking for an apartment, and it's kind of, you know, urgent that I find a place soon, because right now I'm, like, staying on my friend Jen's—I told you about Jen—well, I'm staying on her couch, but she and her husband, they're trying to have a baby, so I need to get out of there, and I was supposed to see this place last night but the broker never showed. But then she called and said if I could meet her at eleven this morning she'd let me in to see the place and so I really have to go, or if I can't go now I need to call her and see if I can meet her after work.

MH: Uh. Yeah. I guess . . . I guess we're through here. Maybe you could leave your contact information with Anne, so if I have any follow-up questions—

KM: Oh, sure. Thanks. It was nice to meet you. I hope I didn't say anything—I mean, I didn't mean to say anything bad about the *Journal*. Or your brother. I'm sure he's, you know. A very nice person.

MH: (*Indecipherable*) Don't worry about it. I'll show you the way out.

Hi, you've reached the voice mail of Jen Sadler. At the tone, please leave your name and number, and I'll get back to you as soon as I can. Bye!

(Tone)

Jen! It's Kate! Oh my God, you are never going to believe—no, I'm sorry. I don't have any spare change. Anyway, I went to that meeting this morning, you know, at Hertzog Webber and Doyle, and I—No, I really don't have any spare change, I'm so sorry. What was I saying? Oh, yeah. I met his brother—you know the T.O.D's fiancée—his brother—and oh my God, he's so cute . . . I can't believe I'm saying something like this about a lawyer . . . let alone a relative of Stuart Hertzog's—Look, here, this is all I've got. Take it. Go ahead. Take it. Oh, my God, I'm not sure this is the best neighborhood, and I don't know where the realtor is, and—No, I'm sorry, I gave all my money to that guy over there. Sorry. I—Oh, here's Paula, thank GOD. I'll call you later. Tell the T.O.D. I'll be back by noon. If I'm not knifed by a crackhead first.

(Click)

Journal of Kate Mackenzie

Oh my God, that apartment was so hideous, I would rather sleep on Jen's couch for the rest of my life than set foot in a place like that ever, ever again. What is WRONG with this city? It's like they penalize you if you're single and can't afford to pay two grand a month for decent housing. Like it's not enough of a stigma, not being in a romantic relationship. No, they have to make it a thousand times worse by making every studio apartment in the city be next door to an OTB and look out over an air shaft.

And oh my God, what did I say to Mitchell Hertzog? It's like I had diarrhea of the mouth, or something, I just kept talking and talking. WHAT IS WRONG WITH ME? I mean, like I don't have enough to worry about without jeopardizing my job, going around, saying the paper fires people unfairly.

It's just that he was so . . . cute! Why did he have to be so cute??? And nice . . . He wears ties his nieces buy for him!

Oh, why couldn't he have been an ogre, like his brother?

Wait a minute . . . he is. He IS an ogre, like his brother. Because what kind of person works for a place like that, a place that takes the side of corporate giants over poor little pie bakers like Mrs. Lopez? What kind of person would work for a place like that?

I know he's going to tell the T.O.D. what I said. Okay, well, maybe he won't—And I don't remember exactly what I said, anyway. Maybe I didn't say anything so bad. . . .

But somehow or other she's going to find out, and I'm going to get fired, and it will be all my own fault, and oh my God, I HATE lawyers, they ruin EVERYTHING for EVERYONE and oh, why did he have to be so cute?

✉

To: Dolly Vargas <dolly.vargas@thenyjournal.com>
Fr: Mitchell Hertzog <mitchell.hertzog@hwd.com>
Re: Kate Mackenzie

I Googled her, but got nada. What do you know about her? Spill it.
You owe me, remember?

Mitch

✉

To: Mitchell Hertzog <mitchell.hertzog@hwd.com>
Fr: Dolly Vargas <dolly.vargas@thenyjournal.com>
Re: Kate Mackenzie

Mitch, darling, what a surprise! How ARE you? It's been ages! I
don't think I ever did thank you properly for getting Julio out of that
little jam with Immigration . . . goodness, it pays to be friends with
a lawyer, doesn't it?

Let me see now, about Kate . . . Isn't that a coincidence? I happen
to be VERY well acquainted with her. She's my HR rep here at the
paper.

Look, why don't I call you in, say, five? I just got my tips done, and
all this typing is not exactly good for them.

Ciao for now. . . .

XXXOOO
Dolly

P.S. She really is a doll, isn't she?

Sleaterkinneyfan: Thank God you're back. It seemed like you were gone FOREVER. Now tell me about Stuart's cute brother. How cute is he? He doesn't have an abnormally large head, does he? It isn't a family trait?

Katydid: Are you CRAZY? Stop I.M.-ing. She's going to catch us. She's been all over me ever since I got in.

Sleaterkinneyfan: Whatever. I'll watch her, and if I see her log on, I'll signal you. So. His head. Cartoonishly gargantuan, or what? How's his butt?

Katydid: Totally normal-size head. I told you, he's cute. I mean, for a lawyer.

Sleaterkinneyfan: Koala-bear cute? Or tie-him-to-the-bed cute?

Katydid: You are sick. But I might tie him to the bed. If I had one. A bed, I mean.

Sleaterkinneyfan: Butt, please.

Katydid: I didn't look at his butt. Are you crazy? He's a LAWYER. I mean, what does it matter what kind of butt he has when he has a job taking advantage of the disenfranchised?

Sleaterkinneyfan: Since when is Ida Lopez disenfranchised? She's in a union, she makes more than I do, probably. Now I would like a description of his ass.

Katydid: What does it matter? It's not like he could ever be interested in me. I'm such a spaz. I mean, I started going off during my interview on this tangent about Dale. I didn't say his name, or anything—Dale's, I mean—but I don't know. Giving a deposition is WEIRD. It's so . . . personal. Everyone is looking at you. I mean, he was

	sitting right there, right across the table. I could have reached out and touched his hand. We DID touch hands at one point, when I spilled my coffee, and we both reached to wipe it off. He has really nice hands. And no wedding ring, either.
Sleaterkinneyfan:	WHO CARES ABOUT HIS HANDS? WHAT ABOUT HIS BUTT?
Katydid:	Okay, okay. Basic stats: height, about six one. Weight, you know, normal for being six one. He looked kind of . . . built, beneath the suit. It was kind of hard to tell. Plus everyone looks built compared to Dale. Nice suit, conservative, but coupled with a tie that had Rocky and Bullwinkle on it. . . .
Sleaterkinneyfan:	You lie.
Katydid:	I beg your pardon, but I do not. Rocky and Bullwinkle, as sure as I'm sitting here Instant Messaging you instead of working on the sexual harassment suit against Dolly Vargas. He says his nieces gave it to him. He's also got dark hair, kind of on the long side, you know, compared to Stuart's. I know because I ran into Stuart on my way out. Mitch is taller than Stuart. Also, his hair isn't thinning like Stuart's. Or graying. Also, he has this dimple in the middle of his chin. And green eyes. Really. Or maybe hazel. But they looked green. Did I say he had really nice hands?
Sleaterkinneyfan:	Butt, please.
Katydid:	I didn't look at his butt!!!!!!
Sleaterkinneyfan:	You lie.
Katydid:	Okay. I looked. It was roundly supple.
Sleaterkinneyfan:	Mmmmmmmmmm

Katydid:	Hey! You're married! You can't be mmm-ming other guys' butts!
Sleaterkinneyfan:	That's what *you* think. So. When are you going to see him again?
Katydid:	I'M NOT! HE'S A MEAN CORPORATE LAWYER. I DON'T DATE MEAN CORPORATE LAWYERS. Or anyone, for that matter. My life is in enough upheaval.
Sleaterkinneyfan:	I thought you said he has nice hands.
Katydid:	He does. But what does it matter? You remember how those guys in law school were back when we were in college. The keggers. The loafers with tassels. Please! And this one's the enemy, remember? He's out to get poor Mrs. Lopez! I could never date someone who made a living defending the likes of Peter Hargrave against the working-class slobs who are just trying to be treated fairly. No matter how tie-to-the-bed-able he might be.
Sleaterkinneyfan:	Liar.
Katydid:	I'm not lying!
Sleaterkinneyfan:	Ladies' room. Now.
Katydid:	No!
Sleaterkinneyfan:	Now. Someone's got to slap some sense into you, and as usual, it looks like that someone's gonna be me.
Sleaterkinneyfan:	logged off
Katydid:	logged off

✉

To: Amy Jenkins <amy.jenkins@thenyjournal.com>
Fr: Courtney Allington <courtney.allington@allingtoninvestments.com>
Re: Last night

Ames, he's a dream. You are SO lucky. And that ring . . . it's gorgeous. We have GOT to get together for brunch and introduce our guys. Brad will just ADORE him. And then maybe you two can come to Aspen with us next December!

Where are you honeymooning? You HAVE to go to St. Bart's. Brad's family has a villa out there. They rent it out when they're not using it—twenty thousand a week—but it comes with a full-time maid, cook, gardener, and chauffeur. It was divine, you simply have to go, it'll be the perfect place to crack out that Burberry bikini you bought at last week's BARNEY's sale. I'll ask Brad when the place is available.

Oh, your hair looks great. Are you still going to Bumble, or have you switched to Fekkai?

Love,
Courts

✉

To: Amy Jenkins <amy.jenkins@thenyjournal.com>
Fr: Heather van Giles Lester <h.vangileslester@vangilesltd.com>
Re: Mrs. Stuart Hertzog (!!!!)

Oh my God, you and Stuart are SO perfect together. He's tall and broad, and you're so petite. All that jogging is REALLY paying off, Ames. I can't believe you're the same little Ames who packed on all those pounds our frosh year. Then again, you DO have to watch it, coming from a heavy family. How are they, anyway? I hope they aren't still upset over that whole not-being-invited to graduation thing, are they? I mean, seriously, Ames, how COULD you have invited them? They wouldn't have fit at the table.

Anyway, just so you know, I went home and Googled Stuart—I know! I'm so bad!—and found out all about Hertzog Senior, and I'm telling you, you have nothing to worry about, the family's good for ten million at least, maybe even more, if you count the crazy mom's doll collection. They've got a condo in Scottsdale, and another in Tahoe, and a house in Ojai.

Girlfriend, you SCORED!!!

Let's do lunch next week. Oh, did you hear? Courts wants to throw an engagement party for you. But I've got dibs on the lingerie shower!

Kisses,
Heath

....

✉

To: Amy Jenkins <amy.jenkins@thenyjournal.com>
Fr: Mary Beth Kellogg Sneed<mbsneed@sneedenterprises.com>
Re: Congratulations

Ames, I'm so happy for you. He's a real sweetie—I love how he told off that waiter for bringing us the wrong year of that merlot (they really DO think they own the city, don't they?) And your ring is gorgeous. If you want to get matching diamond studs and a pendant, you HAVE to see John at Harry Winston. He's the BEST.

A few things you might want to consider, though: genetic testing . . . you know, just to make sure neither of you are carriers of anything nasty . . . although I'm sure you aren't. But you never know.

And secondly—his name. I mean, HERTZOG? See if he'd be willing to drop the OG. There is nothing wrong with being a Hertz, you know. . . . Look at Hertz rental cars.

Just a couple of things you might not have thought of.

Oh, you're going to be the most beautiful bride! The Pilates is really giving you definition in your upper arms, just like I said it would. I hope you'll enjoy this, the most magical time in your life. Every girl should be as pretty a bride as you're going to be, Ames! Let me know if you want help scheduling an appointment at Vera's. I know her cousin personally.

Toodles,
MB

THE NEW YORK JOURNAL
New York City's Leading Photo-Newspaper

Features Division
The New York Journal
216 W. 57th Street
New York, NY 10019

Human Resources Division
The New York Journal
216 W. 57th Street
New York, NY 10019

We, the undersigned, demand the immediate reinstatement of Ida Lopez to her post in Food Craft Services for the senior-staff dining room. We feel that her dismissal is detrimental to the temperament and overall well-being of the paper's staff. Additionally, this morning there were no muffins or scones to go with our coffee. Some of us were forced to go for Krispy Kreme doughnuts across the street. If pastries continue to be unavailable in the senior-staff dining room, and we are forced to continue to leave the building for Krispy Kremes, HR could find themselves looking at disastrously high insurance rates, due to personnel possibly being struck by buses and/or bicycle messengers while venturing from the building in search of breakfast treats.

Furthermore, the saturated fat content of a single glazed Krispy Kreme is approximately 22 grams, twice that of a whole bag of M&Ms. Continued ingestion of said Krispy Kremes could lead to catastrophic healthcare costs as *Journal* employees are felled by diabetes and/or heart disease.

In conclusion, reinstating Ida Lopez as dessert supplier of the senior staff dining room will save the company millions in health-care and insurance costs, and lower the cholesterol and overall discontent of the paper's staff. Please do what you can to see that Ida Lopez is returned to her post. Thank you.

Melissa Fuller-Trent
George Sanchez
Dolly Vargas
Tim Grabowksi
James Chu
Nadine Wilcock-Salerno

✉

To: Amy Jenkins <amy.jenkins@thenyjournal.com>
Fr: Penny Croft <penelope.croft@thenyjournal.com>
Re: Ida Lopez

Ms. Jenkins:

Mr. Hargrave was somewhat disturbed this morning when he went to the senior-staff dining room and found that Ida Lopez, who normally supplies and runs the dessert cart, was not present. He was even more disturbed when, upon inquiring as to the whereabouts of Mrs. Lopez, he learned she had been let go. Surely this isn't true? You may not be aware of the fact that Mr. Hargrave has quite a sweet tooth, and has become quite fond of Mrs. Lopez's cinnamon rolls. I do hope you can get to the truth of this matter, and let me know when we can expect Mrs. Lopez back at her cart.

Sincerely,

Penny Croft
Assistant to Peter Hargrave
Founder and CEO of
The New York Journal

✉

To: Mitchell Hertzog <mitchell.hertzog@hwd.com>
Fr: Stuart Hertzog <stuart.hertzog@hwd.com>
Re: Ida Lopez

I just received a phone call from Amy. She is extremely upset. She said she just discovered that you'd scheduled a pretrial discovery conference with one of her staff members.

You deposed one of Amy's employees this morning without checking with me first? After I specifically asked you to keep me informed on the status of the case, you went ahead and saw one of Amy's employees behind my back?

Don't think this is the last you're going to hear about this.

Stuart Hertzog, Senior Partner
Hertzog Webber and Doyle, Attorneys at Law
444 Madison Avenue, Suite 1505
New York, NY 10022
212-555-7900

....

✉

To: Stuart Hertzog <stuart.hertzog@hwd.com>
Fr: Mitchell Hertzog <mitchell.hertzog@hwd.com>
Re: Ida Lopez

Stuie, you need to relax. You're going to have a coronary if you keep carrying on this way over every little thing I do. I can give you some breathing exercises I learned from a yogi when I was in India, if you want.

You asked me to take this case for you, and I did. But if you want me to win it in my usual stellar manner, you're going to have to let me do things my own way.

What's the big deal, anyway? So I talked to one of your fiancée's employees without you—or Amy—being in attendance. What, the world is going to end now?

Oh, and when you speak to Dad about me, be sure to bring up—one more time—the thing about how I totaled your Beamer in the tenth grade. Because I really don't think you've run that one into the ground yet.

Give my love to Mom, too, when you speak to her. Which I assume you're going to do as soon as Dad doesn't pick up. You know he never answers his cell when he's on the green.

Mitch

....

✉

To: Stacy Trent <IH8BARNEY@Freemail.com>
Fr: Margaret Hertzog <margaret.hertzog@hwd.com>
Re: Your Brother

Stacy, I received a very disturbing phone call from your eldest brother just now. Apparently, Mitchell is up to his old tricks. He is giving Stuart a very hard time about his fiancée. (You did hear that Stuart is engaged? Janice says you told her. God knows no one in this family ever tells ME anything, but why should they, as I'm only their mother? But anyway, Stuart's marrying that nice Amy Jenkins he brought to your house for Thanksgiving.)

In any case, Stacy, as the only one in the family who has ever had a modicum of influence over Mitchell, I'm asking you—no, telling you— to please try to do something about Mitchell's attitude. He has upset his brother very, very much. And after everything we've been through this year with Janice—did you know she dyed her hair *green*? And is insisting we call her Sean? As if there were anything wrong with the name we gave her—I am very much looking forward to planning this wedding between Stuart and Amy. If anything should happen to put it in jeopardy, I'll probably have to be institutionalized. Please don't allow Mitchell to rob me of the single joy I have left in life.

With love,
Mom

Dear Katie,

Hello! I wanted to say thank you so much for all you have done for me. I know it is not your fault I was fired. So I baked this bundt cake for you. I hope you like it. I have enclosed the recipe. Since I know girls your age don't bake anymore, I tried to make it simple for you. I think if you try making this cake for any man, he will marry you in a second flat. But not that ex-boyfriend of yours, he is no good for you.

All my love,

Ida

1 pkge instant chocolate fudge pudding mix

1/2 cup cooking oil

4 eggs

1/2 cup sour cream

1/2 cup warm water

1 12-oz pkge chocolate chips, semisweet

1 pkge dark chocolate fudge or devil's food cake mix
(not with pudding added)

Grease and flour a bundt or angel food cake pan (use cocoa instead of flour to avoid white coating on cake).

Mix everything together except eggs and chips. Add eggs one at a time, mixing well. Fold in chips. Put in greased and floured bundt or angel food cake pan. Bake at 350° F for one hour. Let cool in pan for 10 minutes. Carefully insert a knife around the edge of the pan to loosen cake. Remove from pan and cool completely. Serve drizzled with melted dark chocolate or covered with powdered sugar.

Serves 12.

✉

To: Jen Sadler <jennifer.sadler@thenyjournal.com>
Fr: Kate Mackenzie <kathleen.mackenzie@thenyjournal.com>
Re: Cake

CAKE! Ida left me cake!
Come have some!

Kate

✉

To: Kate Mackenzie <kathleen.mackenzie@thenyjournal.com>
Fr: Jen Sadler <jennifer.sadler@thenyjournal.com>
Re: Cake

Um, I think that is the best thing I've ever eaten. Why do you get all the luck?

Oh no, here comes Reception . . . It's amazing how they can smell cake from seemingly miles away. They're like cadaver dogs, or something. Only they sniff out dessert.

✉

To: Jen Sadler <jennifer.sadler@thenyjournal.com>
Fr: Kate Mackenzie <kathleen.mackenzie@thenyjournal.com>
Re: Cake

THEY ATE ALL MY CAKE!!!!!!!!!

To: Kate Mackenzie <kathleen.mackenzie@thenyjournal.com>
Fr: Amy Jenkins <amy.jenkins@thenyjournal.com>
Re: Ida Lopez

Please forward I. Lopez's personnel file and all of its contents to me.

Please note that in the future, you are NOT to meet with Mitchell Hertzog, or anyone involved in the Lopez case, without myself present as well.

Please also note that as an employee of this corporation, you are forbidden from accepting gifts and/or food items from current or former clients. It is simply a matter of ethics, Kate. Kindly refuse Mrs. Lopez's cakes in the future.

Amy Denise Jenkins
Director
Human Resources
The New York Journal
216 W. 57th Street
New York, NY 10019
212-555-6890
amy.jenkins@thenyjournal.com

Katydid: Get this! Even if he didn't think I was a complete spaz and asked me out, I couldn't go. The T.O.D. says I can't meet with Mitchell Hertzog again unless she's present!!!!

Sleaterkinneyfan: Please. The T.O.D. can't even find last year's salary-increase recommendations. You really think she's going to know if you're seeing some guy?

Katydid: Still. Where does she get off? Also, she said I can't take any more cakes from Ida. If she makes me any more, that is.

Sleaterkinneyfan: In the ladies' you said you weren't interested in Mitch that way anyway, so what do you care? Except about the cake. That I can understand.

Katydid: I'm not. Interested in him. I mean, why should I be? He clearly thinks I'm this huge Kentuckian loser, the way I was dribbling on about . . . oh my God, chicken in garlic sauce. CHICKEN IN GARLIC SAUCE!!!!!!! I was going on and on about it. What is WRONG with me???

Sleaterkinneyfan: You know, the really amazing thing isn't that you dated Dale for ten years: It's that you two ever got together at all. With your self-esteem issues and his addiction to hallucinogens, you two so should have been voted Least Likely to Hook Up with Anyone, Ever.

Katydid: Hey! Come on!

Sleaterkinneyfan: Sorry. It's the hormones. I swear. But seriously, Kate. This is the first guy whose HANDS you've found attractive since you realized Dale wasn't Mr. Right after all. That has to mean something. I say, go for it.

Katydid:	Go for WHAT? I told you, I am ethically opposed to everything Mitchell Hertzog stands for. And besides which, he thinks I'm a spaz, and Amy says I can't see him again without her permission!
Sleaterkinneyfan:	Oh my God, haven't you been listening to a word I've said? Amy Jenkins is T.O.D., not G.O.D. She's not capable of tracking your every movement—
AmyJenkinsDir:	logged on
AmyJenkinsDir:	Ladies. Have I or have I not spoken to you about Instant Messaging during business hours?
Sleaterkinneyfan:	logged off
Katydid:	logged off
AmyJenkinsDir:	logged off
Sleaterkinneyfan:	logged on
Katydid:	logged on
Sleaterkinneyfan:	I hate her.
Katydid:	She's the one with the self-esteem issues.

THE NEW YORK JOURNAL
New York City's Leading Photo-Newspaper

Amy Denise Jenkins
Director
Human Resources
The New York Journal
216 W. 57th Street
New York, NY 10019
212-555-6890
amy.jenkins@thenyjournal.com

MEMO

To: All Administrative Staff, All Divisions
Fr: Amy Jenkins, Director, Human Resources
Re: Internet Code of Conduct—Statement of Company
Policy

Reminders:

Access to the Internet and the availability of e-mail has been provided for the benefit of employees of the *New York Journal* and its clients. It allows employees to connect to information resources and is a communication tool. Its purpose is for employees to conduct official company business, or to receive technical or analytical advice. E-mail may be used for business contacts and for inter-office communications. Every employee of the company has a responsibility to maintain and enhance the company's public image, and to use the Internet in a productive and professional manner. The following guidelines have been established for using the Internet and inter-office e-mail:

Acceptable Uses of the Internet

Employees accessing the Internet are representing the *Journal*. All communications should be professional. Reading reality-show recaps on *Televisionwithoutpity.com* is not a professional use of the Internet. Ditto rating people on *hotornot.com*. Use of the Internet must not disrupt the operation of the company network. It must not interfere with productivity. Employees are responsible for seeing that the Internet is used in an effective, ethical, and lawful manner.

Communications

Each employee is responsible for the content of all text, audio or images that they place or send over the Internet. Fraudulent, harassing, or obscene messages are prohibited. All messages communicated on the office network should have your name attached. No messages will be transmitted under an assumed name. No abusive, profane, or offensive language is transmitted through the system. Employees who wish to express personal opinions in e-mail may not do so using the Company system, nor during Company time under their own usernames.

Harassment

Harassment of any kind is prohibited. No messages with derogatory or inflammatory remarks about an individual or group's race, religion, national origin, political party affiliation, physical attributes, work performance, or sexual preference will be transmitted via the Company's network.

Violations

Violations of any guidelines herein may result in disciplinary action, up to and including termination.

✉

To: Jen Sadler <jennifer.sadler@thenyjournal.com>
Fr: Kate Mackenzie <kathleen.mackenzie@thenyjournal.com>
Re: Internet Code of Conduct—Statement of Company Policy

DO YOU THINK SHE'S TALKING ABOUT US?????
I think she's talking about US.

Kate

✉

To: Kate Mackenzie <kathleen.mackenzie@thenyjournal.com>
Fr: Jen Sadler <jennifer.sadler@thenyjournal.com>
Re: Internet Code of Conduct—Statement of Company Policy

Well, I highly doubt this was directed at Peter Hargrave.

Doesn't she realize she is slowly draining the life from us, until soon
we'll be nothing but dried husks, formerly known as personnel reps?

God, I wish she'd get hit by a bus.

J

P.S. You should go out with him. If he asks. Soulless-lawyer-for-
corporate-raider thing aside. He had on a Rocky and Bullwinkle
tie. Rocky and Bullwinkle!!!!

✉

To: Stacy Trent <IH8BARNEY@freemail.com>
Fr: Stuart Hertzog <stuart.hertzog@hwd.com>
Re: Mitch

Stacy, I know you have some—though not much—influence over Mitch. Still, that's more than I can say about anybody else in this family. Except for maybe Janice. But the last thing Mom wants is Janice talking to Mitch any more than she does already. Did you know the guy actually told her that a good way to keep her bhang from staining her dorm-room carpet is to Scotchguard the rug before she moves all her stuff in? What kind of person SAYS that to their nineteen-year-old sister?

It's no wonder she had to move back home.

Anyway, I would appreciate your talking to him about this case with the pie lady at the *Journal*. I asked him to take it because I'm personally involved. But Mitch seems to be . . . well, taking it far too seriously. To explain: I mean, he's already dragging Amy's employees into depos. He had a pretrial discovery conference with one of them this morning, and failed to notify either Amy or me: Amy and I didn't know anything about it! Worse, I think . . . I'm almost sure . . . he's interested in her. The employee. Not Amy.

You know that look he had in his eye when he came home from Kuala Lampur? Remember?

Well, I saw that same look in his eye when he was escorting the young lady in question out of Dad's conference room today.

Stacy, you have to do something. If he starts messing around with this girl . . . Well, let's just say Amy's job is already on the line because of this mess. Apparently, Peter Hargrave, the paper's owner, was a big fan of this pie lady's muffins, or something. But how was

I to know that? The woman was completely incompetent, and rude besides.

But if Mitch starts messing with this woman from Amy's office . . . it won't be just Amy who could lose her job. Dad'll probably have another coronary. I'm not kidding, Stace. The last thing Webber and Doyle are going to stand for is one of Dad's kids sticking his you-know-what in the company ink. . . .

So talk to him, would you? Tell him you don't think it's a good idea for him to start seeing anyone right now, with things so up in the air with Janice, Dad's heart condition, my wedding, and so forth. Remind him that it is *especially* unethical to start seeing someone who happens to be involved in one of the cases he's trying. Particularly THIS case. Which could get very, very ugly.

Thanks, Stace. I knew I could depend on you.

Love,
Stuart

Stuart Hertzog, Senior Partner
Hertzog Webber and Doyle, Attorneys at Law
444 Madison Avenue, Suite 1505
New York, NY 10022
212-555-7900

....

✉

To: Stuart Hertzog <stuart.hertzog@hwd.com>
Fr: Stacy Trent <IH8BARNEY@freemail.com>
Re: Mitch

First of all, Janice didn't "have to" move back home. Mom and Dad made her move back home, okay? They made her leave school, and for a reason that is so ludicrous, I don't even want to get into it with you.

Second of all, I will not be drawn in to whatever petty fight you and Mitch are having today. I'm sick of it. I have my own problems. Like how my son positively refuses to use his potty. Okay? Finding diapers big enough to fit a thirty-pound kid? THAT is a problem. Mitch making google eyes at your fiancée's employee? Not my problem.

Besides, what makes you think this is going to be like that time in Kuala Lampur? Mitch was nineteen when he lived in Kuala Lampur. That was ten years ago. I think he's matured a little since then.

So . . . I guess I should say congratulations on the whole wedding thing. So. Congratulations. Are you two planning on a big ceremony, or what? In the city, or here in Greenwich? Or at her family's place? Where's she from, anyway?

Stacy

....

✉

To: Stacy Trent <IH8BARNEY@freemail.com>
Fr: Stuart Hertzog <stuart.hertzog@hwd.com>
Re: Mitch

Stacy, you know how I never told on you that time you locked me in the trunk of Mom's Mercedes?

If you don't do something about Mitch, I will be forced to take more drastic measures.

And if you think Mom's going to leave you her antique Madame Alexander doll collection when she hears about that—especially considering the fact that I had an ear infection at the time—well, you're delusional.

Stuart

P.S. About the wedding, we're still working out the details. But definitely not in her hometown (she's from Texas) as she no longer speaks to her parents, due to a falling out back when she was in college.

Stuart Hertzog, Senior Partner
Hertzog Webber and Doyle, Attorneys at Law
444 Madison Avenue, Suite 1505
New York, NY 10022
212-555-7900

....

✉

To: Stuart Hertzog <stuart.hertzog@hwd.com>
Fr: Stacy Trent <IH8BARNEY@freemail.com>
Re: Mitch

I never wanted Mom's stupid Madame Alexander doll collection in the first place. I don't know where she ever got the idea I did.

P.S. How can someone who works in Human Resources not have spoken to her family since she was in college? I mean, isn't she supposed to be some kind of expert in human relations? To have gotten her job in the first place? And she can't even keep the lines of communication to her own family open?

Who is this girl anyway? Dr. Laura?

....

✉

To: Stacy Trent <IH8BARNEY@freemail.com>
Fr: Stuart Hertzog <stuart.hertzog@hwd.com>
Re: Mitch

All right, you might not want the Madame Alexander dolls (a collection appraised at over $50,000, but fine, if you don't want it, you don't want it).

But I assume you still want Mom to look after Haley, Brittany, and Little John when your anniversary rolls around next month. Weren't you two planning a little April-in-Paris getaway? I wonder how willing Mom's going to be to take in the grandkids when she hears how you wouldn't help me out with Mitch. . . .

I guess you could leave the kids with Jason's parents. . . . Oh, but wait. Isn't his father in jail? And his mother . . . Where is she again? Biarritz? With her third husband? Or is it her fourth? And didn't he just turn twenty-five?

Stuart

P.S. Amy happens to have numerous very loving and warm relationships. Just not with any of her blood relatives. But she gets along great with the families of many of her sorority sisters. Many of whom I met at the Monkey Bar last night, and who are eagerly looking forward to our wedding. Unlike, I might add, my own relations, whose congratulations have been perfunctory, at best. Janice still hasn't even called.

Stuart Hertzog, Senior Partner
Hertzog Webber and Doyle, Attorneys at Law
444 Madison Avenue, Suite 1505
New York, NY 10022
212-555-7900

....

✉

To: Stuart Hertzog <stuart.hertzog@hwd.com>
Fr: Stacy Trent <IH8BARNEY@freemail.com>
Re: Mitch

I hate you.

P.S. So does Janice.

✉

To: Mitchell Hertzog <mitchell.hertzog@hwd.com>
Fr: Stacy Trent <IH8BARNEY@Freemail.com>
Re: Stuart = Satan's Spawn

So. Heard from Mom and Stuart already. Sounds like you've had a busy day.

Stacy

✉

To: Stacy Trent <IH8BARNEY@Freemail.com>
Fr: Mitchell Hertzog <mitchell.hertzog@hwd.com>
Re: Stuart = Satan's Spawn

Busy, and profitable. There are times when I really, really love my job. Today would be one of those times.

Mitch

✉

To: Mitchell Hertzog <mitchell.hertzog@hwd.com>
Fr: Stacy Trent <IH8BARNEY@Freemail.com>
Re: Stuart = Satan's Spawn

I heard. Stuart did happen to mention that you deposed one of Amy Jenkins's oppressed flunkies this morning. I take it it went well. Stuart seems to think you found the flunkie . . . ahem, worth your valuable time. True? False? Or do you plead the Fifth?

Stace

✉

To: Stacy Trent <IH8BARNEY@Freemail.com>
Fr: Mitchell Hertzog <mitchell.hertzog@hwd.com>
Re: Uh-oh

Stuart's making you ask, huh? God, he's transparent. Well, you can tell him from me that I found his fiancée's employee most agreeable.

That ought to kill him.

Mitch

✉

To: Mitchell Hertzog <mitchell.hertzog@hwd.com>
Fr: Stacy Trent <IH8BARNEY@Freemail.com>
Re: Uh-oh

Oh my God. The last woman I heard you describe as agreeable was that stewardess you met in Kuala Lampur. And remember how THAT turned out?
Stace

P.S. Stuart's not the one I'm worried about. It's Dad, actually.

✉

To: Stacy Trent <IH8BARNEY@Freemail.com>
Fr: Mitchell Hertzog <mitchell.hertzog@hwd.com>
Re: Uh-oh

Yes, but I am older and wiser now, and no longer prone to be impressed by surgical enhancement.

Mitch

P.S. Since when does Dad care who I find agreeable? Since when does Dad care about anything except making par?

....

✉

To: Mitchell Hertzog <mitchell.hertzog@hwd.com>
Fr: Stacy Trent <IH8BARNEY@freemail.com>
Re: Uh-oh

Oh my God. You HAVE got it bad. What's her name?

Stace

P.S. Um, does a triple bypass just eight months ago ring a bell?

....

✉

To: Stacy Trent <IH8BARNEY@freemail.com>
Fr: Mitchell Hertzog <mitchell.hertzog@hwd.com>
Re: Uh-oh

Her name is Kate.

Tell Jason I went ahead and reserved an 8 A.M. tee time tomorrow for us at New Canaan. If you'll deign to let him out of the house. And I don't care if it's snowing, we're still going.

Mitch

P.S. Tell Stuart to mind his own business.

✉

To: Mitchell Hertzog <mitchell.hertzog@hwd.com>
Fr: Stacy Trent <IH8BARNEY@freemail.com>
Re: Kate

Screw tee times in New Canaan. Get back to the girl. I'm a house-wife with three kids, one of whom still isn't potty trained. To me, ro-mance is a quickie once a week while the kids are glued to SpongeBob SquarePants. If I'm lucky. Now spill it. What's she like? I thought you hated MBA types.

Stace

P.S. I did. He threatened to tell on me about the Mercedes thing.

✉

To: Stacy Trent <IH8BARNEY@freemail.com>
Fr: Mitchell Hertzog <mitchell.hertzog@hwd.com>
Re: Kate

No, I hate other lawyers. Besides, she isn't an MBA. She's a BA. In social work. And thanks for sharing that SpongeBob SquarePants thing. Because I really needed to know that about my big sister.

And in answer to your query, from what I could tell during the in-credibly brief interlude we shared this morning in Dad's conference room, and what I have gathered from a former client of mine who happens to know her, Kate is kind and pure of heart, and recently broke up with her no-good rock-musician boyfriend, and likes chicken with garlic sauce.

Oh, and she's blonde. And from Kentucky. And probably about as unlikely as any girl I've ever met ever to date a lawyer—especially one who works for a client like Peter Hargrave. Hope that helps.

Tell Jason they swear to me that the snow on the seventh green is melting. Also, if you want, I'll come over afterwards and teach Little John how to pitch. Just so he doesn't embarrass himself when he starts kindergarten, throwing like his dad. I mean, like a girl.

Mitch

P.S. The Mercedes thing? Again? Oh, what, and Mom threatened not to leave you her dolls?

....

✉

To: Mitchell Hertzog <mitchell.hertzog@hwd.com>
Fr: Stacy Trent <IH8BARNEY@freemail.com>
Re: Kate

Um, Mitch, not to burst your bubble, but Little John is two. Okay? He isn't going to start kindergarten for at least three more years.

But of course you're welcome to come by anytime. Fair warning, however: Jason's brother—Little John's namesake—and his wife Mel will be over in the afternoon with their new baby. I know how you tend to feel baby-overload if there is more than one set of Pampers in the room at a time, so I wanted to make sure you had time to prepare yourself mentally.

I know—why don't you ask Kate to come along? She probably doesn't like lawyers because she's never really known one. Once she gets to know you, she'll warm up to you. And what better way to show how sweet and cuddly lawyers can be than to see one in the bosom of his family? She could take the train up, and you can pick her up at the station after your golf game and bring her here. Then we can break out those expensive bottles of wine Stuart had his assistant send us for Christmas, and toast him and his bride-to-be. And it'll be really fun because Stuart and Amy won't actually BE here.

Come on, it'll be great. Say you'll invite her.

Stace

P.S. I'll be sure to pass your assessment of my husband's throwing skills on to him. I'm guessing he'll be immensely flattered.

P.P.S. Yes about the dolls.

....

✉

To: Stacy Trent <IH8BARNEY@freemail.com>
Fr: Mitchell Hertzog <mitchell.hertzog@hwd.com>
Re: Kate

Nice try, but if you think any guy is going to bring a girl he's only met once in a professional setting home to meet his family, then can I just say that you have been out of the singles scene for a very, very long time? No offense, Stace, but I think you and Jason need to dump the kids on Mom and grab a weekend in Miami or something. The whole quickie-during-Spongebob thing has warped your idea of what romance actually is.

Allow me to assure you that the chances of my bringing any girl out to meet you and Jason and the kids . . . not to mention some of your many in-laws—even decent ones like John and Mel—before we've even—

Well, you can forget about it.

And now I have to go over to the offices of our future sister-in-law to inquire of her, in person, why she hasn't returned any of my assistant's calls asking her to schedule an appointment for her pretrial discovery conference.

And if I should happen, upon my way there, to run into Kate, you'll undoubtedly hear all about it from Stuart, who'll get it from Amy, so why should I trouble myself?

See you tomorrow.

Mitch

P.S. Really, Stace. You've got to stop letting them push you around. I'll take care of the freaking kids while the two of you are in Paris next month. Okay?

P.P.S. Yeah, I knew. Mom's been talking about it nonstop. You think I am not aware that she's holding canceling on you like an anvil over your head? Relax. The kids love me. We'll have a blast. And that whole thing with Little John's first word—look, I told you, it just slipped out. The guy came at us from out of nowhere. It's a wonder we weren't killed. And wouldn't you rather your son's first word be of the four-letter variety than some boring Mamma or Dadda thing? Wouldn't you?

New York Journal Employee Incident Report

Name/Title of Reporter:
Carl Hopkins, Security Officer

Date/Time of Incident:
Friday, 3:30 P.M.

Place of Incident:
NY *Journal* Lobby

Persons Involved in Incident:
Dale Carter, no affiliation with the paper, 26
Mitchell Hertzog, outside legal counsel, 29
Kathleen Mackenzie, Human Resources, 25

Nature of Incident:
   D. Carter attempted to enter building to give large
      bouquet of roses to K. Mackenzie. C. Hopkins
      stopped D. Carter at security desk and told him to
      wait for K. Mackenzie to come down to sign him in.
   K. Mackenzie, when contacted, said would not come
      down.
   C. Hopkins told D. Carter to leave.
   D. Carter would not leave.
   D. Carter said would wait until K. Mackenzie exited
      building for the day.
   C. Hopkins informed D. Carter that no loitering in
      lobby allowed.
   D. Carter again said would not leave.
   D. Carter sat down in middle of lobby.
   C. Hopkins contacted K. Mackenzie. Told K.
      Mackenzie that D. Carter would not leave.

K. Mackenzie came downstairs.

K. Mackenzie asked D. Carter to leave.

D. Carter said would not leave until K. Mackenzie listened to his new song.

D. Carter began to sing song (Why Won't You Be With Me, Kate).

M. Hertzog entered building.

M. Hertzog approached K. Mackenzie.

M. Hertzog asked K. Mackenzie if there was a problem.

D. Carter finished song.

K. Mackenzie said Nice song now please leave.

D. Carter said would not leave until K. Mackenzie agreed to move back in with him.

M. Hertzog said I think the lady asked you to leave, now go.

D. Carter said Mind your own business.

M. Hertzog said Are you for real?

D. Carter said Try me and find out, Suit Boy.

K. Mackenzie told D. Carter if he did not leave she would notify local precinct and have D. Carter arrested for trespass.

D. Carter said did not care and would not leave until K. Mackenzie agreed to move back in with him. Also said would hit Suit Boy (M. Hertzog).

K. Mackenzie directed Security to notify local precinct.

Local precinct notified by C. Hopkins.

D. Carter began new song (Kate, Why Did You Leave Me)

Officers from local precinct arrived.

D. Carter finished song.

Crowd in lobby applauded.

D. Carter put under arrest by officers from local precinct.

D. Carter removed from premises by officers from local precinct.

Crowd in lobby booed.

K. Mackenzie requested D. Carter be listed as Persona Non Grata at 216 W. 57th Street.

PNG form filled out by C. Hopkins (see attached).

Follow-up:

Incident recorded, sent to A. Jenkins in Human Resources.

THE NEW YORK JOURNAL
New York City's Leading Photo-Newspaper

Security Division
The New York Journal
216 W. 57th Street
New York, NY 10019
212-555-6890

MEMO
To: All Personnel
Fr: Security Administration
Re: Persona Non Grata The *New York Journal*

<u>Persona Non Grata Notification</u>

Please note that the below-named individual has been classified as Persona Non Grata in 216 W. 57th Street as of the date of this notification, and will continue to remain so indefinitely. This individual is not to be allowed on or near the premises of 216 W. 57th Street at any time during the term of above sanction.

Name: Dale C. Carter
SS#: Unknown
Description: (place copy of ID picture if possible)
White male, 26 years of age
6 feet, 175 lbs
Blond hair, blue eyes
Seeks contact with Kathleen Mackenzie,
Personnel Rep, Human Resources, 3rd floor

This individual is not deemed dangerous, however, is prone to cause disturbances by singing and refusing to vacate premises when asked. Contact Security immediately upon sighting of above individual.

Journal of Kate Mackenzie

Oh my God, I can't believe it, I am totally MORTIFIED. I can't believe Dale did that. That seriously has to be the most humiliating thing that has ever happened to me in my life . . . except for maybe when I accidentally walked in on Jen and Craig going at it in the kitchen the other day. . . .I seriously need to find another place to live.

But anyway. About today. And in front of Stuart Hertzog's brother, too! I mean, he saw—and heard—the whole thing! Suit Boy! Dale actually called him that! He was just trying to help, and Dale called him Suit Boy!

He must think I'm a complete whack job now.

Or worse, he's probably feeling sorry for Dale. He's probably thinking I'm this cold-hearted bitch. "The guy wrote this great song about her and she won't even give him a second chance. Well, I certainly won't make the mistake of asking out someone as mean as she is."

God! Like I ever even had a hope that he might. Ask me out, I mean. I mean, look at me! I'm sitting in a phone booth—A PHONE BOOTH—in the lobby, hiding from my coworkers . . . and from him. What kind of freak does that? Hides in phone booths? I mean, besides Superman? And he doesn't hide in phone booths. He changes clothes in them. Only don't ask me how, there's barely enough room in here for me to move my pen, let alone put on a leotard.

Oh God, WHY can't I ever just behave like a normal person in front of cute guys? Why? Now any hope I might have had of passing myself off as a savvy career woman—not that I probably lost all chance at that during that depo I gave him (chicken in garlic sauce? What was I thinking???)—in front of him is totally gone. Not that I ever thought the two of us—I mean, Mitchell and I—God, it's so weird to think that he's Stuart Hertzog's brother.

Still, I mean, there's no denying the guy is cute, and I thought, well, I just thought, you know, if I saw him again, maybe . . .

Oh God, I don't know what I thought.

But I certainly never thought I'd be standing next to him in the lobby of my place of employment while I was listening to my ex-boyfriend singing about his heartache over my leaving him.

And now, frankly, whatever I thought is completely moot. I mean, cute, high-powered lawyers—even ones with Rocky and Bullwinkle ties given to them by their nieces—don't ask out girls whose lives are in COMPLETE AND UTTER DISARRAY, like mine.

✉

To: Jen Sadler <jennifer.sadler@thenyjournal.com>
Fr: Kate Mackenzie <kathleen.mackenzie@thenyjournal.com>
Re: What just happened downstairs

Please shoot me.

Kate

✉

To: Kate Mackenzie <kathleen.mackenzie@thenyjournal.com>
Fr: Jen Sadler <jennifer.sadler@thenyjournal.com>
Re: What just happened downstairs

Okay, normally I would be saying you are making a mountain out of a molehill, but this time, I think you really do have something to worry about. Is it true he really SANG?

J

✉

To: Jen Sadler <jennifer.sadler@thenyjournal.com>
Fr: Kate Mackenzie <kathleen.mackenzie@thenyjournal.com>
Re: What just happened downstairs

Oh yes, he sang. Jen, what am I going to do?

Kate

To: Kate Mackenzie <kathleen.mackenzie@thenyjournal.com>
Fr: Jen Sadler <jennifer.sadler@thenyjournal.com>
Re: What just happened downstairs

It IS kind of funny. I mean, if you look at it in a certain way. That Mitchell Hertzog should happened to have walked in at that very moment . . .

It's just so . . . you.

J

To: Jen Sadler <jennifer.sadler@thenyjournal.com>
Fr: Kate Mackenzie <kathleen.mackenzie@thenyjournal.com>
Re: What just happened downstairs

Oh, ha, ha, I'm laughing. WHY is it that I can never seem to project a cool and put-together demeanor, like Amy, in front of the people I most want to impress? I mean, do you have to have been born without a soul like the T.O.D. in order to achieve some semblance of professionalism in the workplace? Is that it?

Kate

To: Kate Mackenzie <kathleen.mackenzie@thenyjournal.com>
Fr: Jen Sadler <jennifer.sadler@thenyjournal.com>
Re: Why it is that you can never seem to project a cool and put-together demeanor

I don't know, but here's your big chance. HE just walked in. And may I just say, your description does not do him the slightest justice. I wouldn't have known him, if it hadn't been for the tie. The guy is HANDCUFF-to-the-bed hot!

....

✉

To: Jen Sadler <jennifer.sadler@thenyjournal.com>
Fr: Kate Mackenzie <kathleen.mackenzie@thenyjournal.com>
Re: He who?

What are you talking—OH MY GOD!!!!!!!!!!!
It's HIM!!!!!!!!!!!!
What is he DOING here??????????? Why is he going into AMY's office??????????

....

✉

To: Kate Mackenzie <kathleen.mackenzie@thenyjournal.com>
Fr: Jen Sadler <jennifer.sadler@thenyjournal.com>
Re: Mitchell Hertzog

I don't know what he's doing here—talking to the T.O.D. about the case, probably. But this is your big chance to show him you aren't the world's greatest spaz. Get up and go make some copies, or something. Shake that booty you've worked into such perfect shape running up and down the stairs to my apartment. Thank GOD you wore a skirt today. . . .

GO FILE SOMETHING!!!!!!!!! He's coming out of her office . . .

Go!!!!!!!!!! NOW!!!!!!!!!!!!

✉

To: Jen Sadler <jennifer.sadler@thenyjournal.com>
Fr: Kate Mackenzie <kathleen.mackenzie@thenyjournal.com>
Re: Mitchell Hertzog

EEEEEEEEEEEEEEEEEEEEEEEEEEEEEEEEEEEEEEEEEEEEEEE!!!!!!!!!!!!!!!!
!!!!

✉

To: Jen Sadler <jennifer.sadler@thenyjournal.com>
Fr: Tim Grabowksi <timothy.grabowski@thenyjournal.com>
Re: Mitchell Hertzog

Jen, my spies tell me that Stuart Hertzog's brother is in the Human
Resources offices at THIS VERY MOMENT. Also, that he was somehow involved in the incident in the lobby not too long ago, involv-
ing Kate Mackenzie and her ex. We have a bet going here in
Computers that he's going to ask Kate out, because there is nothing more appealing to a heterosexual male (or so I'm told) than a
woman who needs rescuing. And if there was ever a woman who
needs rescuing, it's Kate.

So. Dish. What's the verdict? Don't let me down, darlin', I got a
fifty riding on this. . . .

Tim

✉

To: Tim Grabowksi <timothy.grabowski@thenyjournal.com>
Fr: Jen Sadler <jennifer.sadler@thenyjournal.com>
Re: Mitchell Hertzog

Could you be more gay? Actually, he apparently came in to have a little powwow with the T.O.D. She looks pretty upset about it, so it must have been about Ida Lopez. You know she's been getting grief about that from the 25th floor. In fact, she's on the phone right now, probably to her fiancé, complaining about his brother's cavalier attitude.

Mitchell just came out of her office and bumped into Kate, who was on her way to the copier. They are exchanging pleasantries.

Will that win you your fifty? Wait, were you for or against?

ComputerGuy: SPILL! What're they saying now?

Sleaterkinneyfan: Tim! Is that you?

ComputerGuy: Who else would it be? No time for pleasantries. Of course I couldn't be more gay. I AM gay. Now what are they talking about? Has he asked her out yet?

Sleaterkinneyfan: Oh my God. You computer people have no life. Okay, wait, let me just lean over here a little. . . .

She's apologizing for the lobby scene. He's saying, "You mean guys don't show up in your lobby bearing roses and singing love ballads to you every day?"

ComputerGuy: Oooooooooooooo. Is it true he's over six feet tall and has a full head of hair?

Sleaterkinneyfan: Yes. And I should add, he's quite buff. For a lawyer.

ComputerGuy: WHY ARE ALL THE GOOD ONES STRAIGHT?????????

Sleaterkinneyfan: Now Kate's laughing. Oh, God, she's nervous as hell. She keeps tossing her hair.

ComputerGuy: Hair tossing is good. What now?

Sleaterkinneyfan: Shit! Kate's 4:30 appointment just walked in. Dolly Vargas.

ComputerGuy: NOOOOOOOOOOOOOOOOOOO!!!!!!!!!

Sleaterkinneyfan: Oh, yes. Like a heat-seeking missile, Dolly's already got Mitchell in her sights . . . she's centering on him . . . oh yes, and going in for the kill.

ComputerGuy: Abort! Abort! Don't just sit on your ass, Sadler! DO something!

Sleaterkinneyfan: What am I supposed to do, Tim? Dolly's the Style Editor. She's wearing stiletto boots with a freaking Prada leather trenchcoat, and knowing Dolly, I can't promise you she has anything on underneath it.

	The guy is going down. . . .
ComputerGuy:	Our fair Kate will prevail! Because she is modest and cares about others. . . . Aw, hell, because Dolly's pushing 40 and starting to look it.
Sleaterkinneyfan:	Wrong! He's leaving. With Dolly.
ComputerGuy:	No!!!!!!!! Has a date with our fair Kate been secured?
Sleaterkinneyfan:	Ew, Dolly's taking his arm. She is escorting him to elevators!
ComputerGuy:	HAS DATE BEEN SECURED?
Sleaterkinneyfan:	Can't let you know till after Kate's meeting with Dolly. . . . No . . . wait . . . Kate's looking this way. She's signaling. . . .
ComputerGuy:	WHAT?????? DON'T LEAVE US HANGING HERE.
Sleaterkinneyfan:	Negative. That's a negative. He did not ask her out. Repeat. He did not ask her out.
ComputerGuy:	The horror. Oh, the horror.
Sleaterkinneyfan:	Hey, we tried, okay? We'll get him next time, champ.
ComputerGuy:	Next time? I can't go through this again. Oh, God, I need a Campari.
	I am actually moist beneath the pits.
Sleaterkinneyfan:	Dolly is returning from elevators. She has a sly, cat-who-swallowed-canary look on her face. . . .
ComputerGuy:	Are you surprised? We all know she swallows.
Sleaterkinneyfan:	Ew! This conversation is over.
Sleaterkinneyfan:	logged off

To: Kate Mackenzie <kathleen.mackenzie@thenyjournal.com>
Fr: Dolly Vargas <dolly.vargas@thenyjournal.com>
Re: You

Katie, sweetie, it was LOVELY seeing you this afternoon. I didn't
know you were friends with Mitch Hertzog. Isn't he a lamb? He
helped me out of the most horrendous jam with one of my exes. . . .
I met him at a benefit for heart disease. Mitch, not the ex. Hertzog
Senior's a longtime Heart Association benefactor . . . although
more, I think, because he's hoping to benefit from the research himself more than because he actually wants to help others. Mitch is
the black sheep of the family—a *major* disappointment to his parents, from what I understand. You know, he worked for a few years
as a public defender. He tried very hard to give all manner of horrible people the vigorous defense they so badly needed but could
not afford. Something about giving back to the community.

Still, in spite of that little lapse in judgment, he's yummy. SO unlike
his loathsome older brother. Did I tell you Stuart Hertzog once
nearly got into a fistfight with a city councilwoman at a Trent (of the
Park Avenue Trents, darling—Stuart and Mitchell's sister is married
to one) fundraiser? A FISTFIGHT, darling . . . something about the
New York City school system, I can't remember what. I think Stuart
felt like, since he didn't have kids, why should he pay so much in
taxes for upkeep of the public school system? So the councilwoman
told him because the schools were educating today's children to be
tomorrow's doctors, and didn't he think he'd need healthcare in his
old age, and Stuart said over his dead body would he ever go to
a doctor who'd received a public-school education. Well, you can
see why she wanted to hit him).

Anyway, darling, why didn't you TELL me that you and your scruffy
little musician had broken up? I feel just awful, regaling you daily
with stories of my own romantic conquests, never knowing that you

were sitting there the whole time with your poor little heart all broken to bits. Is it true he caused that ruckus in the lobby today? I thought at the very least we'd had a bomb threat. But how perfectly ROMANTIC (if what I hear is true) that yummy Mitchell came to your rescue! Well, Mitch and the paper's crack security staff, anyway.

And what is this I hear about you sleeping on various people's couches since you left the little parasite—I mean, Dale? Sweetie, you're insane. Come stay with me and Peter! We have plenty of space—there's a guest room and everything. And you needn't worry . . . Peter's hardly ever there. He's got shared custody with the kiddies from the first wife . . . or maybe his second . . . well, anyway, he's only in our little pied-a-terre a few days a week. The rest of the time, he's in Scarsdale with the junior Hargraves. It'd be a THRILL to have a roomie. We can have oodles of girl talk, order in horrible fattening foods, and watch Candida Royale videos all night long. . . . Oh, say YES!

You can move in tonight. Peter's got some school function to attend with one of the kiddies. Let me know when you'll be coming by, so I can tell Xavier (the doorman, sweetie).

XXXOOO
Dolly

....

✉

To: Jen Sadler <jennifer.sadler@thenyjournal.com>
Fr: Kate Mackenzie <kathleen.mackenzie@thenyjournal.com>
Re: Tonight

Listen, DON'T GET UPSET, but Dolly Vargas has invited me to stay at her place for a few days, and I think I'm going to take her up on it. You and Craig deserve a break from houseguests. I mean, from what I saw in the kitchen the other day, you guys really need some privacy. . . .

I'll come home with you to pick up my stuff, then be out of your hair by 9, I SWEAR.

Kate

....

✉

To: Kate Mackenzie <kathleen.mackenzie@thenyjournal.com>
Fr: Jen Sadler <jennifer.sadler@thenyjournal.com>
Re: Tonight

Are you INSANE? You're moving in with DOLLY VARGAS????
Jesus, Kate, I know our couch isn't all that comfortable, but aren't you going a bit overboard? I mean, the woman was wearing a MINK VEST the other day. INDOORS.

I can understand your being tired of all the Ramen and wanting some lobster bisque, but really, Kate. Do you honestly think she's going to let you sit through an entire episode of *Charmed* without asking you a half million times if she looks fat in whatever new outfit she's planning on wearing to whatever fabulous party she's attending that night?

At least *I* let you get your daily dose of Alyssa Milano without interruption.

Come on. Stay. I know East End is tempting, but really, everybody here on West 83rd loves you, too.

J

To: Jen Sadler <jennifer.sadler@thenyjournal.com>
Fr: Kate Mackenzie <kathleen.mackenzie@thenyjournal.com>
Re: Nice Try

Come on. You know having me constantly underfoot is putting this total crimp in your baby-making. And I am perfectly aware of the fact that it's NCAA championship time, and that all Craig wants is his couch back.

Besides, maybe if I'm not there, Dale will stop, you know, terrorizing every delivery man who walks into your vestibule. And Dolly's got a doorman, so even if Dale finds out where I'm staying, it's not like he's going to be able to get into the building.

Really, Jen, it's just better for everybody, all around.

Well, except maybe for Dolly.

Is the T.O.D. still crying? Has anybody figured out what Mitch said to her?

Kate

To: Craig Sadler <csadler@terminator.com>
Fr: Jen Sadler <jennifer.sadler@thenyjournal.com>
Re: Tonight

Oh my God, you have got to do something!!!! Kate is threatening to move out! She's throwing herself on the mercy of the paper's Style Editor, Dolly Vargas. Dolly Vargas, who is sleeping with the founder and CEO of the paper I work for. While I'd like to think she's moving in with Dolly in order to subtly hint to Hargrave that he should hire back Ida Lopez and can the T.O.D., I can't help feeling she's doing it because our couch sucks so much.

E-mail her and tell her she's NOT getting in the way and that you want her to stay.

PLEASE?

J

....

✉

To: Jen Sadler <jennifer.sadler@thenyjournal.com>
Fr: Craig Sadler <csadler@terminator.com>
Re: Kate

Um, why would I want to do that? Convince Kate to stay, I mean? Don't get me wrong, I like Kate—of all your freaky friends, she is the ONLY one I could stand sleeping on my couch for the past four weeks.

But, Jen. It's been a month. I know Kate doesn't have much money and the NYC real estate scene is crazy. I am not blaming Kate AT ALL for not having been able to find a decent place to live. But I would really, really, really, really like to have my couch back.

And our privacy.

Come on, Jen. We're trying to make a baby here.

And frankly, this stuff with Dale? Getting REAL old, Jen. I mean, I had limited patience with him back in school, when he was always leaving those pizza boxes lying around and scratching his balls in front of everyone—like because the guy's a musician, he has some right not to act like a civilized human being.

The constant phone calls, notes slid under our door, harassment of our neighbors until they buzz him in, and, though you and Kate were at the movies at the time, his singing "Ice Weasels Gnaw My Brain" from the street at the top of his lungs? Not cute, gifted musician or no.

Let her go. Maybe she'll be able to convince this Hargrave guy to give YOU the T.O.D.'s job. Kate can be very persuasive, when she pulls that corn-fed Kentucky farmgirl thing.

Kate moving out is a GOOD thing, Jenny. Remember that. It's a GOOD thing.

Craig

From the Desk of
Kate Mackenzie

Hi, Amy. Your phone seems to be on send all calls. Tried knocking, but you didn't answer. Just wanted to let you know that I met with Dolly Vargas re: the Hector Montaya thing, and she's agreed to go through the sexual harassment workshop one more time. Hopefully third time will be the charm, and it will stick!

Hope you have a good weekend, and see you on Monday. And I'm so sorry, again, for what happened in the lobby this afternoon. I promise it won't happen again. At least, I don't think it will. Well, I hope it won't.

Kate

Kathleen A. Mackenzie
Personnel Representative, L–Z
Human Resources
The New York Journal
216 W. 57th Street
New York, NY 10019
212-555-6891
kathleen.mackenzie@thenyjournal.com

To: Mitch Hertzog <mitchell.hertzog@hwd.com>
Fr: Dolly Vargas <dolly.vargas@thenyjournal.com>
Re: Kate

Well, darling, it's all settled. She's coming over tonight. I feel positively *giddy* with self-congratulation at how easily I managed it. The girl is simply *desperate* for 8 hours of uninterrupted sleep.

I guess a month in someone's living room can do that to a person.

So tell me the truth—you owe me that much, because you know it isn't every day I open my doors to a human resources representative, even if she *is* a perfect treasure, with her "you all's" and "fixin' some suppers"—are you in love with her? Because I understand you only just met her, so maybe things are moving a little fast, even for me.

On the other hand, I perfectly understand the attraction. There's nothing a big hulking man like you finds harder to resist than little damsels in distress like our own Mayberry miss. Speaking of hulking . . . You've been working out, haven't you, sweetie? Don't try denying it. Are you still on that paraplegic basketball team, or whatever it is? The one where you pretend like you're in a wheelchair and play ball with all of those boys who really *are* in wheelchairs? Well, let me just say, it's working, you've got some real upper-body definition going on under that Tweety Bird tie or whatever it was you had on. I wish you'd ask Peter to join your little team, or whatever it is. He needs a hobby, poor thing.

And God knows, he could use the workout.

God! This is so FUN! Promise you won't break her heart, though. Because that would be a real buzz kill. Kind of like when Peter brings his kiddies over.

Oh, God, I've got the Prada show. Ciao for now.

XXXOOO
Dolly

....

✉

To: Dolly Vargas <dolly.vargas@thenyjournal.com>
Fr: Mitch Hertzog <mitchell.hertzog@hwd.com>
Re: Kate

There is no licentious motive behind my request that you offer Ms. Mackenzie a place to stay. She merely seems like a person who needs a helping hand . . . and *whose* hands are more competent than *yours*, Dolly?

Thanks again.

Mitch

....

✉

To: Mitchell Hertzog <mitchell.hertzog@hwd.com>
Fr: Stuart Hertzog <stuart.hertzog@hwd.com>
Re: Amy

Just what are you trying to do, anyway? You had no right to go to Amy's office today and attempt to intimidate her like that. She is a sweet young woman, not one of those hardened criminals you're used to dealing with. She will schedule an appointment with you for pretrial discovery when I say she can . . . and that will be when she is good and ready to, and not before.

And what is this letter you keep going on about? Amy keeps impeccable records, so whatever this letter is you keep nagging her about, I'm certain it's in that pie lady's file.

God, you are SUCH an asshole. I really thought Stacy might have been able to get through to you, but I see now that you're too far gone.

Which is a pity. You had real potential.

But now I know you're just as depraved as those pimps and murderers you helped put back out on the street.

Stuart Hertzog, Senior Partner
Hertzog Webber and Doyle, Attorneys at Law
444 Madison Avenue, Suite 1505
New York, NY 10022
212-555-7900

....

✉

To: Stuart Hertzog <stuart.hertzog@hwd.com>
Fr: Mitchell Hertzog <mitchell.hertzog@hwd.com>
Re: Amy

That's funny. I thought *you* were the depraved one. After all, aren't you the one who made your fiancée fire a woman, merely because she wouldn't give you a piece of pie?

Ms. Jenkins seems to be somewhat nervous concerning her case against Mrs. Lopez. I understand that while a verbal warning was issued, a written letter of warning, however, was not. I believe that, according to her collective bargaining agreement, the delivery— and acknowledgment—of such a letter is necessary before steps toward permanent dismissal can be taken.

But Mrs. Lopez says she never received such a letter. Strange, isn't it, that she was fired anyway?

And not to spoil your illusions, sporto, but your "sweet young girl" can fight her own battles. She has a mouth on her like a long-shoreman. She actually called me a fucker, if memory serves. . . . Oh, and wait, it does, since I taped our brief but oh-so-illuminating conversation in her office.

Hey, wouldn't it be fun if I played this tape for Mom? Oh, yeah! I'm going to give Mom a call right now!

Love ya
Mitch
aka The Fucker

Hello, you've reached the Hertzog residence. Margaret and Arthur can't come to the phone just now. Please leave a message, and one of us will be happy to get back to you.

(Tone)

Mom? Hi, it's Stuart. Listen, I just want to say . . . Well, Mitch says he's going to call you, and I just want to make sure you know, before he does, that the tape he says he's going to play for you . . . Well, it's fake. It's a fake, and—

(Click)

"Hello?"

"Mom?"

"No. It's Sean. Is that you, Stuart?"

"Yeah. Janice, let me talk to Mom."

"Mom's not here. And I've asked you before. Don't call me Janice. It's Sean."

"Okay, Sean, whatever. Just tell Mom when she gets home—"

"Hey, is it true?"

"Is what true?"

"About that Amy girl."

"You mean that I'm marrying her? Yeah, it's true. And I hope, Janice, that you'll join us on our special day—"

"No. I mean about her calling Mitch a fuckhead."

"Janice. Is the answering machine still recording?"

"Yeah. I think so."

"Hang up the phone, Janice."

"The name is Sean, I *told* you."

(Click)

✉

To: Jen Sadler <sleaterkinneyfan@freemail.com>
Fr: Kate Mackenzie <katydid@freemail.com>
Re: Paradise

Hey. It's me. I'm e-mailing you, and on a WEEKEND. That's because I'm e-mailing you from Dolly's laptop at her place, and she
has DSL. Oh my God, you guys would DIE if you saw this place.
Dolly lives in a penthouse, overlooking the East River. You can see
BOATS going by. BOATS.

And that's not all. She's got THREE bathrooms—THREE—and three
bedrooms, each the size of your living room, and a living room the
size of your whole apartment, and a terrace—a *terrace*—the size
of your building's roof. This place is SO NICE.

I mean, not that your place isn't nice. Because it totally is. Your
place is nice and comfy and lived in. I mean, seriously, that bean-
bag chair is way comfier than any of the chairs Dolly has.

But the cool thing about Dolly's place is that, you know. I'm not in
anybody's way. Not even Dolly's. Because she's never even here.

Well, I mean, she's here now. I can hear her shower running. But I
don't know what time she came rolling in. She went to some big party
last night. She wanted me to come, too, but I have to admit, I was kind
of more interested in her TV. Jen, she's got a 50-inch plasma screen
with HD and three hundred channels! And that's just in the living
room! In my room, there's a 36-incher, and even though it isn't HD,
it's still flat-screen. I found channels on it I'd never even HEARD of.

I know what you're probably saying. That I should have gone to
the party with Dolly. I mean, she even offered to let me borrow her
clothes. She had a leather halter top all laid out for me. Just like the
kind Alyssa Milano wears.

But I don't know. I just didn't feel like going to a party with a bunch of people I don't know. I know style editors do it all the time, but human resources representatives? Not so much. So I ordered in chicken in garlic sauce and watched the Travel Channel. Yeah! A whole channel, devoted to travel! Did you know that in Thailand, you can hail a public bus like you do a cab here in New York? Well, you can. You just stick out your hand and they stop for you. Could you imagine if we tried that here, with the M1? They would just mow us down.

Ooops, Dolly's coming out of her room. I mixed up a big batch of pancake batter, so I can fix her breakfast. I figure it's the least I can do because she's been so nice to—

Oh, wait a minute. That's not Dolly—

....

✉

To: Kate Mackenzie <katydid@freemail.com>
Fr: Jen Sadler <sleaterkinneyfan@freemail.com>
Re: Paradise

Oh my God, you can't leave me hanging like this. WHO IS IT?

Also, although you clearly aren't missing us, we're missing you. Craig's first words when he stumbled out of the bedroom this morning were, "What? No pancakes?"

See? You're missed.

So. Spill. Did you just have breakfast with PETER HARGRAVE, founder and CEO of the esteemed publication for which we work?

Tell me the truth: boxers or briefs?

J

To: Jen Sadler <sleaterkinneyfan@freemail.com>
Fr: Kate Mackenzie <katydid@freemail.com>
Re: Paradise

Um, no, I did not just have pancakes with Peter Hargrave. Because Peter Hargrave was not who just came wandering out of Dolly's bedroom. The person who just came wandering out of Dolly's bedroom was someone I've never seen before. He was about our age, with shoulders out to here, and probably one of the more attractive men I've seen in a while. Like model attractive. Which, if you like that kind of thing, can be nice. I guess. Although I wouldn't want to go out with someone who was prettier than me.

He just went, "Uh, hi," when he saw me . . .
AND THEN HE LEFT!!!
Just LEFT!!!!!!!!!!

I do not want to cast aspersions on Dolly's reputation, but I think . . . well, I think Peter Hargrave might have some competition.

Oops, here's Dolly. Explanation hopefully forthcoming.

Katie

⊠

To: Kate Mackenzie <katydid@freemail.com>
Fr: Jen Sadler <sleaterkinneyfan@freemail.com>
Re: Paradise

WHO WAS HE?????

And I just want to apologize for the fact that Craig and I were unable to provide you with plasma screens, the Travel Channel, your own bathroom, and a river view. Not to mention strange, broad-shouldered men wandering through the apartment on Saturday mornings.

Now. WHO WAS HE?????

....

✉

To: Jen Sadler <sleaterkinneyfan@freemail.com>
Fr: Kate Mackenzie <katydid@freemail.com>
Re: Paradise

Um, Dolly doesn't appear to know his name. She just calls him Skiboy. Because he is a skiing instructor.

She met him last night. SHE MET HIM LAST NIGHT!!!!! AND SLEPT WITH HIM ALREADY!!!!!!

I don't want to sound like some girl from Kentucky, but excuse me, what happened to getting to know someone before getting horizontal with them? She could have at least found out his NAME, for crying out loud.

But when I mentioned this to Dolly, she just went, "Who cares about his *name*, darling, when he's got those *shoulders?*"

And so Skiboy I'm afraid he is destined to remain.

I asked Dolly what about Peter Hargrave, and she told me she and Peter have had an open relationship ever since his third marriage.

Dolly really likes my pancakes. After this we are going jogging (!) around the reservoir in order to keep our girlish figures. Then we're going to some new opening at the Met. Want to join us?

Katie

P.S. Really, your place is much better than Dolly's. All she has in the fridge is champagne and yogurt. Really. I had to use Better Butter to make the pancakes, so they are a bit runny.

....

✉

To: Kate Mackenzie <katydid@freemail.com>
Fr: Jen Sadler <sleaterkinneyfan@freemail.com>
Re: Jogging

Um, thank you for the invitation, but I am trying to get pregnant, remember? The last thing I need is for my uterus to fall out, which is always what I fear is going to happen whenever I go jogging.

Have fun with your new little friend. Craig and I will probably just go to the movies, or something. Not all of us can lead glamorous jet-setting lives with Skiboys trailing in and out of our penthouse.

J

P.S. Dale left four messages on the machine and finally settled for throwing a can of Del Monte peaches with a note wrapped around it onto our fire escape. Do Del Monte peaches have some kind of symbolic meaning for the two of you? Or do you think he just couldn't find a brick? Anyway, near as I can decipher—his hand-writing is execrable, I suppose because he's a musical genius, or whatever—the note says:

> Katie, sorry about what happened at your office. Please don't be mad. I swear I'll never do it again. But I really need to know: Have you seen my bowling shoes? You know, those ones I accidentally wore home from

Chelsea Piers that one night? Because I really need them for a gig. They go great with my plaid pants.

Love always,
Dale

P.S. Who was that guy in the Bugs Bunny tie, or whatever it was, who kept looking like he wanted to hit me? Is he like your new boss or something? What happened to the T.O.D.? Anyway, I don't like that guy very much. That's all. Dale

Such a charmer. Hey, maybe Dolly'll share Skiboy with you! Have fun at the concert.

J

What is the sound of one hand clapping?
What is the weight of a single grain of
sand? The answer is: Equal to my interest
in the message you are about to leave.
So make it short.

(Tone)

Mitch. Oh my God. It's Stace. I never in
a million years expected him to just
stop by like that. I mean, he's never
done it before. It must be *her* influence.
I was totally at a loss. Trust Stuie not to
think he has to call first. I mean, who
wouldn't want the great Stuart Hertzog
to grace them with his presence? Anyway. What did he say to you, exactly,
out in the garage? Jason said he walked
in while he was putting his clubs away,
and you two were going at it. Jason says
he never saw anybody who looked more
like he wanted to take a swing at someone. Stuart, I mean. At you. Oh . . . No,
sweetie, I don't know where Mermaid
Barbie went. Did you leave her in the
hot tub again? Check there. . . . Anyway,
it was great to see you. You look good.
Call me back so we can talk bad about
her.

(Click)

What is the sound of one hand clapping?
What is the weight of a single grain of

sand? The answer is: Equal to my interest in the message you are about to leave. So make it short.

(Tone)

Mitchell. This is your mother speaking. I don't know what kind of game you think you're playing with your brother, but I can tell you I for one do not find it very amusing. Stuart is extremely, extremely hurt. I want you to call and apologize to him. It's bad enough that you're sullying Amy's reputation by implying she dismissed this muffin lady wrongly or without just cause. But just what, exactly, did you mean today when you asked her—in front of your sister, and her in-laws, and everyone, if I hear correctly—if the Pi Delts were going to perform any sort of initiation rites on Stuart? Were you implying that Pi Delta is some sort of Satanic group? Just because no Greek society would ever accept you as a member is no reason to malign the organization. Especially given that your own father was a Delta Upsilon. I am tired of having to clean up your messes, Mitchell. I want you to call your brother and apologize not only for the slight against Amy, but also for making up this ridiculous rumor that she called you a nasty name. So I want you to say you're sorry. That's all. Just pick up the phone and call your brother and say you're sorry. Don't think your father isn't going to hear about all of this, if you don't.

(Click)

What is the sound of one hand clapping?
What is the weight of a single grain of
sand? The answer is: Equal to my interest in the message you are about to
leave. So make it short.

(Tone)

It's Sean. Dude, you are in so much
trouble. I've never seen Mom so pissed
off. She says this is the last straw. She
says you're always putting her in the
middle, and that she feels like she has
to make a choice between you and Stuart, and she's choosing Stuart, because
she says you're mentally unstable. Oh,
and did Amy Jenkins really call you a
fuckhead? Dude, that is just *so* sweet.
Call me.

(Click)

What is the sound of one hand clapping?
What is the weight of a single grain of
sand? The answer is: Equal to my interest in the message you are about to
leave. So make it short.

(Tone)

I would thank you to keep your opinions
on the Greek system and my engagement to yourself, Mitch. You don't need
to be sharing them with Stacy's in-laws

and everyone else in Greenwich. Nobody's interested in your observations on the traditions of my fiancée's sorority. Furthermore, your assertion that Amy did not follow proper protocol when dismissing that idiot pie lady is completely absurd. As director of Human Resources, Amy can hire and fire whomever she chooses. I think you're forgetting just which side you're working for in this case. You are being employed by Peter Hargrave, NOT Ida Lopez. I'd thank you to remember it. And don't you ever, ever waltz into my fiancée's office and demand to see paperwork, as if she were one of those common criminals you used to defend and with whom, I'm told, you still occasionally socialize. Amy is a far better person than the sort you're used to, and deserves to be treated not just as a law-abiding citizen, but as a future member of your family. Understood?

God, I ask you to take on a simple case of wrongful termination, and you manage to turn it into some freaking conspiracy against the working man—my God, Mitch! Just do the job you were asked to do and stop overthinking everything, as you are so wont to do. Some people just deserve to lose their jobs, you know! Unless you want to be one of them, get off Amy's case. And don't even TRY to say that I couldn't get Dad to let you go if I wanted to. We both know who Dad's favorite is, and it's not you, buddy.

(Click)

✉

To: Stacy Trent <IH8BARNEY@freemail.com>
Fr: Mitchell Hertzog <mitchell.hertzog@hwd.com>
Re: Today

Tried to call but your line's been busy. This wouldn't have anything to do with Haley and Brittany's discovery of the Powerpuff Girls' hotline, would it?

Anyway, sorry to have caused tumult at Finca Trent. I don't know why Stuart got so bent out of shape. All I meant was that, back at U of Michigan, the Pi Delts had this practice of stripping naked any man who became engaged to one of their own, and leaving him chained that way to the Pi Delta sign in their sorority house's front yard, for the ogling of passersby. I just wondered, you know, if Amy's Pi Delt sisters were going to perform a similar act on Stuart, for the benefit of New Yorkers. I merely suggested that Stuart might be stripped and chained to the *New York Journal* sign outside 216 West 57th Street. I don't have the slightest idea why that would upset her so much. Do you? I mean, if you can't take the heat, hand back the lavaliere, is what I say.

Tell Jason I had a good time on the greens today . . . well, what you could see of them, beneath all the snow. Maybe going golfing in March isn't the best idea I've had recently.

Won't be around if you call later, I've got to go to some benefit at the museum for Dad. Can't say I mind, really. Rubbing shoulders with people who have more money than they know what to do with beats hanging out with people who can't stop talking about how adorable it was when little Taylor spat her ubby across the church at Richard Junior's christening.

No offense.

Mitch
aka The Fucker

Welcome to the opening of the Gregory Shearson French Nineteenth-Century Drawing Collection at the Metropolitan Museum of Art

Why did I come to this? Oh my God, I'm so bored, I think I'm going to die. I mean it's not like I

Entertainment provided by the Chamber Music Society of Lincoln Center

would rather be back at Dolly's watching the Travel Channel, because I wouldn't. At least, I don't

Gregory Shearson's collection touches on many of the trends in French drawing of the time: the heroic Neoclassicism of David; the refined classicism of Ingres; Delacroix's expressive Romanticism; the richly textured landscapes of the Barbizon School; Seurat's luminous sheets of shaded crayon; and the jewel-like watercolors of Paul Signac and Henri-Edmond Cross.

think I would. I don't know. If I were still with Dale, I'd be sitting in some smoky bar in the East Village right now, waiting for him to go on. Correction, I'd be running around the apartment, helping him find his bowling shoes, since the band wouldn't be going on until after midnight, and no way would Dale be ready to go by now. And I'm not saying I wouldn't rather be here, because this is way better than your typical East Village bar, I mean, no one smoking or asking if they can smell my hair. But I don't feel like I fit in, even with Dolly's borrowed duds.

The selection captures another facet of the taste of a great American collector famous for the range

and depth of his interest in the history of European art.

I mean, first of all there's the fact that my hair is way bigger than anybody else's here—but Dolly said it looks good curly. I *so* should have blown it out. And second of all, well, I think I am the only person here with less than ten grand in my 401K. I might be the only person here who even HAS a 401K—besides Dolly, I mean. I seem to be the only one here without a DATE. I mean, Dolly didn't exactly mention she was meeting up with Skiboy here. But there he was, waiting for her, right by the red carpet. And can I just say, his shoulders look even BROADER at nighttime.

**This exhibition was made possible by
a grant from the Gregory Shearson Foundation.**

Okay, one more champagne, and I am out of here. Where is that waiter? Where—OH MY GOD! OH MY GOD, WHAT IS *HE* DOING HERE?

AND WHO IS THAT *WITH* HIM? Oh my God, Mitchell Hertzog is here with a date. A DATE! Oh, and look at her. Just look at her. SHE had a blow-out. SHE didn't take the advice of the style editor for the *New York Journal. She* looks great. Well, if by "great" you mean seven feet tall and a hundred pounds. She actually looks like a praying mantis, if you ask me.

Oh God, why did I eat all those leftover cold sesame noodles for dinner?

Chamber Music Society of Lincoln Center program

Maybe I can slip out before he sees me with my hair like this. If I get behind that pillar

Quintet for Clarinet and Strings in A Major, K. 581...........Mozart

and slither over to the coat-check thingie, I can probably make it. Oh please God let me make it

Sextet for Clarinet, String Quartet and Piano..................Copland

NOOOOOOO! He's seen me! What do I—

Quintet for Two violins, Viola, Cello, and Piano in F Minor, Op. 34..Brahms

Why is it that every time I see Mitchell Hertzog I manage to make a total and complete ass of myself? If I'm not dribbling along about chicken in garlic sauce, I'm dealing with my lunatic ex-boyfriend or acting like I know something about art and classical music, when clearly, CLEARLY, I do not.

And he looked SO nice, too. I mean, really, really, really nice, in his tuxedo. He looked SKIBOY nice. Seriously, even Skiboy's shoulders paled in comparison to Mitchell Hertzog's.

He acted nice, too. He was all, "What are YOU doing here? I would've thought a girl like you would have something better to do than hang at a thing like this."

Like I was too glam for the place, or something. Ha, I wish. I told him I'd just come to keep Dolly company, on account of her having an extra ticket.

He looked around for Dolly, but of course she had gone off with Skiboy. The two of them were behind the cellist with their hands down each other's pants.

And then, me, idiot girl I am, I can't leave it at that. Oh, no. I keep foaming away at the mouth:

Me: Oh, yes, well, Dolly and I, we go way back. In fact, right now we're roomies, can you believe it?

Him: Roomies? Really? How did that happen?

Me: Well, you know, I'm between apartments right now, and Dolly, she has that big penthouse, way up on East Eightieth and East End Avenue and I don't know, she asked and I jumped. . . .

LAME LAME LAME LAME I'm sure the Praying Mantis is a better conversationalist. At least until she bites his head off after they're done mating (it's praying mantises that do this, right?)

Then he went, "Well, it's probably good you're in the penthouse. That way your musical friend might find it a little harder to serenade you. Since you don't seem to find his serenades all that appealing."

Dale! God! I'd managed to forget all about Dale. I'd managed to forget for a minute there that the last time I saw this man, I was begging the NYPD not to use their nightsticks on my psychotic ex.

"Oh," I said, trying to sound all—what's the word? Je ne sais quoi, I guess. I'm sure the Praying Mantis would know. "That. Yes. Thanks so much for your help with that, by the way. Um, Dale and I, we, well, we broke up, and he's not, um, taking it well."

And he went, "So I gathered. Listen, if you need anything, any kind of legal help with that, a restraining order, or something—"

Oh my God! He wants to help me get a restraining order! Against Dale! I mean, I probably should. Only I don't want Dale to go to jail. I just want him to go away.

But still. Like if I ever needed a restraining order, I'd go to HIM! I mean, Hertzog Webber and Doyle charge like five hundred bucks an hour, or something. Maybe even more. I could use up my entire savings account for what this guy charges in three hours.

But I swear to God, there I was, standing there thinking, "If I don't take him up on his offer, he'll think maybe I'm not serious about breaking up with Dale, and then he'll never ask me out."

Mitchell Hertzog, I mean.

Yeah. That's what I was thinking. About Mitch Hertzog. While I was standing there talking to him at an opening to which he had CLEARLY BROUGHT A LONG, BLONDE, SLINKY DATE! Who was staring right at me from over by the Ingres (which she did not exactly not resemble, if you get my drift. I wonder if Ingres used praying mantises as models for his subjects)!

God, I am pathetic. Give me a guy in a tux—even a guy who is clearly taken—and all I can seem to think about is sharing the Sunday Times and strolls through Central Park.

So then, just to make things REALLY awkward and lame, I laughed all breezily and went, "Well, you know, ha ha, I'm on a human-resources-department salary, I really doubt I could afford you."

Then Mitchell said the nicest thing. I mean, seriously, the nicest thing. He said, "I'd be happy to do it at no charge. Why don't you stop by my office on Monday and we'll talk about it? Say, lunchtime?"

But then he added, "I know a great place for chicken in garlic sauce."

I have to admit, for a minute I was so shocked I just stood there staring at him, probably with my mouth hanging open. I was trying to figure out what to do—whirl around and make a beeline for the door, or tell him where to get off—when it was like he realized I wasn't laughing and he poked my arm and went, "Whoa. Joke. That was a joke. What, they don't joke in human resources?"

And the thing is, the last thing I want to do is fall for a lawyer. And I seriously don't want to get a restraining order against Dale—I mean, he isn't a threat to me—my ego, maybe, but not my body.

But Mitch just smiled so nicely when he said the word joke, and he seemed sincerely to want to help me, and, well, he poked me. Like a friendly poke. How many lawyers give people friendly pokes? I mean, really?

And I will admit that maybe all of that—and the fact that the Praying Mantis was glaring so hard at me—caused me to, I don't know, lose my head all of a sudden. Because the next thing I knew, I was promising him I would do it, I would have lunch with him on Monday, even though he's a lawyer and his brother is the most heinous man in the world and he has a seven-feet-tall, hundred-pound girlfriend already and the T.O.D. SPECIFICALLY SAID I WAS NOT TO SEE MITCHELL HERTZOG AGAIN UNLESS SHE WAS PRESENT!

Except that I'm not meeting him about Mrs. Lopez. I'm meeting him about Dale. Which is, you know, totally un-work-related. Well, except for when Dale shows up at my workplace with a bouquet and a new song for me. But whatever.

I just thought that was the sweetest thing—I mean, this very high-powered lawyer, offering to help me with my stupid, boring problem. . . .

Well, I practically started crying right there on the spot. If he had offered me a lease on a studio apartment for nine fifty a month, utilities included, within walking distance of my office, I could not have been more touched.

And then of course, I had to go and ruin the moment by saying, "Well, okay, yeah . . ." and then because he was still standing there and I was still standing there and Miss Praying Mantis in a Dior wraparound evening dress was also still standing there, having seen the whole thing—you know, her date make a date with me, even though it wasn't really a date, because it was lunch, and work-related—for him, anyway—I couldn't just leave it, I had to be all, "Aren't you going to introduce me to your friend?"

And Mitchell looked kind of startled—really, like he'd forgotten she was even there—and went, "Oh, of course. Clarissa, this is Kate Mackenzie. I'm working with her on a breach-of-contract arbitration. Kate, this is Clarissa Doyle."

And then the Praying Mantis came slinking over and stuck her creepy overlong Ingres-like hand at me and went, "So nice to meet you. You must be with Substantiated Oil, then," and I went, "Um, no. The New York Journal. Mitchell—I mean, Mr. Hertzog—I mean, Mitchell—is helping us with a wrongful termination suit."

Which of course caused the Praying Mantis to just look at me and go, "Breach of contract, you mean. There is no wrongful termination in the state of New York." And then she looked at Mitchell from beneath her eyelashes—she must spend a fortune at Sephora because they were super long . . . her eyelashes, I mean—and then there was one of those embarrassing silences, during which I guessed that Mitch must have met Clarissa through work.

And then I put two and two together, and remembered that the name of Mitch's firm was Hertzog Webber and Doyle, and that Clarissa had to be the Doyle. Or a Doyle, anyway. And then I thought how happy, you know, it would probably make everybody, if she and Mitchell got married, because then they could start a little lawyer empire, like France, or something, and then, I don't know, the thought of it made me wish I hadn't drunk so much champagne, because suddenly I got a very bad headache, which I guess Mitch must have noticed, since he went, "Are you all right, Kate?"

I said I was, because, you know, you have to lie about that kind of thing, and then, to deflect the attention off me, I asked him how his family liked Amy, although I almost called her the T.O.D.

"Uh, everyone seems to like her just fine," Mitch said. "Are you sure you're all right?"

"Just peachy," I said. I couldn't believe those words came out of my mouth. But there they were, floating like a bubble over my head, like in a Peanuts cartoon. It was as though even Clarissa was stretching her Praying Mantis neck to look at them.

And of course that only made my headache about ten times worse, and the damn Brahms didn't help much, either.

Then it was like a nuclear bomb went off inside my head, because who should I see standing not twenty feet away but Stuart Hertzog and the T.O.D.!!!!

I about swallowed my tongue. I mean, if the T.O.D. caught me fraternizing with Mitch, after expressly forbidding me from doing so, I would be demoted to the mailroom quicker than you could say Staff Assistance Program. . . .

I don't think Mitchell saw them, but he saw my face, and all of a sudden, he went, "Kate, you look done for. Let me get your coat and a cab home. Clarissa can tell Dolly you decided to go on home without her."

To which Clarissa replied, looking more like a Praying Mantis than ever, "Yes, of course I will."

And even though I was all, "No, it's all right," he got my coat tag from me. I have to say, I didn't exactly fight him on the whole getting-me-out-of-there, and-fast thing. We managed to slip right by the T.O.D. without her even noticing (she was busy picking at an hors d'oeuvre and I think mentally tabulating how long she'd have to work out on her treadmill before she'd burn off all the calories in it).

Anyway, next thing I know, Mitch and I were standing in the drizzle in front of the Met, and he was flagging down a cab for me.

"It must be the champagne," I said lamely, because I didn't want to admit that it was the sight of my boss that had caused me to go green around the gills. Because, you know, after all, my boss is his future sister-in-law, and even if he will eventually find out for himself how heinous she is, I can't be the one to tell him. "Really, I'm not used to it. And Dolly and I went on a run around the reservoir today, and I'm not used to that, either, and . . . It must have been the champagne."

And then Mitch said, "Really? I thought it was the crowd, myself. I can't stand all the glad-handing."

And then a cab pulled up, and Mitch opened the door for me and put me inside and told the driver where to go. Then he looked at me, and went, "See you on Monday, Kate."

I had time to say only, "See you on Monday, and thanks—" before he shut the door on me. And then the driver took me home.

And so now I'm lying here—Dolly and Skiboy aren't back yet. Maybe they won't come back tonight. Maybe they'll go to his place. Though I can't imagine Skiboy's place is better than Dolly's—and I'm wondering to myself . . .

Well, just how did Mitch Hertzog know Dolly's exact address, anyway? Because he did. He gave it to the cab driver.

I wonder if HE ever wandered around this place in his tightie whities.

No. Surely not. He is definitely a boxers man.

To: Mitchell Hertzog <mitchell.hertzog@hwd.com>
Fr: Clarissa Doyle <clarissa.doyle@hwd.com>
Re: Your little waif

Well, haven't you gone all Galahad. Your little Lady Elaine is adorable. But you ought to tell her it isn't good form to leave the ball before midnight. She missed all the fireworks between you and Stuart. What WAS he so upset about?

I can't say much for that creature he's marrying. She looks like somebody shoved a Manolo Blahnik up her ass.

When you can drag yourself away from Cinderella, sweet prince, do you think you could give me a call about the Brinker-Hoffman case?

C

To: Mitchell Hertzog <mitchell.hertzog@hwd.com>
Fr: Haley and Brittany <WELUVBARNEY@trentcapital.com>
Re: You

Uncle Mitch! We had fun yesterday. You should come over more often. We really liked how red you made Uncle Stuart's face, when he was yelling at you in the garage. Can you do that again, next time you come?

So Uncle Stuart is marrying that lady? Mom says she's going to be our aunt Amy. She's okay, except she wouldn't try any peanut butter M&M chocolate chip fudge cookies. They were good—you ate five, remember? But she said she was on a special diet, and couldn't eat something called carbs. We told her we didn't put any carbs in our cookies, just M&Ms, but she said M&Ms were carbs.

Uncle Mitch, what's carbs?

Well, that's all. Thank you for the Barbie video, we put it on and turned it up REAL loud this morning, just like you said. You were right: Daddy does look funny when he runs downstairs screaming with his hair all standing up.

Love,
Haley and Brittany
(and Little John, too little to work the computer)

....

✉

To: Mitchell Hertzog <mitchell.hertzog@hwd.com>
Fr: Stacy Trent <IH8BARNEY@freemail.com>
Re: You

Heard from Stuie this morning. He says he saw you at the museum last night with Clarissa Doyle. Tell me you two are not dating again. I thought you guys figured out you were completely incompatible way back in 9th grade, when she deflowered you behind the pool house.

Naughty.

Stace

Hi, you've reached Kate and Dale. We can't come to the phone right now, but please leave a message at the tone, and we'll get back to you.

(Tone)

Hi, Katie! It's Mom again! You never returned my call. I just wanted to let you know, Charlie and I are in Sante Fe. Sante Fe, New Mexico. Oh, it's just lovely here, you and Dale have to come visit us sometime. The air is so—

"H-hello?"

"Hello? Dale? Is that you? It's Carol, Dale."

"Oh. Mrs. Mackenzie. Hey. How's it going."

"Did I wake you, Dale? I'm so sorry. The time difference. Let's see, it's noon here, which means it must be . . . three in the afternoon there. Dale, what are you still doing in bed at three in the afternoon?"

"I had a gig last night. I didn't get home till five."

"Oh. I see. Well. Is Katie there? Let me talk to Katie, and you can go back to sleep."

"Mrs. M., Katie moved out."

"What?"

"Yeah. Like a month ago."

"Katie moved OUT?"

"Yeah. I thought . . . you mean, you haven't heard from her?"

"No. No, not since Colorado. Right, Charlie? Didn't we talk to Katie in Denver? But that was only last week, and she didn't say anything about—"

"She probably didn't want to worry you."

"Oh. Oh, dear, you're probably right. Well, what happened, Dale? Did you two have a fight?"

"Yeah. I guess so. I don't know. She started talking all crazy about marriage, and wasting the best years of her life, and wanting a commitment and shit. But you know, Mrs. M. I gotta take it one day at a time."

"Well, of course you do, Dale. You don't want to be tied down, any more than I want to be tied down, or Charlie. That's why we're driving cross-country, never staying in any one place too long. But you know, Katie's always been a little on the conventional side. She never liked it when we traveled, not even the time we went to Disneyworld."

"Yeah. She said she wouldn't go on tour with us. If we ever get a tour, I mean."

"Hmmm. That sounds like Kate. Well, tell you what, Dale. Give me her number. Is she staying with Jen? I'll give her a call—"

"She *was* staying with Jen. But Jen said she moved out. So now I don't know where she's staying."

"Wait a minute. You don't know where Kate is?"

"No. And Jen won't tell me. On account of how I did something kinda dumb the other day. I mean, I thought it was the kinda thing Kate'd want me to do, kinda romantic and shit. But I guess she didn't think it was so romantic, since she had 'em call the cops on me. . . ."

"Just give me Jen's number, Dale. I'm sure Jen'll tell me where Katie is staying. And Dale, really, try not to take this too personally. You and Katie were meant for each other. I mean, you haven't been together since the eleventh grade for nothing, now, have you?"

"Naw. I guess not. Okay. Jen's number is 555-1324. That's 212. And Mrs. M.?"

"Yes, Dale?"

"If you talk to Kate, tell her . . . tell her I love her. I mean, I can't be who she wants me to be—'cause I can only be myself. You know? But I still love her."

"Of course I'll tell her, Dale. That is just so sweet—"

"And can you ask her where she put the coffee filters? 'Cause like, we can't find 'em anywhere. We've been using a pair of Scroggs's socks, and socks don't make real good coffee filters, it turns out."

"Of course I'll ask her, Dale. Love you. Buh-bye!"

"Bye."

(Click)

To: Kate Mackenzie <katydid@freemail.com>
Fr: Jen Sadler <sleaterkinneyfan@freemail.com
Re: Your mother

Bad news: your mom just called. She finally reached Dale, and he told her you two split up. She sounds really upset. I told her I don't have your number, but that I could get it. I said I left it at work. A little fib, I know, but hey, it doesn't hurt anyone, and it buys you some time.

So. What do you want me to do? I tried calling you, but the line's been busy for hours. What are you guys doing over there? Pranking all the eligible bachelors in New York?

J

To: Jen Sadler <sleaterkinneyfan@freemail.com
Fr: Kate Mackenzie <katydid@freemail.com>
Re: My mom

Aaargh. I knew she'd figure it out sooner or later. She LOVES Dale. I am never going to hear the end of this one.

I had to take the phone off the hook, because Dolly and Skiboy are still asleep. Or at least, they're still in her bedroom. With the door closed.

Whatever, you don't have to give her this number. She can call me at work tomorrow. I mean, now that the cat's out of the bag.

So. Did you and Craig have fun without me this weekend?

✉

To: Jen Sadler <sleaterkinneyfan@freemail.com>
Fr: Kate Mackenzie <katydid@freemail.com>
Re: Peter H Alert!!!!

Peter just came in! I'm serious! And Dolly is still in bed with Skiboy! I'm doing my best to distract him—he seemed a little surprised to see me here—but I'm running out of stuff to do. I already showed him how I can play "Slave for U" on Dolly's baby grand.

Now he's poking around, looking for the mail. Any second now, he's going to burst in on Dolly, and then there'll be murdered Skiboy everywhere! Or at least an awkward silence. What do I—

Too late.

✉

To: Kate Mackenzie <katydid@freemail.com>
Fr: Jen Sadler <sleaterkinneyfan@freemail.com>
Re: Peter H Alert!!!!

DON'T LEAVE ME HANGING HERE!!!! WHAT HAPPENED????

✉

To: Jen Sadler <sleaterkinneyfan@freemail.com>
Fr: Kate Mackenzie <katydid@freemail.com>
Re: Peter H Alert!!!!

Well. Guess what? It turns out Skiboy is MY boyfriend. Who knew?

At least, that's Dolly's story, and she seems to be sticking to it.

Though what MY boyfriend was doing in DOLLY's shower is a mystery—but apparently not one Peter Hargrave feels necessary to get to the bottom of. He and Dolly are currently snuggled up on the couch, reading the Sunday *Times* and making fun of it. Skiboy kept shooting them dirty looks until I finally told him I had to go to Pilates (!) and kissed him good-bye.

I don't know how much longer I can take this. I mean, Peter Hargrave OWNS my place of work. Can I really go around lying to him like this?

I guess, for free rent, it's a small price to pay. Still, I snagged the Real Estate section, and am going to hit the streets in a bit. There are a lot of studios I can afford, it turns out . . . in NEW JERSEY!!!!

TTYL
Kate

East 94th St.—rent-stabilized studio,
no fee, no appl. fee, no ba.
Steps from Central Park,
prewar building, hi ceils,
windows in kit. & bath,
live-in super, $1395 imm.
212-555-9966

Taken. Of course.

1 AVE/OFF HOUSTON NO FEE
BRITE AND AIRY STU $1095
All units have marble bath,
HWF, new appl.'s and video intercom.
Call Armand 212-555-1790

Fee.

27th St. East, charming studio $1395
Recent Renov. Hi ceils, large closet,
hwd. flrs, all appl.'s new,
OPEN HOUSE TODAY
call for appt. 646-555-0650

Taken.

Ave. A off Houston low fee,
500 sq ft studio, $1300
hwdflrs, sep kitchen, D/W
call 212-555-0003

LIES! ALL LIES!!!!!!!!!!!
Oh God, I hate everyone. Wish I was dead.

✉

To: Kate Mackenzie <katydid@freemail.com>
Fr: Dale Carter <imnotmakinganymoresandwiches@freemail.com>
Re: Us

Hey. Scroggs's brother is letting me borrow his computer. I'm still allowed to e-mail you, aren't I? I mean, I know you won't take my calls. And I guess you don't like me dropping by your office, either.

But the thing is, Kate, I gotta talk to you. I mean, this is really messed up. I'm not used to not having you around. It's like . . . weird.

And okay, I know I screwed things up, but I think you're being a little harsh with this whole moving out thing. I mean, come on, Kate. You're my—what's it called—my lodestone. I can't think about anything but you. It fully blows. I mean, remember when we were back in Luxor and we were all dreaming about coming to New York, how great it was going to be, and all? Well, I realize it didn't turn out to be all that great, but Kate, it still can be. To-morrow the guys and I are signing our record deal. We're gonna be RICH, Kate. But it's like I can't even get jazzed about the bling, because you won't be there to help me spend it.

I know I can't give you what you want, Kate, but we could still have a really, really, really good time. I mean, the record company, they own a place in Baha. BAHA, babe! Think about it.

Well, anyway. That's it. Peace out, and don't let the man keep you down.

Dale

To: Dale Carter <imnotmakinganymoresandwiches@freemail.com>
Fr: Kate Mackenzie <katydid@freemail.com>
Re: You

Touchstone, not lodestone. Baja, not Baha. And you can't spend bling. Bling is what you spend money *on*.

Dale, trust me on this. I have come to the conclusion that I am just not cut out to be a rock musician's girlfriend. I'm not sure what I'm supposed to be instead. But I'm pretty sure it doesn't involve going to Baja. I'm sorry, but that's just the way it is. The sooner you accept that and move on, the happier you'll be, Dale.

Love,
Kate

To: Devon Hildenbrandt
      <devonhildenbrandt@hildenbrandtindustries.com>
Fr: Amy Jenkins <amy.jenkins@thenyjournal.com>
Re: The earrings

Devon, you're a goddess. Thanks so much for the loan of your sapphires for last night. They looked perfect with my Barney's shell.

Sorry I missed you at the soiree, but the place was packed. Did you see who WAS there, though? The supermodel Vivica! Although I thought she looked a little bit fat in that dress, didn't you?

Anyway, I had a blast . . . except for the fact that I caught a glimpse of one of my employees there . . . one I've been having particular problems with lately. She's apparently all cozied up with Dolly Vargas, the style editor. You know, it can be a little aggravating . . . I've worked at the *Journal* for almost five years, and I've never been asked out for so much as a cup of coffee with any of the editors, let alone anyone else on the staff. Well, I guess it just goes to show, you can pick your friends, but not your coworkers. Still, it's a little irksome. She's only been working for me for less than a year, but already she knows more people than I do.

But whatever. Like I was saying, thanks for the loan of the earrings. Fair warning: I'm going to be asking for a similar pair from Stuart for our first anniversary. They should go great with the sapphire cocktail ring I'll be expecting after the birth of Stuart Jr., LOL!

I'll see you at next week's cocktail hour—it's at Pop downtown, right? I'll get your sapphires back to you then.

Kisses,
Amy

Amy Denise Jenkins
Director
Human Resources
The New York Journal
216 W. 57th Street
New York, NY 10019
212-555-6890
amy.jenkins@thenyjournal.com

✉

To: Stacy Trent <IH8BARNEY@freemail.com>
Fr: Mitchell Hertzog <mitchell.hertzog@hwd.com>
Re: Clarissa

What Clarissa and I did or did not do in that pool house is none of your concern. I went to the opening the other night because her current flame—some investment banker—is out of town, and she asked me to go with her, and as Michigan wasn't playing, I thought, why not? I like art as much as the next guy.

So tell Mom not to get her hopes up. There's not going to be any double wedding for me and Stuart.

Now, if you will excuse me, I have a week's worth of Travel Channel to catch up with.

The Fucker

✉

To: Kate Mackenzie <kathleen.mackenzie@thenyjournal.com>
Fr: Amy Jenkins <amy.jenkins@thenyjournal.com>
Re: Dress Code

Kate, as I'm sure you're aware, we at the *Journal* do try to maintain a professional demeanor.

That said, I don't feel that the skirt you're wearing this morning is quite an appropriate length for the office. Please see that it is taken out of the weekly rotation from this day forward.

Amy

Amy Denise Jenkins
Director
Human Resources
The New York Journal
216 W. 57th Street
New York, NY 10019
212-555-6890
amy.jenkins@thenyjournal.com

This e-mail is intended only for the use of the individual to which it is addressed and may contain information that is privileged and confidential. If you are not the intended recipient, you are hereby notified that you have received this transmission in error; any review, dissemination, distribution, or copying of this transmission is prohibited. If you have received this communication in error, please notify us immediately by reply e-mail and delete this message and all of its attachments.

Katydid:	The T.O.D. says my skirt is not appropriate officewear!
Sleaterkinneyfan:	NO!!! What is wrong with that skirt? I'll admit, it's a bit on the short side, but I think you look adorable! The T.O.D. is just jealous because she doesn't have the guts—or the imagination—to wear anything shorter than knee length.
Katydid:	Either that or she just straight-out hates me. Dolly loaned this skirt to me. It's Dolce and Gabbana! Suede!
Sleaterkinneyfan:	I know how you are about suede. And joy of joys, no one has peed on that one. Unless Skiboy . . . No, that is going too far. Any particular reason you are clad in Dolly-wear today? Or did she stop you at the door and force it on you?
Katydid:	Well, I AM having lunch with Mitch Hertzog. But it is a BUSINESS lunch.
Sleaterkinneyfan:	I have bad news for you. That isn't a very businessy skirt. Are you sure Dolly got the part about its being a business lunch?
Katydid:	I explained to her that Mitch and I are meeting to discuss taking out a restraining order against Dale—
Sleaterkinneyfan:	Oh. Well, in that case, it all makes sense. That looks like a restraining-order skirt if I ever saw one. But back to this lunch. When did this happen?
Katydid:	Oh. When I saw him Saturday night at the opening.
Sleaterkinneyfan:	Describe.
Katydid:	Nothing to describe. He was there with a girl. A very pretty girl. She looked like a praying mantis. And she's a Doyle, as in Hertzog Webber and Doyle.

Sleaterkinneyfan: Oh. Still, he's having lunch with you, not her.

Katydid: A BUSINESS lunch.

Sleaterkinneyfan: Ergo, that ultra-businessy skirt.

Katydid: SHUT UP! Is it really that slutty? Will you trade skirts with me?

Sleaterkinneyfan: Are you kidding me? Then I'll have to take a restraining order out against Rob the copy guy. Hey, did you get a load of the T.O.D.'s earrings?

Katydid: Yes. They are blinding me. A gift from Stuart, perhaps?

Sleaterkinneyfan: You know it. I can't believe he's giving her that kind of stuff, and they aren't even married yet. It's not even her birthday! You know the last present Craig gave me? A scale. Nice, huh?

Katydid: Hey, the last present Dale gave me was a drumstick. He said it was Flea's. But I'm not so sure.

Sleaterkinneyfan: How was the apartment hunting?

Katydid: Well, if I had ten grand in my savings account for first and last month's rent plus a security deposit, I'd be golden. But since I don't, I guess it's just going to have to be me, Dolly, Peter, and Skiboy. At least until I get my tax refund—and the lease runs out on my place with Dale, and I get my half of the deposit back. And I'm able to hock one pair of peed-on suede boots and my very valuable collected works of the Bangles.

Sleaterkinneyfan: Ouch. You know there's always room at Chez Sadler.

Katydid: Thanks. You're the best. I—Uh-oh, phone call. More later.

✉

To: Jen Sadler <jennifer.sadler@thenyjournal.com>
Fr: Kate Mackenzie <kathleen.mackenzie@thenyjournal.com>
Re: My mother

I thought mothers were supposed to be sweet and supportive, and love you unconditionally. In fact, I distinctly remember Professor Wingblade telling us that mothers are the ONLY people who can be counted on for unconditional love.

So how come MY mother, instead of feeling badly for me that my boyfriend refuses to commit, is yelling at ME for putting too much pressure on him? I swear to God, my own mother likes my ex more than she likes me.

Kate

✉

To: Kate Mackenzie <kathleen.mackenzie@thenyjournal.com>
Fr: Jen Sadler <jennifer.sadler@thenyjournal.com>
Re: Your mother

That's just because she hasn't seen you in that skirt yet.

No, seriously, your mother is currently driving across the country in an RV with a man ten years her junior who likes to whittle bird whistles. Okay? Like you're really going to score points with this woman for breaking up with your soon-to-be-rock-star boyfriend. Did she tell you that you should have just let yourself get "accidentally pregnant" and then you'd have been set for life? Ten to one she did. Is this the sign of a woman playing with a full deck?

J

✉

To: Jen Sadler <jennifer.sadler@thenyjournal.com>
Fr: Kate Mackenzie <kathleen.mackenzie@thenyjournal.com>
Re: My mother

YES! Oh my God, did you get struck by lightning, or something? Because you're clairvoyant.

Like I would want to get a husband THAT way. Like having a husband is even that important to me. I mean, you can be a fully rounded human being and not be married, you know. In fact, remember how Professor Wingblade told us that the overall happiness level of marrieds vs. singles was higher in singles? What does THAT say to you?

Oh, sorry. I forgot you were married there for a second.

But I'm just saying. It isn't because I want to be married that I broke up with Dale. It's because if he doesn't love me enough to want to marry me, then he doesn't love me at all.

Or something like that. Know what I mean? God, I HATE talking to my mother, she always gets me confused.

Kate

✉

To: Kate Mackenzie <kathleen.mackenzie@thenyjournal.com>
Fr: Jen Sadler <jennifer.sadler@thenyjournal.com>
Re: Your mother

I get what you mean. Hey, shouldn't you be meeting your lunch date round about now? It's almost 12:30.

J

To: Jen Sadler <jennifer.sadler@thenyjournal.com>
Fr: Kate Mackenzie <kathleen.mackenzie@thenyjournal.com>
Re: My mother

EEEEEEEEEEEEEEEEEEEEEEEEE!!!!!!!!!!!!!!

I'm late!

Wu Liang Palace

Authentic Sichuan Cuisine

Oh my God, I knew I should have made Jen switch skirts with me, I must look like the biggest slut in the world, it's no wonder he took that call on his cell and has been out in the restaurant lobby

South Sea Shark's Fin for Two	$19.95

for so long, he's probably embarrassed to be seen with me, and who can blame him, I look like Alyssa

Crab Meat Asparagus Bisque for Two	$8.95

Milano on *Charmed* or whatever. He's probably scared of me, oh God why did I ever

Fish Maw Chowder	$8.95

say I would have lunch with him? I mean, he's a LAWYER, after all, and I've always sworn . . .

Fish Filet in Broth for Two	$7.95

but he's just so *nice*, and the chicken in garlic sauce IS really good here, and I'm sure his call must

Chengdu Wonton in Broth	$3.50

be really important, and he DID look really annoyed when he saw who it was on the caller ID.

Hot and Sour Soup	$3.50

Probably it's about a really important case or something. I hope it's not that Clarissa girl, I really don't

Chicken Corn Egg Drop Soup	$3.50

think he'd have taken it if it was, although maybe, who knows? It's kind of funny, I really don't think he likes Amy all that much. He says people who exercise that many times a day scare him, which is good

Pan-seared Dumplings	$4.95

because God knows I could barely move yesterday after that run around the reservoir the day before.

Steamed Vegetable Dumpling	$4.95

Not that it was much of a run considering the fact that Dolly stopped every 60 seconds to talk to

Spareribs	$6.95

someone who was going by, God she knows everyone in the world, it seems like. Plus he likes the

Fantail Shrimp	$6.95

Travel Channel, which means we already have something in common, not that we like it for the same

Cantonese Roast Duck	$5.95

reason, he likes it because he's been to all those places, I like it because now I don't have to go, since I

Shanghai Vegetable Spring Roll	$2.50

saw it already on TV. But still that's something, anyway, more than I had in common with Dale, except

Chilled Noodles with Spicy Vinaigrette	$4.50

that we grew up together and both like, you know, sex. And he was the nicest boy in the whole school,

Stir Fried Chicken with Lettuce Taco	$6.95

and the only one who was even remotely interested in anything besides football. And he's

Sichuan Pork Dumpling with Chili Vinaigrette	$4.50

not a businessy type of person (Dale, I mean), because I don't know if I could be with someone who is

Fried Taro Toast $3.95

always worried about the bottom line or whatever, at least Dale was in a creative profession. Not like I'm going out with Mitch Hertzog, or anything. I mean, I WISH. It's just lunch, for God's sake. To talk about taking a restraining order out on Dale.

Only he's SO NICE—Mitch, I mean—and he smells good, too, and he has on a Spiderman tie today. He says his nieces gave it to him, too. God, I hope it isn't serious between Mitch and that Praying Mantis girl. OH MY GOD

IS THAT SCROGGS????

✉

To: Mitchell Hertzog <mitchell.hertzog@hwd.com>
Fr: Kate Mackenzie <kathleen.mackenzie@thenyjournal.com>
Re: Lunch

Please let me apologize one more time. I AM SO SORRY ABOUT
YOUR SUIT. I don't know what came over Dale, I really don't. I
guess he thought we were out on a date or something, ha ha! Well,
you know he's a little unstable. But really nonviolent. Except toward
suits, apparently.

PLEASE, you've got to send me the dry-cleaning bill. I owe you that
much at least.

Kate

✉

To: Kate Mackenzie <kathleen.mackenzie@thenyjournal.com>
Fr: Jen Sadler <jennifer.sadler@thenyjournal.com>
Re: You

What happened????? You look white as a sheet. Did one of those
video voyeurs get a shot up that skirt of yours as you were coming
down the steps outside the building? Because we can track down
the guy and have a blanket party on his head if you want. I know
people who can make it happen.

J

✉

To: Jen Sadler<jennifer.sadler@thenyjournal.com>
Fr: Kate Mackenzie<kathleen.mackenzie@thenyjournal.com>
Re: What happened

Oh, just the USUAL. I made a complete and utter fool of myself. WHY can't I EVER pass myself off as a cool-headed business-woman? WHY???

Of COURSE we were having a perfectly nice time—well, except that he got this call in the middle of the meal, but whatever, it was prob-ably some multimillion-dollar deal he's working on, or something—when who should come in to the restaurant but DALE, and the whole rest of the I'm Not Making Any More Sandwiches crew, and he starts making this big deal out of how I'm there, like it's kismet or something, only he kept calling it *schism*, and then Mitch walked up and was like, "Sorry about that," and sat down across from me, and next thing I knew, Dale had thrown the entire platter of chicken in garlic sauce on Mitch.

So there I am, lamely trying to wipe it off him, which meant, of course, that I actually had to touch him, although it was through a napkin, but can I just take a moment to say hubba-hubba? I mean, I could FEEL his muscles through all the stir-fried rice. How does a lawyer get all built up like that? I mean, Dale plays guitar, but you know, his chest practically caves in and he mostly looks ane-mic. . . .

But anyway.

It was just mortifying, all right? What do I DO??? I made Dale apol-ogize, but you could tell he didn't mean it. And I guess I can't really blame him, we WERE talking about taking out a restraining order against him, but really, it's all Dale's fault. I mean, Del Monte peaches? Who DOES that?

What do you think I should do? Send flowers? Or candy? That seems sort of . . . not right. For a guy, I mean. What would you do? I mean, if it had been Craig. And you two weren't married. But you still thought he was way hot and wanted him to like you. Even though he's a soulless corporate drone. Who likes Spider-man.

I mean, I e-mailed him, but it doesn't seem like enough. Know what I mean?

I really, truly wish I were dead.

Kate

....

✉

To: Kate Mackenzie<kathleen.mackenzie@thenyjournal.com>
Fr: Jen Sadler<jennifer.sadler@thenyjournal.com>
Re: What happened

You did the right thing. Believe me, if this guy is interested, he'll forgive you.

But what about Dale? Are you going for the restraining order or not? Seems like YOU'RE not the one who should file for it. Mr. Muscle should.

Could you tell if he had a six-pack?

J

✉

To: Jen Sadler<jennifer.sadler@thenyjournal.com>
Fr: Kate Mackenzie<kathleen.mackenzie@thenyjournal.com>
Re: What happened

The restraining order! Oh! I forgot all about it!

Definite six-pack. The guy is cut.

Oh my God. I can't believe I just wrote that.

Kate

✉

To: Kate Mackenzie<kathleen.mackenzie@thenyjournal.com>
Fr: Jen Sadler<jennifer.sadler@thenyjournal.com>
Re: What happened

God dammit. Blondes really do have more fun.

J

✉

To: Kate Mackenzie <kathleen.mackenzie@thenyjournal.com>
Fr: Mitchell Hertzog <mitchell.hertzog@hwd.com>
Re: Lunch

You don't owe me anything. Look, really, don't worry about it. How were you to know the label would pick THAT restaurant, out of all the restaurants in Manhattan, to take your ex-boyfriend's band to lunch after signing their big deal? It IS midtown, and there ARE a lot of record companies in Manhattan.

And I thought he comported himself very well, after the initial surprise.

The garlic sauce will come out.

If anyone should be apologizing, it's me. I am so sorry about that horrifically long phone call. It's just that my little sister is home from college, and there've been some issues between her and my mother, and somehow, I always seem to get caught up in the middle. . . .

Anyway, if you'd really like to make it up to me, we can try again. How about dinner Friday night?

Let me know.

Mitch

P.S. Actually, considering what happened today, I think it might be safer if we were to eat in. My place okay? I make a mean shrimp scampi.

P.P.S. Want to give me a clue as to why your ex's band is called I'm Not Making Any More Sandwiches? Not that I'm aching to go out and buy their new album. Just curious.

....

✉

To: Mitch Hertzog <mitchell.hertzog@hwd.com>
Fr: Kate Mackenzie <kathleen.mackenzie@thenyjournal.com>
Re: Dinner

I would love to have dinner at your place, if you're sure it's not too much trouble. And you have to let me bring something. Dessert all right? Thanks for asking . . . and for being so understanding about Dale.

The reason his band is called I'm Not Making Any More Sandwiches is because Dale used to work in the only bagel shop in downtown Luxor, Kentucky, where we both grew up, and people used to come in all the time and ask for bagel sandwiches—you know, like ham and cheese on a bagel, or peanut butter and jelly—and Dale didn't think that was right, because he thinks bagels don't make good sandwich bread, because they're too thick and you can't get a good bite without scraping your gums or whatever, so he went on this kind of strike and would only put traditional things on the bagels, like smoked salmon and cream cheese, and the manager got mad and asked him what he was doing, and Dale yelled, "I'm not making any more sandwiches," and so they fired him—unjustly, he felt.

Anyway, the local newspaper heard about the bagel controversy, and they ran a big front-page story on it, along with a big photo of Dale. The caption read, *I'm Not Making Any More Sandwiches.* And the phrase just caught on around town, and so the guys in the band, to capitalize on the modicum of celebrity Dale had, started calling their band that, and the name just stuck.

Wish I could chat more, but I have a staff meeting to attend. Talk to you later!

Kate

New York Journal
Human Resources Division Staff Meeting

Agenda:

> Oh my God, could this be more boring? I can't believe the
> T.O.D. dragged me from an e-mail from Mitch for this.
> —K

Review of Unlawful Harassment Policy
The Company is committed to providing a work environ-
ment free of unlawful harassment.

> So. Mitch, is it now? You like him!
> —J

Company policy prohibits harassment because of sex (which
includes sexual harassment, gender harassment, and harassment
due to pregnancy, childbirth, or related medical conditions)—

> Shut up.

> You do. Admit it.

—and harassment because of race, religious creed, color, national origin or ancestry, physical or—

> He did ask me over for dinner on Friday night.

—mental disability, medical condition, marital status, political affiliation, age, sexual orientation—

> OVER for dinner? SEXY. It had to have been the skirt. It
> couldn't have been the garlic sauce down his pants, now could it?

—or any other basis protected by federal, state, or local law or ordinance of regulation. All such harassment is unlawful. Prohibited unlawful harassment includes, but is not limited to, the following behavior:—

Shut up. God, I hate this. By the way, I said I'd bring dessert. Can I have your lemon-bar recipe?

Does Mitch really strike you as the lemon-bar type? I think he's more seven-layer cookie, myself.

Verbal misconduct such as epithets, derogatory jokes or comments, slurs or unwanted sexual advances.

Seven-layer cookies are too heavy.

For what? For a little apres dinner—

Visual misconduct such as derogatory and/or sexually oriented posters, photography, cartoons, or gestures, including those accessed or sent via e-mail.

SHUT UP!

How did you know what I was going to write?

Physical conduct such as assault, unwanted touching, blocking normal movement or interfering with work because of sex, race, or any other protected basis.

Because I know you. God, this is so BORING!

You're telling me. Why is she wearing tan pantyhose? Are we all supposed to believe she went to Aruba for the weekend, and only her legs got tan?

Threats and demands to submit to sexual requests as a condition of continued employment, or to avoid some other loss, and offers of employment benefits in return for sexual favors; and—

> *She must have run out of nude ones. And I know for a fact that she didn't go to Aruba for the weekend.*

—retaliation for having reported or threatened to report harassment.

> *I saw her at the Met Saturday night.*

If you/one of your clients believe you/he/she have/has been unlawfully harassed, provide a written or verbal complaint. Your complaint should include details of the incident(s), names of the—

> *Do you suppose she and Stuart went home afterwards and had torrid sex?*

> *Ew! Thanks for the visual.*

—individuals involved, and names of any witnesses. The Company will immediately undertake—

> *Well, that must be the only reason he likes her, right? She has no other redeeming qualities. I mean, she's a power-hungry, back-stabbing, two-faced uber bitch.*

—effective, thorough, and objective investigation of the harassment allegations. If the Company determines that unlawful harassment has occurred, effective remedial action—

> *The B word! You can't use the B word on the staff meeting minutes! My God, what's wrong with you, Jen?????*

—will be taken in accordance with the circumstances involved. Any employee determined by the Company to be responsible for unlawful harassment will be subject to appropriate disciplinary—

> Well, you know it's true. It has to be the sex. She must just give BJODs all day long.

—action, up to and including termination. Whatever action is taken against the harasser will be—

> Wait . . . what are BJODs again?

—made known to the employee lodging the complaint and the Company will take appropriate—

> Oh, my little Kentucky innocent. Blow jobs on demand.

—action to remedy any loss to the employee resulting from harassment. The Company will not—

> EW!!!! Would you stop???? Besides, it's not like he's such a great catch himself. I mean, he's no George Clooney in the looks department, and does he even HAVE a personality? Or a sense of humor? It's not just anyone that Mrs. Lopez refuses to serve pie to, you know. She's very discriminating.

—retaliate against you for filing a complaint and will not tolerate or permit retaliation by management, employees or coworkers. The Company encourages all employees to report any incidents of harassment forbidden by this policy immediately so that complaints can be quickly and fairly addressed.

> Yeah, well, so's Amy. And she is not the type to get engaged to anybody worth less than a million a year. I mean, you got

that kind of money coming in, you can overlook any bald spot and inordinately small unit.

Would you stop??? Not in the middle of trust games!!!!

I hate these frigging trust games. What the hell are they supposed to establish?

Um. That would be trust. Amongst your coworkers.

Please. I wouldn't trust Amy to warn me not to cross the street in the path of an oncoming bus. Do you really think I'm going to trust her to catch me as I fall backwards?

That's not the one we're doing today. And besides, we're supposed to be learning them so that we can go around to the different divisions and have them do it. You know. Little trust workshops amongst the staff.

Please. Can you imagine doing the lap sit in Features? George Sanchez would crush everyone beneath his massive girth.

As a Human Resources representative, Jen, you are not supposed to show bias against weight-challenged individuals.

Whatever! George just needs to lay off the Krispy Kremes. Which he wouldn't be half so tempted by, if the T.O.D. hadn't fired Mrs. Lopez. Wait. WHAT did she just say we're supposed to be doing?

Oh my God, you so need to be off those hormones. We're supposed to be dividing up into groups and building shelters for ourselves—

Don't even tell me. Using those old back copies of the *Journal* she's got lying over there?

Yes. But we aren't allowed to use tape or scissors.

Motherf******!

JEN!

Seriously, this is the stupidest—

Uh-oh, she's dividing us into groups now.

I'd better be in your group, or—

✉

To: Amy Jenkins <amy.jenkins@thenyjournal.com>
Fr: Stuart Hertzog <stuart.hertzog@hwd.com>
Re: Ida Lopez

Sweetheart, I have done everything I can to prevent it, but the fact
is, I simply can't get you out of a pretrial discovery conference with
Mitch. He is insisting that it be sometime this week, and so I thought
tomorrow would be best. . . . That way we can get it over with.
And you don't have to worry, because I'll be right by your side the
whole time.

He wants Kate Mackenzie there, as well. God knows why. I've
given up trying to second-guess my brother. He is, not to put too
fine a point on it, a freak of nature. If it were not for the fact that I
remember our mother being pregnant with him, I would suspect he
was adopted. I promise you none of the other Hertzogs are like
Mitch.

Well, except for possibly my sister Janice. But she's young enough
that hopefully any defects in her character can still be cured.

But like I said, he is a fine, fine lawyer. Remember, I love you, and
would never let anyone or anything hurt you.

After the depo, I'll take you to lunch, anywhere you want to go.

All my love,
Stuart

Stuart Hertzog, Senior Partner
Hertzog Webber and Doyle, Attorneys at Law
444 Madison Avenue, Suite 1505
New York, NY 10022
212-555-7900

✉

To: Kate Mackenzie <kathleen.mackenzie@thenyjournal.com>
Fr: Jen Sadler <jennifer.sadler@thenyjournal.com>
Re: Trust Games

Told you we'd trounce those losers.

J

✉

To: Jen Sadler <jennifer.sadler@thenyjournal.com>
Fr: Kate Mackenzie <kathleen.mackenzie@thenyjournal.com>
Re: Trust Games

Yeah, but, Jen, we've known each other since college. The Reception staff turns over every six months. Did you really think they were going to have their house up faster, or that it would be more secure than ours?

Kate

✉

To: Kate Mackenzie <kathleen.mackenzie@thenyjournal.com>
Fr: Jen Sadler <jennifer.sadler@thenyjournal.com>
Re: Trust Games

Come on! They're younger than we are! And we kicked their asses! Even when Amy came by and tied that scarf around your head, we STILL beat them. With one of our team members BLIND!

And what about the Budget staff? Some of them have worked to-gether for YEARS, and we still beat them. WE RULE!!!

J

✉

To: Jen Sadler <jennifer.sadler@thenyjournal.com>
Fr: Kate Mackenzie <kathleen.mackenzie@thenyjournal.com>
Re: Trust Games

I'd forgotten about this competitive side of yours. It's been a while since we played Scrabble, I guess. It isn't really a very attractive trait, Jen.

Kate

✉

To: Kate Mackenzie <kathleen.mackenzie@thenyjournal.com>
Fr: Jen Sadler <jennifer.sadler@thenyjournal.com>
Re: Trust Games

Who cares? WE WON!!!!! I am telling you, it is only a matter of time until we take over this place, you and me. It'll be Kate and Jen's Free Therapy Clinic in no time! Just you wait and see!

J

✉

To: Jen Sadler <jennifer.sadler@thenyjournal.com>
Fr: Kate Mackenzie <kathleen.mackenzie@thenyjournal.com>
Re: Trust Games

Um, yeah, okay, CALIGULA.

I just got a call from Amy. She wants me in her office STAT. She actually said that. What does she think this is, anyway, an emergency room? Is she defibrillating a heart in there, or just filing people's 1099s?

I hope we open up Kate and Jen's Free Therapy Clinic soon.

Kate

....

✉

To: Kate Mackenzie <kathleen.mackenzie@thenyjournal.com>
Fr: Amy Jenkins <amy.jenkins@thenyjournal.com>
Re: Tomorrow

To review what we just discussed, tomorrow morning you and I will appear at 9 A.M. in the offices of Hertzog Webber and Doyle to be further deposed in the matter of Lopez vs. the *New York Journal*. You will be dressed in a professional manner. You will answer all questions put to you in a truthful manner. You will not, however, say anything that could be construed as not reflecting positively on your employer.

This is a serious matter, Kate, and I am counting on you to handle it in that way, and not allow whatever personal feelings you might have for the employee involved to cloud your better judgment.

Amy

Amy Denise Jenkins
Director
Human Resources
The New York Journal
216 W. 57th Street
New York, NY 10019
212-555-6890
amy.jenkins@thenyjournal.com

✉

To: Mitchell Hertzog <mitchell.hertzog@hwd.com>
Fr: Sean <psychodramabeautyqueen@freemail.com>
Re: Mom

Look, I'm sorry I interrupted your important business lunch or whatever it was, but seriously, I don't know how much longer I can put
up with this. She is a FREAK, all right? A FREAK.

Guess what she did NOW. Go on. Guess. I go to the mall for one
frigging hour to see if they have the new *X-Men* comic in, and what
does she do? WHAT DOES SHE DO?

She sprays everything in my room with that drug-detecting spray.

I am not even kidding. You know that spray you can buy on TV for
like $19.95 or whatever? That spray that turns a color if there's
drug residue on whatever object you're spraying?

Well, she sprayed that shit ALL OVER my room.

And OF COURSE I don't do drugs—at least, not at HOME, I'm not
a MORON—so OF COURSE the shit didn't turn a color.

But guess what? EVERYTHING IN MY ROOM IS STICKY. Seriously.

It's like Stacy's freaking twins have been here. I mean, even my LEATHER JACKET is sticky! The leather jacket I had to save for MONTHS to buy, because you know Mom won't let me go near the money Gramps left me. I mean, I had to work the graveyard shift in the quad store for that jacket.

And now it's like one of those adhesive fly strips. I'm not kidding. There was actually a moth stuck to it already by the time I got home.

I confronted Mom about it, and she says—get this—STUART told her to do it. STUART. Mr. Just Say No himself.

I can't stand it here anymore, Mitch. I think there's a very good chance I might go completely mental and take her goddamn Madame Alexander doll collection and put it out with the rest of the garbage where it BELONGS!!!!

Or do you think I'm overreacting? But think about it, Mitch: My UN-DERWEAR is sticky. And not because I've been having any fun in them!!!!

Sean

....

✉

To: Sean <psychodramabeautyqueen@freemail.com>
Fr: Mitchell Hertzog <mitchell.hertzog@hwd.com>
Re: Mom

Thanks for those last couple of lines about your underwear. That's really something every guy wants to know about his little sister. Not.

Look, I told you, you're welcome to stay with me anytime you want. But keep in mind the only way you're going to convince Mom and

Dad that you're all right to go back to college is if you play it their way for a few months. If you cool it on the hair dye and the diatribes at the dinner table against gross materialism, you should have them eating out of your hand by the time apps for fall semester come rolling around.

Keep your chin up, and send everything to be dry-cleaned . . . at Mom's expense, of course.

Mitch

....

✉

To: Kate Mackenzie <kathleen.mackenzie@thenyjournal.com>
Fr: Dolly Vargas <dolly.vargas@thenyjournal.com>
Re: You

Darling, it was SO sweet of you to pretend to be Skiboy's girlfriend yesterday. You really are an INVALUABLE little roomie. I can't imagine what I ever did without you.

Now, I'm going to have a late night tonight—the fall shows, don't you know—so if you wouldn't mind just letting Skiboy in when he shows up—it will probably be around nine—I'd love you forever. He's had some entanglement with his landlord—I don't know what, I try not to pay attention when he talks, he's so dull. But those shoulders! Oh!

He promises not to be any trouble. And no need to worry about Peter, he's got his golf lesson at Chelsea Piers tonight, so we won't be seeing him until Wednesday at the earliest.

Ciao!
XXXOOO
Dolly

✉

To: Kate Mackenzie <kathleen.mackenzie@thenyjournal.com>
Fr: Dale Carter <imnotmakinganymoresandwiches@freemail.com>
Re: Lunch

Okay, so I know I owe you an apology for that whole thing today
at the restaurant. I'm really sorry. In fact, I'm so sorry, I already
wrote a song about it. It's called "Chicken a la Kate." Will you
PLEASE come to our gig tonight so you can hear me sing it? We'll
be playing over at Bryant Park, for one of the designers for the fall
fashion runway shows. It's our first official gig with our new label.

And in spite of what Scroggs thinks, we are not sellouts to be playing at a fashion show. I mean, isn't that what life is, really? A fashion show?

So was that guy I poured chicken on really your lawyer? Or is he
like your new boyfriend? Because it looked to me like he likes you
as more than just, you know, somebody he's lawyering for.

Dale

✉

To: Dale Carter <imnotmakinganymoresandwiches@freemail.com>
Fr: Kate Mackenzie <kathleen.mackenzie@thenyjournal.com>
Re: Chicken

Client. The people lawyers do their "lawyering" for are called
clients. And that is what I am to Mitch Hertzog. His client. That's
all.

But Dale, you seriously have to give up on the whole trying-to-get-
me-back thing. Because I'm not coming back. I'm not saying I don't

still love you—there's a part of me that will probably always love you. But during this time I've spent away from you, I've realized something, and that's that I'm not *in* love with you anymore. I don't think I have been for some time.

And it's not just because you won't make a commitment. It's because I realize now you and I have completely different values and goals in life. I mean, really, Dale, what am I going to do when you and the band go on tour? Follow you around the country? I'm not a groupie. That wouldn't make me happy. What makes me happy is helping people.

And don't say that YOU need my help and that that should be enough for me. I'm not talking about looking after someone's bowling shoes or keeping the apartment stocked with coffee filters. I'm talking about helping people to make career and life choices. I know it may not seem like it sometimes, but ultimately, when things are going the way they should, that's what I do here at the *Journal*. And I really really love it.

But even you have to admit that my job and your job are totally incompatible. I mean, how many rock stars have you seen on *Behind the Music* who are married to human resource representatives? Not even one.

So Dale, please, please, please move on. I'm not coming back, not ever, and I know that, in time, you'll see this is for the best.

Love,
Kate

Journal of Kate Mackenzie

According to Professor Wingblade, all human beings have worth and dignity. But I wonder if he would still feel that way if he met the T.O.D. I mean, she really is reprehensible. A little while ago, when we met up here in the outer office of Hertzog Webber and Doyle, she took one look at me and was like, "Well, it's about time you dressed like a professional." Right in front of the receptionist and Stuart and everything!

Thank God Mitch wasn't here yet. But still. I guess she thinks we can ALL afford to raid TSE anytime we want. Maybe if I were making seventy grand a year like her, and not forty, like me, I could. But on my salary, it's Ann Taylor Loft or nothing.

And she's been so mean to poor Mrs. Lopez! I have to admit, I was kind of surprised to see her here—in Mitch's office, I mean. I guess I forgot this whole thing revolves around her, and not the T.O.D. She does have a way of making everything be about her—the T.O.D., I mean.

Like when Mrs. Lopez was all happy to see me and offered me a slice of carrot cake from this pan she'd brought along, the T.O.D. gave me the dirtiest look for actually taking it. The cake, I mean. Maybe she was just jealous because Mrs. Lopez didn't offer her cake. . . . Probably she'll turn it into a whole big thing about how I've let the department down or something by siding with staff instead of management. I bet I'll be playing trust games from now until the end of time.

I don't care, though. This cake is heaven. If only I could make something as good for dessert when I go over to Mitch's. Mrs. L gave me the recipe. And they say the way to a man's heart is through his stomach. . . .

He has on a Wonder Woman tie today. I love Wonder Woman. SHE would never let a tyrannical office despot make her feel guilty for eating cake.

What's really weird is, when he showed up, Mrs. Lopez gave HIM cake, too. Not Stuart. She didn't offer STUART one. But she did his brother.

Which means Mrs. Lopez's whole thing about Stuart (whatever it is) isn't because of a Hertzog FAMILY trait.

Why I should find this so comforting, I hardly know. But for some reason, the fact that Mrs. Lopez likes Mitch makes me not feel so bad about liking him, too.

Oops, here comes his assistant. I guess it's my turn.

Ida Lopez's Carrot Cake

Preheat oven to 350° F. Butter and flour two 9-inch cake pans.

Sift together and set aside:

2 cups flour
2 1/2 teaspoons baking soda
2 teaspoons cinnamon
1 teaspoon salt

In a separate bowl, combine one cup canola oil and 1 1/2 cups sugar. To the oil/sugar mixture add three eggs and the dry ingredients. Then add:

1 cup unsweetened apple sauce
3–4 cups grated California carrots (squeeze out the juice using cheesecloth)
1 cup walnuts

Mix on low speed until just incorporated (do not overmix). Divide batter between the two cake pans. Bake for 40 to 50 minutes. Give pans a quarter turn every 15 minutes.

To make the frosting, cream together 13 oz. cream cheese (room temperature), 5 oz. butter (room temperature). 1 1/2 cups confectioners' sugar, and 1 tablespoon lemon juice.

Appearances:
Kathleen Mackenzie (KM)
Mitchell Hertzog (MH)
Amy Jenkins (AJ)
Stuart Hertzog (SH)
Ida Lopez (IL)
Jeri Valentine (JV), attorney for the plaintiff
Recorded by Anne Kelly (AK) for later comparison with
   stenographer's transcript
Miriam Lowe, Shorthand Reporter and Notary Public within
   and for the State of New York

MH: Ms. Mackenzie, thank you so much for being here
   today. Ms. Mackenzie, Mrs. Lopez's attorney and I have
   just been discussing the case of Ida Lopez with your supervisor, Ms. Jenkins, and there seems to be a disagreement that I hope you can settle, if you'd be amenable
   to that.
SH: Objection.
MH: Stuart, you can't object. This is pretrial discovery, not
   the courtroom.
SH: Well, you didn't listen last time I tried to interrupt.
MH: Maybe because you shouldn't be interrupting.
SH: When it comes to the protection of my client, I most

certainly will interrupt, as often as I deem necessary, if doing so will get us to the truth.

JV: Pardon me for interrupting, gentlemen. But don't you two have the same client?

SH: You'd think so, wouldn't you? We're supposed to be working to get at the truth here, Mitch. For our *client*.

MH: But that's what I'm trying to do. Get to the truth.

SH: By asking Ms. Mackenzie about a letter she can't possibly remember writing?

MH: I am willing to give Ms. Mackenzie more credit than you are. I believe she is capable of remembering documents that she sent out under her own name. Most people are.

SH: Yes, but most people don't, as Ms. Mackenzie does, have several hundred employees about whom she writes letters every day.

MH: She doesn't write several hundred letters a day, however. Do you, Ms. Mackenzie?

KM: No.

JV: Don't look at me, Stuart. *I'm* certainly not going to object.

SH: Mitch—

MH: Ms. Jenkins, do you maintain that Ms. Mackenzie writes several hundred letters a day?

AJ: No, certainly not. But I do maintain that the document in question might—

MH: Let's just ask Ms. Mackenzie, shall we? Ms. Mackenzie, I'm going to ask you about a certain document that you allegedly wrote, and I want you to tell me what you can about it.

KM: Well, I'll try.

MH: Great. The document in question is a letter of written warning that Ms. Jenkins alleges Ida Lopez received before her dismissal last week. Do you remember writing such a letter?

KM: I remember writing a *rough draft* of a warning letter to

Mrs. Lopez after an incident that occurred prior to the one for which she was dismissed.

AJ: See? I told you!

JV: Excuse me, Ms. Jenkins. I believe, Ms. Mackenzie, you said you *drafted* such a letter?

KM: Yes. But I never finished it.

AJ: That's a lie!

JV: Please, Ms. Jenkins. Mr. Hertzog, would you please control your client?

MH: Hey there, Amy. Simmer down.

SH: This is ridiculous! Ms. Jenkins is understandably upset. The letter in question was undoubtedly finished and sent, as we have the signed copy right here, initialed by Mrs. Lopez to indicate she received it—

IL: And I tell you, I didn't sign any such letter!

KM: She's right. Mrs. Lopez couldn't have initialed the letter I was writing to her, because I never finished it. I got interrupted, and right after that, the T.O.D—I mean, Amy—called, and said I was to dis—

AJ: I did not!

KM: —miss Mrs. Lopez. Amy, what are you talking about? Yes, you did.

AJ: This is a complete fabrication, a campaign by an incompetent employee to cover her ass because SHE screwed up!

KM: What are you talking about? You told me—

AJ: She's lying! Stuart, she's obviously lying. How could she not be, when the very fact that the letter exists AND was initialed by Mrs. Lopez—

IL: I didn't initial anything! No one ever gave me anything!

MH: There's an easy way to clear up this disagreement, don't you think, Jeri? Why don't you show a copy of the letter in question to Ms. Mackenzie—

AJ: This is an outrage! Stuart, are you going to let him do this to me? Are you going to take the word of someone with a clear grudge against the paper over mine?

JV: Ms. Mackenzie has no reason to harbor a grudge against the paper. Do you, Ms. Mackenzie?

KM: No, of course not.

JV: Fine. Now, if you would just look at this paper here that was found in Mrs. Lopez's personnel file. . . .

SH: Mitch, could I please see you in the hallway?

MH: Hang on a minute, Stuie. I want to see what Ms. Mackenzie has to say.

SH: Mitch. The hallway. Now.

JV: Mr. Hertzog, could you please be quiet? Ms. Mackenzie is trying to concentrate.

SH: Oh, you have got to be shitting me with this, Jeri.

JV: I beg your pardon, but I'm not. Part of my client's case against the paper includes the fact that proper procedure for dismissal—in this case as stipulated by her union—was not followed. And yet, miraculously, this piece of paper, which my client says she's never seen before, has appeared in her file. I just want to verify that Ms. Mackenzie did indeed write and send it. Ms. Mackenzie? Did you indeed write and send the letter of written warning you are holding in your hand right now?

AJ: You can't ask her to remember every piece of paper that crosses her desk. She's just a paper pusher, after all—

JV: Again, Mitch, I'd like to ask that you control your client.

MH: Amy. Cool it.

SH: Cool *this*, Mitch.

MH: Miriam, could you please let it be noted in the transcript that counsel for the defense just gave his fellow counsel for the defense what is known in the vernacular as "the finger"?

ML: Yes, sir.

SH: Miriam, strike that.

MH: Too late. Isn't it, Miriam?

ML: Yes, sir.

JV: Ms. Mackenzie.

KM: Yes?

JV: The paper you're holding. Do you remember writing it?

KM: Um. Well, I remember starting it . . . or one like it.

AJ: See? See, I told you she couldn't remember. Can I go now?

JV: Please, Ms. Jenkins. Ms. Mackenzie?

KM: But I didn't write this.

AJ: She's lying!

SH: Really, Jeri, can't you see what she's doing? This young woman has a grudge against her employer because Ms. Jenkins had to reprimand her yesterday for wearing a skirt of an inappropriate length to the office, and she's just trying to—

JV: Is that true, Ms. Mackenzie?

KM: Well. Yes, about the skirt. I mean, Amy issued me a warning letter about it.

MH: That skirt you had on yesterday? That black suede one you wore to the restaurant?

KM: Um. Yes.

MH: I liked that skirt. What was wrong with that skirt?

SH: Would you PLEASE stick to the topic at hand, Mitchell? We're talking about forgery here. Because if that girl is saying she didn't send the letter she's holding, that is a very serious accusation—

MH: Did you sign this letter, Kate?

KM: That looks like my signature. But I didn't write—or sign—this letter.

AJ: That's impossible!

MH: And you didn't hand that letter to Mrs. Lopez to initial?

KM: At no time did I hand any document of any kind to Mrs. Lopez to sign.

JV: Thank you very much, Ms. Mackenzie. Mr. Hertzog,

Ms. Jenkins, looks like I'll be seeing you both in court. Ida, let's go.

SH: Hold on just a minute, here! Jeri, put your damned briefcase down. We aren't done yet.

MH: Really? I think we are.

SH: Excuse me, Ms. Mackenzie. Do you realize the seriousness of what you're saying?

MH: Do you think we're done, Jeri?

JV: Very much so, Mitch.

SH: You're implying, Ms. Mackenzie, that somebody has committed forgery.

KM: Well. I don't know about that. All I know is, I didn't write that letter. And I didn't give it to Mrs. Lopez to sign.

MH: Thank you very much, Ms. Mackenzie. You may go now.

SH: No, she may not fucking go, Mitch.

JV: Well, my client and I are fucking going.

SH: Nobody is going anywhere. Ms. Mackenzie, how long have you worked at the *New York Journal*?

JV: Stuart, Ms. Mackenzie has already been deposed. I'm not interested in—

SH: Yes, but you asked that she be brought here today, to help clear some things up—your words, no?

JV: Yes, but—

SH: Well, that's all I'm trying to do. Help clear things up. Now. Ms. Mackenzie, you've been with the paper for a little less than a year, correct?

MH: Stuart, this is my case, I believe, not yours.

KM: Um. Yes?

SH: Right. And I believe you were hired on the strong recommendation of your friend, Ms. Jennifer Sadler. Is that correct?

KM: Jen told me about the opening in her office, yes, and I applied. . . .

MH: I believe your exact words, Stuart, were that you were

too personally involved in the case to want to get involved. . . .

SH: And so you were hired, is that correct, Ms. Mackenzie? And you and Jen, as you call her . . . Would you say she is your best friend?

MH: Stuart, where the hell are you going with this?

SH: Excuse me. I ask only to be extended the same courtesy I extended to you, Mitchell. Were you not, Ms. Mackenzie, living with Ms. Sadler until recently?

KM: Well, I . . . I mean, I've been having some trouble finding a place, and so I was staying at Jen's until I could find somewhere I could afford on my own. . . .

SH: And do you and Ms. Sadler—whom I believe you met in college—sometimes gossip in the workplace?

MH: Stuart. Really. What does this—

SH: Oh, that will become apparent. Don't you two like to pass notes, and Instant Message each other, and e-mail back and forth between your computers on an almost constant basis, Ms. Mackenzie?

KM: Well, Jen and I . . . I mean, we maintain a close working relationship, and she helps me with many work-related projects—

SH: Work-related. Is your commenting on the apparel of your supervisor, Ms. Jenkins, work related?

KM: Well, apparently her commenting on mine is—so, yes.

MH: Touché.

SH: What about referring to Ms. Jenkins as . . . What is it again? Oh, yes. The T.O.D. Is that work related?

KM: How did you—

MH: Stuart. Cut it out.

JV: I agree with Mitch. What does any of this have to do with the fact that your client—or at least someone in her office—forged my client's initials on a document she never even saw?

SH: I'm getting to that. What does T.O.D. mean, Ms. Mackenzie?

KM: Um. It means . . . It means Tough On Doubters. Because Amy's always very tough on people who doubt . . . her ability.

SH: Tough on Doubters.

KM: Uh-huh.

SH: You realize you're supposed to be telling the truth here, don't you, Ms. Mackenzie?

KM: (inaudible)

SH: What was that, Ms. Mackenzie?

KM: Nothing.

SH: Isn't it true that you and Ms. Sadler dislike Ms. Jenkins, and spend most of your time at the office every day making fun of her?

KM: No. That's not true at all.

SH: Isn't it also true that you are friendly with a number of *New York Journal* employees who'd like nothing better than to see Mrs. Lopez reinstated?

KM: Well, yes. I mean, everybody loves Mrs. Lopez, and we all miss her very much—

SH: That is an inaccurate statement right there. Not everyone at the *New York Journal* loves Mrs. Lopez. Not everyone believes she is entitled to get her job back. Not everyone agrees she even MAKES the best key lime pie in the city—

MH: Stuart. Come on. This is getting personal now, and I don't think—

SH: YOUR friends are the only ones who feel that way, isn't that so, Ms. Mackenzie? Including the woman you are now living with, Ms. Dolly Vargas. Who happens to be involved—and I mean in the romantic sense—with the owner of the *New York Journal*, Peter Hargrave, who ALSO expressed regret at the loss of Mrs. Lopez's baked goods. Isn't that so, Ms. Mackenzie?

KM: Isn't what so? That I'm living with Dolly, or that Peter likes Mrs. Lopez's cinnamon buns?

SH: Isn't it true, Ms. Mackenzie, that you and the entire

staff of the *New York Journal* are so addicted to this woman's baking that you are lying about not having written that letter of warning in order to afford her a loophole with which she might win back her post?

KM: No!

MH: Stuart. Come on.

SH: Isn't it true that your dislike of Amy Jenkins is so strong that you would do anything to get her into trouble with her superiors—such as deny having written a document that has what even you stated appears to be your signature on it?

KM: No! I mean, yes, it looks like my signature, but it's not. I never even got a chance to finish writing it. Amy e-mailed me and said—

SH: That's all. No more questions.

KM: But it's not true. About the letter. I mean—

SH: I said no more questions, Ms. Mackenzie.

MH: I have a question for you, Stuart. How do you sleep at night?

SH: Better than you will, when Dad hears about this. Come on, Amy. We're done here.

I'm in trouble. BIG trouble.

Oh my God. Oh my God, I don't understand any of this. Mitch says it's nothing, but I think he's just saying that to make me feel better. It's not nothing. It's clearly not nothing. I mean, my boss just accused me of being a liar. How can that be nothing?

And I can see how from her point of view it would be more beneficial for me to be perceived as a liar than, you know, her. Which is basically what she is. I mean, ONE of us is lying, and if it's not me, it has to be her. Because I certainly never wrote that letter, and I certainly never had Mrs. Lopez sign it.

So who did?

At least I have Mrs. Lopez to back me up. She says she didn't sign it either.

Except . . .

I'm sorry, Mrs. Lopez is very sweet, but she's not the most reliable witness. I mean, she definitely has an agenda, which is getting her job back. Mine is apparently that I want to get back at AMY, but for what? I mean, it's true I think she's a big, shallow loser and it's true we call her the T.O.D., but how did she find out? Jen's going to freak when she hears Amy knows, and the last thing I want is to freak out Jen, she's got enough problems as it is with the fertility thing and—

OH!!! I've got to get control of myself. Think about something other than Stuart Hertzog. Think about kittens and rainbows. Oh yuck, that won't work. Think about the Travel Channel. Yes, the Travel Channel, teal blue seas and yawning blue sky overhead, little huts on stilts above the water, like in Bali . . .

Oh my God, I can't believe my boss basically accused me of being a liar in front of Mitch Hertzog, the one person in the world I wanted to impress with my cool professionalism. So far I've blathered about chicken and garlic sauce to him, had my ex-boyfriend THROW chicken in garlic sauce on him, nearly gotten sick in front of him, had my ex sing ballads in front of him, and now my boss is calling me a liar in front of him. . . .

Mitch says all I have to do is go back to my office and find the e-mail Amy sent me—the one telling me to skip the written warning—and forward it to him. Also forward him the draft of the letter I was writing to Mrs. Lopez but never finished. He seems to think this will make everything all right.

But how will it make everything all right? Sure, it'll prove I didn't have anything to do with that letter. But it won't help the *Journal* win Mrs. Lopez's case against it. And isn't Mitch supposed to be on the paper's side, not Mrs. Lopez's? I mean, isn't the *Journal* paying his fees?

But it's like . . . it's like he *wants* Mrs. Lopez to win. Like he set up this whole thing to make Amy look like the big, fat liar she is.

Which is fine, except that . . .

Amy KNOWS we call her the T.O.D. She KNOWS.

I mean, that's not going to make working with her slightly UN-COMFORTABLE or anything. . . .

Oh, WHY did we ever start calling her that? I mean, she IS a tyrannical office despot, but we ought to have kept it to ourselves. It isn't nice to call people names, even if they deserve it. All human beings have worth and dignity, that's what Professor Wingblade always said. All human beings have worth and dignity. Except maybe for Nazis. And Al-Qaeda. And tyrannical office despots. . . .

STOP IT! Amy is not as bad as Hitler! She hasn't killed anyone. THAT WE KNOW OF.

I will never call her the T.O.D. again. I will never call her the T.O.D. again. I will never call her the T.O.D. again. I will—

Oh, God, my cab is a block away from 216 W. 57th even as I write. Please God, don't let Amy be there when I walk in. Please let me get to my desk and forward the e-mail and the draft and get my stuff and go home sick for the rest of the day. . . . Please please please please please . . .

$4.50, plus $1 tip for cab. Don't forget to send the T.O.D. a reimbursement form!

Wait . . . Why is Carl Hopkins standing by the door?

THE NEW YORK JOURNAL
New York City's Leading Photo-Newspaper

Security Division
The New York Journal
216 W. 57th Street
New York, NY 10019
212-555-6890

MEMO
To: All Personnel
Fr: Security Administration
Re: Persona Non Grata

Persona Non Grata Notification

Please note that the below-named individual has been classified "persona non grata" in 216 W. 57th Street as of the date of this notification and will continue to remain so indefinitely. This individual is not to be allowed on the premises of 216 W. 57th Street at any time during the term of above sanction.

Name: Kathleen A. Mackenzie
ID#: 3164-000-6794
Description: (photo attached)
White female, 25 years of age
5 feet, 4 inches, 120–130 lbs.
Blonde hair, blue eyes

Contact Security immediately upon sighting of above individual.

cc: Amy Jenkins, Director, Human Resources

Hello, you've reached the voice mail of Jennifer Sadler. Sorry I can't take your call right now. At the tone, please leave your name and number, and I'll get back to you as soon as I can.

(Tone)

Jen? Jen, where are you, it's Kate. I'm in the lobby downstairs. They won't let me up. They say I'm PNG'd. I told them there has to be some kind of mistake, but they say there's not, and they even showed me the form. It says I weigh a hundred twenty to a hundred and thirty pounds. Do I really look like I weigh that much? I only weigh one seventeen. I'll bet Amy wrote this! That would explain it. . . . Do you know what's going on? I'm . . . Oh, wait, here comes Amy. She's holding . . . Oh my God, she's holding a box of my stuff. That's my Disneyland snowglobe from on top of my computer monitor. Why does the T.O.D. have my Disneyland snowglobe? Oh . . . my . . . God. . . .

(Click)

THE NEW YORK JOURNAL
New York City's Leading Photo-Newspaper

Amy Denise Jenkins
Director
Human Resources
The New York Journal
216 W. 57th Street
New York, NY 10019
212-555-6890
amy.jenkins@thenyjournal.com

Kathleen A. Mackenzie
Personnel Representative
Human Resources
The New York Journal
216 W. 57th Street
New York, NY 10019

This letter serves to inform you that as of today's date, your employment at the *New York Journal* has been terminated. Your belongings from your work station have been inventoried and packed. You are to be escorted from the premises by Security, and have been listed as Persona Non Grata at this location. Should you need to speak to anyone regarding the termination of your position at the *New York Journal*, you will need to do so by telephone. Your initials below indicate receipt of this letter.

Amy Jenkins
Director, Human Resources

Well, it's happened. I'm fired. I'm actually fired.

I've never been fired before. Even when I was the salad-bar attendant at Rax Roast Beef back in Luxor, and my manager, Peggy Ann, said I was the worst salad-bar attendant they'd ever had, because I picked the cauliflower out of the dressing canisters instead of stirring it to the bottom, I still never got fired for it.

Until now.

How could this have happened? I don't understand how any of this could be happening. This morning I had a job. This morning I had no boyfriend, or place of my own to live. But I still had a job. I had a job that I even sort of liked.

And now I have no job. I have no boyfriend, I have no place to live, and I have no job.

Oh my God. I'M HOMELESS!

It's true! Except for the fact that I'm sitting in a penthouse suite (that doesn't actually belong to me), I have become a statistic—one of New York's many unemployed homeless.

Oh God! Soon I'll be living in a cardboard box! In Alphabet City (except Alphabet City has become totally gentrified—I bet even a cardboard box there costs $1200 a month . . . and they probably want first and last and a security deposit on it, too).

What am I going to do? I mean, seriously. I have no job to go to, no place to live. . . . WHAT AM I GOING TO DO????

I guess I could ask Dale for a loan. He just came into millions. Or however much they pay members of bands that have just been signed to a major label.

But if I ask Dale for a loan, I'll actually have to talk to him. And I don't want to talk to him. Not after the chicken-with-garlic-sauce incident. Plus he'll just feel all superior—*Oh, she couldn't make it without me.*

Ditto Mom. I mean, she isn't about to touch a penny of what Dad left her when he died . . . not the principal, anyway. And besides, she'll just tell me to go back to Dale again. I swear, she'd be prouder of me if I followed Dale and the band around wearing nothing but a hand-knitted poncho than she'll ever be over my having a job or my own place to live.

Jen? No, I can't to go to Jen, she has her own problems. I can't keep running to Jen every time I suffer a financial or emotional setback.

Mitch? Mitch? How can I even think about going to Mitch? I mean, this is all his fault, anyway! He KNEW Amy forged that letter! He knew she forged it, and he wanted Mrs. Lopez's lawyer to see that, because for some reason Mitch is on Mrs. Lopez's side and not the paper's. Which is all well and good, since Mrs. Lopez is a sweet lady and all, and none of this is her fault, anyway.

EXCEPT THAT NOW I HAVE NO JOB!!!!!!!!!!! Is that what he wanted? For me to get fired????

No wait. Mitch is a reasonable person. A decent person, even. A reasonable, decent person would never get a girl fired because her ex threw chicken on his pants.

I should have have just quit my stupid job in the first place in protest over what happened to Mrs. Lopez. Seriously, this is like karma, or something. Because I didn't quit my job, as I knew I morally should have, my job has been taken away from me.

And hey, don't I get severance pay? Or at least unemployment? I should AT LEAST get unemployment. Why didn't I read the personnel handbook more closely? Let's see, I'm administration, not staff, so that means I get . . . two weeks pay as severance? Or is it four weeks? WHY couldn't I have been union? Then the T.O.D. wouldn't have dared fire me without issuing both a verbal and written warning first. . . .

Let's see . . . unemployment for someone who was making $40,000 a year is . . .

Oh God. Skiboy just walked in. He says Dolly told him to meet her here after work. They're going to some benefit dinner, or something. Doesn't Skiboy look nice in a tux? Yum. Not as nice as Mitch Hertzog, but . . .

OH MY GOD, I CAN'T BELIEVE I WROTE THAT!!!! I am never thinking another kind thought about Mitch Hertzog again. THAT GUY GOT
ME FIRED!!!!!!!!!!

Skiboy just asked me what I'm doing here in the middle of the day.
I told him that I was fired on account of standing up for my convictions
at work. He seems impressed. He says this calls for a celebration.

And really, if you think about it, I SHOULD celebrate. I am free of
the oppressive rule of the tyrannical office despot! I don't know where
I'm going to find a new job, let alone scrounge up first and last
month's rent, plus a security deposit for a place of my own while living
on unemployment checks, but I'm free! Liberated! Why shouldn't I celebrate by drinking a vodka and tonic in the middle of the day?

"Yes, we SHOULD celebrate," I just told Skiboy. And he is breaking
out the Grey Goose now.

Really, things aren't SO bad, are they? Yes, I have no job, no life, no
place to live, etc. And I can't even move back home with my parents,
because my father is dead and my mother is driving cross-country in
an RV the size of Dolly's terrace.

But I have what few are given—ooooh, Skiboy makes strong drinks—I
have what you called the greatest gift of all: the opportunity to make a
whole new start in life. Really, I could be anything. I could be a doctor—
well, if I could get money for med school. And if the sight of blood
didn't make me feel all sweaty. I could be a politician—really, I'd be
very good at that, you know, because I know what it feels like to be
trod upon and broken, like the people of Jersey City or wherever. I
could be a lawyer—

Oh, no, bleech, a lawyer, never! I never want to be like Stuart Hertzog.
I HATE him. As much as I hate Amy Jenkins. The two of them deserve
each other. I hope they both enjoy their country-club wedding and
their Sandals honeymoon and their house in Westchester and their 2.1
kids and no dog because of the kids' allergies and their gas-guzzling,
environment-destroying—Yes, thank you, Skiboy, a refill would be

lovely—SUV, and their two weeks in Aspen and their summer on the Cape and their JP Tods and their Tse cashmere sweaters on their two-year-old, and preschools that cost ten grand a year for two mornings a week and then the right elementary school because God forbid Junior doesn't get into the right college so he can get the right job so he doesn't end up like ME, A BIG FAT HOMELESS UNEMPLOYED FREAK THAT NO ONE LOVES AND WHO IS GOING TO DIE PENNILESS, BITTER, AND ALONE. . . .

Okay, one more drinkie, then I have to hite the pavement, becauge I am woman hear me rihatibgrmvn

✉

To: Dolly Vargas <dolly.vargas@thenyjournal.com>
Fr: Jen Sadler <jennifer.sadler@thenyjournal.com>
Re: Kate

Dolly, something AWFUL has happened. Kate's been fired! Amy gave her the old heave-ho right before lunch. I don't know what went down at the meeting they went to this morning, but Amy came tearing in here with SECURITY, cleaned out Kate's desk, confiscated her computer, and that was that. I haven't been able to reach Kate—I don't even know where she is. She left a message a little before noon, but since then. . . .

Dolly, you've GOT to talk to Peter about this. Kate is a GOOD employee. If she's been fired—and like this—it must be a mistake. It probably has to do with Mrs. Lopez. PLEASE PLEASE ask Peter to look into it.

And if she shows up at your place, can you ask her to call me? I'm really worried about her.

Jen

✉

To: Jen Sadler <jennifer.sadler@thenyjournal.com>
Fr: Dolly Vargas <dolly.vargas@thenyjournal.com>
Re: Kate

Darling, don't worry. I just called home, and Kate's safe with Ski-boy. He says he's taking good care of her.

Of COURSE I'll talk to Peter, only you know he flew to San Francisco this morning to check on his vineyard. I mean, I'm happy to

Boy Meets Girl   235

see if I can do anything to help our poor little Miss Moppett, but I'm not sure Peter's going to be able to be of any help until he gets back.

Tell you what, though, if it makes you feel any better, I'll call Mitch Hertzog. He'll know what to do. After all, from what I hear from Kate—and it's hard to tell, with all the slurring—he's the one who got her fired. He can damn well get her hired back.

Got to run—so many new designs, so few adjectives to describe them. . . .

XXXOOO
Dolly

Hola, darling! It's me, Dolly! I'm not home at the moment—or possibly I am, but I'm . . . indisposed. Anyway, leave a message, and I'll get back to you just the second I can. Ciao!

(Tone)

Kate? Kate, it's me, Jen. Dolly says you're home. How come you're not picking up? Kate, come on, pick up. I know you're upset—hell, I would be, too. But this is not over, okay? Dolly and I are going to get your job back, don't you worry. We're not going to let that fucking T.O.D. win. We're all in this together, Kate, and we're going to get your job back. Did you hear me? Well, call me as soon as you get this message. I'm really worried about you, Kate.

(Click)

Hola, darling! It's me, Dolly! I'm not home at the moment—or possibly I am, but I'm . . . indisposed. Anyway, leave a message, and I'll get back to you just the second I can. Ciao!

(Tone)

Kate? This is Mitch Hertzog. I just heard. Look, I am so—I don't even know how to begin to say how sorry I am. I had no idea—I mean, I suspected she was up to something, but I never in a million years thought that she'd stoop to—Listen, I am not going to let them do this to you. All I need is that e-mail Amy sent you and a draft of that letter you wrote, and we have them, okay? I'll get your job back in no time. If you can just get one of your coworkers to forward those documents from your computer, we're golden. Kate? Are you there? If you're there, pick up. If not . . . well, call me as soon as you can. You have my numbers. Just . . . God, I can't believe she did this. I'm so sorry. Call me.

(Click)

✉

To: Stuart Hertzog <stuart.hertzog@hwd.com>
Fr: Mitchell Hertzog <mitchell.hertzog@hwd.com>
Re: Kate Mackenzie

Well, I hope you're satisfied. Your fiancée, obviously acting under your instructions, just dug her own grave. That's right, Stu. Because I am going to bury Amy for this. Bury her. I hope this won't interfere with your wedding plans too much. Don't worry, she'll probably still marry you, since she's going to NEED to change her name by the time I get through with her. She won't be able to get on a guestlist in town with the name Jenkins.

Oh, and tell her from me—she doesn't know the meaning of the word *fucker*. But she will, shortly.

Mitch

✉

To: Dolly Vargas <dolly.vargas@thenyjournal.com>
Fr: Mitch Hertzog <mitchell.hertzog@hwd.com>
Re: Kate

What do you mean, "Not to worry, she's home safe with Skiboy"? What the hell is a Skiboy?

Mitch

Journal of Kate Mackenzie

Vodka and tonic is good. I loves my vodkja tonic!!!!!!!! I love= Skiboy for mkiokhkin vosah toiniubc and fir dskoiwn k khiohmvu kjh ojjng bdf Skikjfioh vodkaolsj is goodnkjn oi dks Boy knlskn Mliktch nsk JSen ihds Skibooy knlsknf DOlly knds i liek lijnf pretty kndnvloucds skibod friend!!!!

Har hahr

✉

To: Mitchell Hertzog <mitchell.hertzog@hwd.com>
Fr: Stuart Hertzog <stuart.hertzog@hwd.com>
Re: Kate Mackenzie

Hey, don't blame ME for the fact that your little girlfriend got her ass canned. If she doesn't know how to play the game, she shouldn't be playing with the big kids now, should she? Besides, the only person you SHOULD be blaming for what happened is yourself. You're the one who brought up that stinking letter, friend, not me, and not Jeri.

The real question is . . .

Why'd you do it? Was it really out of some vestigial White Knight desire to see that Lopez woman get her job back? Or were you just trying to make Amy look bad? Are you really so jealous of my having found a woman so perfect that you can't stand to see me happy? Is that it, Mitch?

Well, hope you're satisfied. That Lopez bitch isn't getting her job back, Amy's probably going to get promoted over this, and your little blonde is going to have to head on down to the food-stamp line.

Good times, bud. Good times.

"Stuie"

Stuart Hertzog, Senior Partner
Hertzog Webber and Doyle, Attorneys at Law
444 Madison Avenue, Suite 1505
New York, NY 10022
212-555-7900

Hello, you've reached the mobile phone of Arthur Hertzog. I'm on the links at the moment—or maybe at the bar—and can't get to my phone. But leave a message, and I'll be back to you in a flash.

(Tone)

Dad, it's Stuart. You have to come home. I mean it. I know you're probably enjoying yourself, and God knows, you deserve a vacation, just like the rest of us. But Mitch is out of control. I really mean it. I'm worried he actually might do me—or worse, my fiancée—bodily harm. Dad, I've had to barricade myself in my office because just now in the hallway—right in front of Clarissa— right in front of the receptionists—he actually took a swing at me. A swing at me, Dad. He tried to physically strike me. You know he's always been bigger than me. You HAVE to do something. Call me tonight, I'll be home.

(Click)

Hello, you've reached the mobile phone of Arthur Hertzog. I'm on the links at the moment—or maybe at the bar—and can't get to my phone. But leave a message, and I'll be back to you in a flash.

(Tone)

Arthur, it's Margaret. You know I would never deliberately disturb you when you are on one of your interminable lost boys' retreats. But if you would deign to check your messages once in a while, you would see that all hell has broken loose back home. Mitchell physically assaulted Stuart—assaulted him!—in the hallway. I understand that law enforcement was not called in, but only because Stuart didn't want the reputation of the firm tarnished by controversy. You've GOT to do something, Arthur. Oh, and your daughter Janice hasn't been any joy to live with these past few days either. You might want to give her a call, too, and tell her that drugs kill! THAT's why I violated her privacy. Because I don't want HER to end up like Mitch. You do know he smoked marijuana when he was in Thailand, don't you? I swear it's residual THC that's making him behave this way. Oh, for God's sake, Arthur, put down the highball and come HOME!

(Click)

Hello, you've reached the mobile phone of Arthur Hertzog. I'm on the links at the moment—or maybe at the bar—and can't get to my phone. But leave a message, and I'll be back to you in a flash.

(Tone)

Dad, it's Sean. Seriously. I'm going to kill her. If she comes in my room one more time, I won't be held responsible for my actions. Also, Stuart's girlfriend is a tool. That's all.

(Click)

Hello, you've reached the mobile phone of Arthur Hertzog. I'm on the links at the moment—or maybe at the bar—and can't get to my phone. But leave a message, and I'll be back to you in a flash.

(Tone)

Hi, Daddy, it's Stacy. Look. You might be getting some messages. . . . I'm not saying I really understand what's going on, but if I were you, I'd just ignore them. It's just Stuart, being a jerk. How's the weather? It snowed here last night. Just a dusting, but still. Snow! In March! The girls say hi, and so does Little John. Love you.

(Click)

✉

To: Mitch Hertzog <mitchell.hertzog@hwd.com>
Fr: Stacy Trent <IH8BARNEY@freemail.com>
Re: Kate

Okay, okay, slow down. I could barely understand your message. Apparently, you've left the office now, and you aren't answering your cell, so I'll try Blackberrying you. So you had a meeting with Stuart and his girlfriend and the ever-attractive Kate this morning, and then Amy apparently fired Kate, and now you can't find her (Kate) because she's run off with someone named Skiboy?

Well, really, Mitch. She doesn't sound as if she was all that stable to begin with if she's hanging out with people named Skiboy. Maybe you're better off.

Although it was mean of Amy to fire her. Why'd she do it, anyway?

Little John said his first full sentence today, in case you're interested. It was, "Up yours, dickhead." Apparently, he heard it from his "Unca Mitch," who said it to his "Unca Stu" last Saturday. So thanks for that.

All my love,
Stace

✉

To: Stacy Trent <IH8BARNEY@freemail.com>
Fr: Mitch Hertzog <mitchell.hertzog@hwd.com>
Re: Kate

Thanks, got your message. Don't worry, though, I found her. Well, "we" found her, actually—I ran into Kate's friend Jen in the lobby of Dolly Vargas's building. Apparently, she was as concerned as I was about Kate, and we both came rushing over here, in separate cabs. We finally convinced the doorman to let us up, since no one was answering the intercom.

Thank God he did, too. Apparently "Skiboy," Dolly's latest "friend"—not Kate's—got Kate completely plowed on vodka and tonics. He doesn't seem to see what the problem is, being pretty well sloshed himself. But he's not the one we found facedown on Dolly's bearskin rug.

Good thing they're both still fully dressed, or I'd be wiping the smarmy grin off his face.

By the way, his real name is Gunther. He doesn't know why everyone seems to call him Skiboy.

Anyway, Jen and I are currently trying to sober Kate up, although she is not being very receptive to this plan. Jen's trying to get her to down some Vitamin B right now.

Sorry about the alarming phone call—I guess I just needed to talk to someone sane for a minute. But this Jen girl seems surprisingly lucid, for a human-resources type.

I'm just going to ignore that little barb of yours about Kate being unstable.

Oh, and congratulate Jason for me. I'll be proud as punch the day MY boy first uses the word *dickhead* in a sentence.

Fucker

To: Mitch Hertzog <mitchell.hertzog@hwd.com>
Fr: Stacy Trent <IH8BARNEY@freemail.com>
Re: Kate

<Good thing they're both still fully dressed, or I'd be wiping the smarmy grin off his face.>

You like her, you like her, you really, really like her.

Sorry. I was momentarily transported to second grade there.

So. You're in love with the instable little lush, aren't you? It's okay, you can admit it to your big sis. You always did have a bit of a rescue complex where girls were concerned. You just LOVE rushing in to play the big hero.

But do you really think you can get her job back? I mean, no offense, but you're not the one engaged to her boss.

And, uh, just a word of warning: when she sobers up, she might not like you anymore. You DID get her fired, from what I understand.

Stace

P.S. I am so getting you back when you have kids of your own. Their first words are gonna be "I love my uncle Stuart."

To: Stacy Trent <IH8BARNEY@freemail.com>
Fr: Mitch Hertzog <mitchell.hertzog@hwd.com>
Re: Kate

Re: your accusation that I have some sort of "rescue complex" when it comes to choosing my romantic partners: I must disagree. Admittedly, there have not been many, but the women I have chosen to date have all been fiercely independent, with very definite goals and lives of their own. Even the flight attendant you mentioned—the one in Kuala Lampur—aspired to own her own gym someday. Her body was important to her, and she worked hard to keep it trim, and longed to help other women do the same. . . .

Sorry, I'm being flippant when I meant to be serious. The fact of the matter is, Stuart's girlfriend really pulled a number on us both. Kate and me, I mean. Well, mostly on Kate. I suspected, but wasn't sure, that Amy falsified a document—and forged Kate's name on it. I will admit that I hoped to force Ms. Jenkins to own up to it at the depo today. I figured I'd rub Stuart's nose in the fact that his future wife isn't the innocent young flower he'd like all of us to believe she is. You know, make him admit Amy's capable of calling me a fucker, and all of that. In fact, I was hoping I could get her to do it in front of him.

But damned if Ms. Jenkins—with Stuart's help—didn't turn the tables. I've seen dirty dealing in my day, but even some of the pimps I've defended in the past couldn't have held a candle to those two for pure subterfuge. Amy's now saying Kate is the one lying about it, and used that as grounds for firing her.

Thing is, Amy seized Kate's computer, so the chances of proving Amy wrong are slim to none. Still, the urge to see justice done is pretty strong, considering the whole damn thing's my own fault—and where there's a will, there's a way, and yadda yadda yadda. . . .

You know us rescue-complex types. We're all the same.

Hey, did you talk to Stuart at all? I almost got off a good one right in his face, but I tripped over one of those damned potted ferns Dad's got all over the lobby. Then he barricaded himself in his office and wouldn't come out. Big baby.

Better go, my battery needs recharging, and Kate seems to be coming around. . . .

The Fucker

....

✉

To: Margaret Hertzog <margaret.hertzog@hwd.com>
Fr: Stuart Hertzog <stuart.hertzog@hwd.com>
Re: Mitch

I tried calling you, Mother, but no one is picking up. Are you speaking to Dad, perhaps? I put a call in to him, but got no response. I hope you're having better luck.

Seriously, Mother, I'm worried. I think Mitch needs to be on medication. Clearly he has anger management issues, as today's violent outburst so eloquently illustrated. I suggest we sit down with the therapist you've been sending Janice to and ask if he can do some sort of intervention on Mitch. The man is clearly suffering from some sort of delusion. I almost wonder if it could be post-traumatic stress syndrome left over from his days as a public defender. You know he saw some grisly photos during that time, death and dismemberment and she-males and who knows what all else.

And really, he can't think any of it—the sacrifices, the time—was ultimately worth it, because all he was doing was trying to defend lowlifes who were never meant to function in society in the first place, and probably should never have been born at all.

Maybe Mitch just needs a vacation. Maybe Dad could arrange for Mitch to use the condo in Aspen for a few weeks. I think if we could just get him out of the office for a while, he might be okay.

Think about it, Mother. He's been acting strangely ever since you made Janice come home from college—not speaking to you, except to accuse you of interfering where your help's not wanted or needed, that kind of thing. Almost as if he were on JANICE's side.

He's screwed up his own life so badly, it's no wonder he thinks it's fine if Janice screws up hers. Thank God Dad was able to bail Mitch out by offering him a position with the firm. Think what he'd be doing by now if Dad hadn't been so generous. Probably working for the Legal Defense Fund, or worse.

Well, anyway, call me, Mother, as soon as you can. We really need to do something about Mitch before it's too late.

Stuart

P.S. Amy sends her love. We looked at the loveliest apartment today, a three-bedroom on Fifth Avenue, complete with a maid's room and eat-in kitchen. We also had blood taken for genetic testing to make sure neither of us is a carrier of any inherited disorders. You know Dad's side of the family has always been a little sketchy—I mean, everything that happened prior to great-grandad's arrival at Ellis Island. It will be interesting to discover if there is any form of psychosis that might possibly run through our family. Because I'm convinced that is what's wrong with Mitch.

Stuart

Stuart Hertzog, Senior Partner
Hertzog Webber and Doyle, Attorneys at Law
444 Madison Avenue, Suite 1505
New York, NY 10022
212-555-7900

✉

To: Kate Mackenzie <katydid@freemail.com>
Fr: Vivica <vivica@sophisticate.com>
Re: Your Ex

Dear Kate,

Hi, you don't know me, but the other night I did a runway show (I am
a model) in Bryant Park for Marc Jacobs and I met your ex-boyfriend,
Dale Carter, lead singer for the band I'm Not Making Any More
Sandwiches (isn't that the funniest name for a band? Dale told me why
he calls his band that, and I think it's just the CUTEST story).

Anyway, I think Dale is pretty hot, and all. I mean, I have always
wanted to have a boyfriend who could perhaps immortalize me in
song. Like that Alison girl that other guy sings about, or the Lady in
Red. Or Layla. Or that lucky-duck showgirl Lola, for that matter.

But the thing is, due to an unfortunate experience two years ago in-
volving a man I learned was actually a murderer (well, attempted,
currently serving twenty years to life), I have given up on dating
men who don't come with references, particularly from their exes.
I would really like to get to know Dale better, because he is a fox—
I love his little goatee!—and a musician and all. But I told him, "No
way will I ask you out, buster, unless you give me your mother's
phone number and the names and e-mail addresses of the last five
girls you've dated."

Well, you can imagine I was pretty surprised when I found out
Dale's only been with one girl in the past ten years! I mean, I
haven't even had the same HAIR COLOR for that long, let alone
DATED anyone. I think it is pretty impressive that Dale and you
went out for that long, even if, like Dale says, you ultimately
stabbed him in the back by demanding a commitment and then left
him, rendering him into the broken shell that he is today.

I, however, am not looking for commitment, since I am only twenty-fo—
three years old, and as I said, I am a model, and so I travel quite
a bit between New York and Milan and Paris, and the last thing I
want is a ball and chain. Know what I mean? I mean, I did get a
dog, finally, but Pedro is a Maltese and fits into my wallet, practically. If you could get a wallet-sized boyfriend I so would, but you
can't, so I am stuck looking for ones who don't mind a girlfriend
who travels a lot. But since Dale will be touring with his band for
the next eighteen months, he says my traveling is cool with him.

So if you don't mind, Kate, could you call me on my cell at your convenience? The number is 917-555-4532. And if you could just answer true or false on the topics below, I would really appreciate it.

Love,
Vivica

1) My ex has never attempted to murder someone for the inheritance money.
T or F

2) My ex is appreciative of the fine arts, such as driftwood sculpture.
T or F

3) My ex would never have sex with a hotel maid while I was at
the beach.
T or F

4) My ex would never lie about having a job and then try to borrow my money and never pay it back.
T or F

5) My ex has never borrowed my Christian Dior thong and
stretched it all out.
T or F

6) My ex enjoys exotic cuisine, such as onion blossoms from TGI Friday's.
T or F

7) My ex is fond of animals.
T or F

8) My ex is respectful of his mother/sisters/aunts.
T or F

9) My ex has never asked another person to pose as him in order to dupe a reporter into thinking he is somewhere he is not.
T or F

10) My ex does not snore.
T or F

Thanks bunches!

V

....

✉

To: Kate Mackenzie <katydid@freemail.com>
Fr: Mitchell Hertzog <mitchell.hertzog@hwd.com>
Re: Hi

Remember me? Okay, stupid question.

Wait, before you hit the Delete button, hear me out—or read me out, anyway.

I had absolutely no right to do what I did. And I can't even begin to tell you how sorry I am. I completely and totally screwed up. My intention, for what it's worth, was twofold—and I could probably be disbarred for admitting this, but what the hell: 1) to get Ida her job back—no one who makes brownies like that should be out of work, and 2) to show my brother what kind of girl he's marrying, by forcing my future sister-in-law into revealing what kind of two-faced liar she really is.

I should have known Ms. Jenkins would react the way she did. She is, after all, cut from the same cloth as my brother.

I know you didn't write that letter, Kate. I know Amy wrote it, forged your signature and Ida Lopez's initials on it, and then stuck it in Ida's file. I'm betting she didn't do it until after Ida filed for breach of contract, when Amy must have realized she'd been a little too cavalier with union regulations in her zeal to appease my brother's wounded pride.

What I'm really writing to say—besides I'm sorry—is that I don't want you to worry about any of this, because I'm going to get your job back.

And then we'll see how your boss likes being on the receiving instead of the sending end of a letter of termination for a change.

Listen, we really should get together and talk about this. What are you doing tonight? If you're not feeling too vodka-and-tonicked out, why don't you come over to my place for dinner? It might be safer than dining out. At least for my wardrobe.

Please don't say no. I owe you dinner, at the very least.

Mitch

Journal of Kate Mackenzie

Help.

Pain. Intense pain, radiating from behind eye sockets. Can barely move.

What HAPPENED? Oooooh, writing in capitals is hurting my eyes. But really . . . what DID happen last night? It's all starting to come back, but only in patches. I remember . . . Skiboy. I remember Skiboy being really nice to me.

But why? Why would Skiboy be nice to me? He's Dolly's boyfriend. Something to do with my job, I know but . . .

Ooooh. That's right. I have no job. I have no job anymore. Which is good, because it's . . . 12:45 in the afternoon, which means if I did have a job, I would be three hours and forty-five minutes late for it now.

Amy. Amy fired me. That stupid cow. I can't believe she did that.

Jen. Did Jen come over last night? I seem to dimly remember—

Oh. My. God.

Jen did come over last night. To check on me. But so did—

MITCH HERTZOG!

Mitch Hertzog came over last night to check on me. Only I was PLASTERED. And . . . oh my God. I think I threw up on him.

Okay. Okay, deep breath. Just get to the phone. Just get to the phone to call Jen and see if I really did throw up on Mitch Hertzog. Maybe it was all a bad dream. . . .

It wasn't a dream. I just got off phone with Jen. I really did throw up on Mitch Hertzog. On his shoes, no less.

Oh! And he had on really nice shoes! They were wingtips. Jen says there were chunks of vomit stuck in the little punched-out places. . . .

To which all I can say is . . . Good.

Oh, God. If I had anything left to throw up, I'd throw it up now.

WHY did I let Skiboy fix me all those drinks? Why didn't I just say no? Oh my God, now on top of being homeless, jobless, and boyfriend-less, I'm an alcoholic. They're going to have to send me to the Betty Ford Clinic.

Only I can't afford to go there, because I don't have any health insurance, because I lost my job.

Jen says Mitch was really very kind and concerned about me last night. Great. The person who is responsible for getting me fired was kind and concerned about me last night. As I was yakking on his shoes.

WHY didn't I see any of this coming? Not the being-hung-over-from-drinking-with-Skiboy thing. The losing-my-job thing. My God, I just WALKED into it, didn't I? Amy's little trap.

Of course, I had an excellent guide steering me along . . . Mr. Mitch Hertzog.

Hertzog. God. It even sounds as if I'm hurling up an evening's worth of vodka and tonics when I say it. Hertzog. Hertzog. Amy HURTS OGG.

Oh God, I wish I were dead.

A Note from
Dolly

Good morning, roomie! Just a note to say I know you probably feel like <u>merde ce matin</u>. Never fear, I'm the queen of hangovers. There's tomato juice in the fridge, and Vitamin B in my medicine cabinet.

And don't worry about the bathmat. Hortense comes on Thursdays. She's a whiz with stains of any kind.

Skiboy said he had a fabulous time last night. Apparently you are very entertaining when you're sloshed. He said you sang him the Kentucky State song. We should make a point to go out for karaoke one night—you and me and Skiboy. It'll be a blast!

Anyway, be a lamb, and if any packages come for Skiboy via UPS, make sure you hide them away somewhere, just in case Peter comes home unexpectedly. I don't want any unpleasant surprises, if you know what I mean.

Feel better, and use my Jacuzzi, if you think it will help.

Ciao,
XXXOOO
Dolly

To: Kate Mackenzie <katydid@freemail.com>
Fr: Jen Sadler <jennifer.sadler@thenyjournal.com>
Re: You

Hey, you. You okay? How you holding up? You had a lot of people worried about you. Your lawyer friend seems like a really nice guy. Attentive, too. Call me if you want to talk.

J

⊠

To: Jen Sadler <jennifer.sadler@thenyjournal.com>
Fr: Kate Mackenzie <katydid@freemail.com>
Re: Me

Yeah, a real nice guy. A real nice guy who got me fired.

Oh, and as if things weren't bad enough, guess what I got this morning? I mean, besides an apology from Mitch—which is not anywhere near groveling enough, in my opinion. He had the nerve to ask me to dinner. Yeah! Dinner! Like that's going to help get my job back.

I got an e-mail from VIVICA. You know, the supermodel? The one who does the Victoria's Secret ads on TV?

Yeah. Guess who she's interested in dating? Dale. But she wanted my input first. I'm Not Making Any More Sandwiches played at a fashion show, and she met him there. She wants to go out with him, but she doesn't want to pursue it any further unless he likes driftwood sculptures, or something. I don't know. I was too hung over to read her e-mail properly.

God. I should have just stayed in Kentucky. Seriously.

Kate

....

✉

To: Kate Mackenzie <katydid@freemail.com>
Fr: Jen Sadler <jennifer.sadler@thenyjournal.com>
Re: You

No, you should not have stayed in Kentucky. If you had stayed in Kentucky, you never would have stopped wearing blue eyeshadow. Seriously, Kate, it was not a good look for you.

Also . . . you might never have met Mitch.

Kate, I know you might not believe this, but the guy was really hurting last night. He feels TERRIBLE about what happened with you and Amy. I really don't think he saw it coming. I don't know what exactly went down at the deposition—he told me a little about it—but his intention was NEVER to get you fired. I really think he's on our side in all of this, Kate. I think he wanted to help get Mrs. Lopez's job back . . . because he thought that's what YOU wanted.

I think he also wanted to make Amy look like a liar, but whatever, that one backfired pretty badly, too.

I know you probably don't feel too forgiving right now, but really, I think the guy meant well. And he didn't even blink about his shoes. Your *barf* isn't even gross to him. That has to mean something.

You know what he does, to stay in such great shape? Mitch, I mean? He volunteers at the Y. That's how he got all those muscles

you told me about. He plays wheelchair basketball. With para-
lyzed guys, you know?

Would a guy like that REALLY purposefully try to make a girl lose
her job? No.

Now snap out of it. We're going to get your job back. I promise.

And call the guy and say you'll go to dinner with him.

J

‥‥

✉

To: Jen Sadler <jennifer.sadler@thenyjournal.com>
Fr: Kate Mackenzie <katydid@freemail.com>
Re: Me

Are you HIGH???? I'm not going to have dinner with Mitch Hertzog. Even if it is true about the wheelchair basketball. Or are you
just saying that to get me to like him? Because if I find out it's not
true . . .

Not that it matters. THE GUY GOT ME FIRED, JEN.

And okay, maybe you're right, and he didn't mean it, and genuinely feels bad about it. But the fact is, I DON'T HAVE A JOB. Or
a PERMANENT ADDRESS. Or . . . ANYTHING.

So even if he DOES like me and my barf, what do I have to bring
to the relationship? Yeah, that'd be a big zero.

So what's the point of having dinner with him? Because what

would a totally PERFECT, WHEELCHAIR-BASKETBALL-PLAYING GUY LIKE THAT EVER SEE IN A JOBLESS REJECT LIKE ME????

Going to put my head in the oven.

Kate

....

⊠

To: Kate Mackenzie <katydid@freemail.com>
Fr: Jen Sadler <jennifer.sadler@thenyjournal.com>
Re: You
Fwd: ⊠ Say it isn't so! ⊠ Kate ⊠ Kate

Well, before you kill yourself, check out these e-mails from your personnel. Do these sound like they're from people who think you're a reject? DO THEY?

....

⊠

Fwd: <katydid@freemail.com>
To: Jen Sadler <jennifer.sadler@thenyjournal.com>
Fr: Nadine Wilcock-Salerno <nadine.salerno@thenyjournal.com>
Re: Say it isn't so!

Is it really true? Kate got the axe? But WHY? She was the nicest personnel rep this stupid company ever had (present company excluded, of course)!

This REEKS of Amy Jenkins. Is she behind this? I knew that bitch was up to something the other day in the staff dining room, when I saw her actually lift a piece of buttered bread to her lips. I haven't seen her go off Atkins in two years . . . I should have known she was celebrating.

What can I do to help get Kate back? Because if Amy thinks we're lying down for this one, she's high. She can tell us to be sweeties and wipe the seaties, and she can take away our Dessert Lady. But she can't fire Kate and get away with it. No way.

Nad:-(

....

✉

Fwd: ✉ <katydid@freemail.com>
To: Jen Sadler <jennifer.sadler@thenyjournal.com>
Fr: Mel Fuller-Trent <melissa.trent@trentcapital.com>
Re: Kate

Oh my God! Is it really true? Amy fired Kate? Why? Not for tardiness, I hope.

Jen, this is awful. Kate was SO nice to me when they were giving me that grief about going part-time. We have to DO something! What can I do? The Trents love holding benefits. Can we hold a benefit? For Kate? Just let me know, PLEASE!!!!

Mel

....

✉

Fwd:<katydid@freemail.com>
To: Jen Sadler <Jennifer.sadler@thenyjournal.com>
Fr: Tim Grabowski <timothy.grabowski@thenyjournal.com>
Re: Kate

I just heard. This means war. The T.O.D.'s aware of that, isn't she? That in firing Kate, she's alienating the entire Tech Dept? Because there isn't a guy here who wouldn't walk over hot coals for Kate.

She's the only one in that damn office (not including you, Jen) who treated us computer guys with anything remotely resembling respect. Not to mention compassion.

And she used to come to our *Farscape* marathon parties, too.

What can we do to get her back? Just let us know, and it's done.

Tim

....

✉

To: Kate Mackenzie <katydid@freemail.com>
Fr: Jen Sadler <jennifer.sadler@thenyjournal.com>
Re: You

Do those sound like e-mails from people who are happy to see you go? No, they don't. People here like you, Kate. MITCH likes you, too, barf on his shoes or not. Now cheer up.

Besides, you can't put your head in Dolly's oven, I just checked with her, and it's electric. The worst that can happen is that you'll bake yourself.

J

....

✉

To: Jen Sadler <jennifer.sadler@thenyjournal.com>
Fr: Kate Mackenzie <katydid@freemail.com>
Re: Me

Thanks for the e-mails. I guess they made me feel better. A little.

I'm going out to buy a paper. I need to start looking for a new job. Not to mention a new apartment. But first things first.

Did I mention I hate everyone in the whole universe? Present company excluded, of course.

Kate

Please. I don't even own a bicycle.

I can't believe I went to college so I could file.

Or knock on doors.

Fundraising/Devmt EOE MFDVSO
THE LESBIAN, GAY, BISEXUAL &
TRANSGENDER COMMUNITY
CENTER Seeking exp'd counselors. Post-
op transgenders preferred. Qualified
applicants should fax cover letter stating
sal history & desired pos: 212-555-2657

Great. The only way I'd qualify for this one is if I turn into a she-male.

ELECTRICIAN Expd Mechanic w/
following skills: Plan-install-wiring for
installation of panels, fixtures, outlets,
comm'l air conditioning & refrigeration,
low voltage wiring, intercoms, security &
fire alarm systems, motor controls &
installing motors, fans & pumps. $1000+
week. Fx res: 212-555-1460

WHY didn't I become an electrician?????

HEALTH FOOD HELP—PT/FT
Produce workers/Deli Juice Bar Person &
Cashier wtd. Health Food Store Exp.
Required. No Phone Calls. Please apply
at Yoga Yogurt, 229 W. 13th St (btw 7th
& 8th Aves)

Food service. Might as well move back to Kentucky and ask if I can have my old job at Rax Roast Beef.

LIFEGUARDS Wanted—
Free conditioning & training for great
summer lifeguard jobs at NYC beaches
and pools. Employment after successful
completion of training course, final test
and background check. By date of hire
must be 16+. Call 212-555-7880 EOE

Ha! I WISH!

To: Jen Sadler <jennifer.sadler@thenyjournal.com>
Fr: Mitchell Hertzog <mitchell.hertzog@hwd.com>
Re: Kate

Hi, Jen. I tried to call, but all I got was your voice mail.

Have you heard from Kate this morning? How's she doing? I e-mailed her, but I haven't heard back.

Let me know if you've heard anything.

Mitch

✉

To: Mitchell Hertzog <mitchell.hertzog@hwd.com>
Fr: Jen Sadler <jennifer.sadler@thenyjournal.com>
Re: Kate

She's fine. Ornery, but fine.

I don't think it will come as too much of a shock to you if I tell you that you are not one of her favorite people this morning, either. She doesn't seem to remember too much about what happened last night. How are your shoes, anyway?

J

✉

To: Jen Sadler <jennifer.sadler@thenyjournal.com>
Fr: Mitchell Hertzog <mitchell.hertzog@hwd.com>
Re: Kate

My shoes are fine. And it's great to hear that Kate's all right. Not so great, you know, that she hates my guts, but I can't say I blame her.

Listen, do you have access to Kate's computer at work? I was wondering if you'd be willing to commit a little white-collar crime for me. Nothing major, just check Kate's e-mail IN box and see if that note from Amy Jenkins—the one telling Kate to quit writing the warning letter to Ida Lopez—is still there. Could you do that for me, and let me know? I'd appreciate it.

Mitch

✉

To: Mitchell Hertzog <mitchell.hertzog@hwd.com>
Fr: Jen Sadler <jennifer.sadler@thenyjournal.com>
Re: Kate

Sorry to be the one to break it to you, but Kate's workstation has been cleared, and her computer's hard drive replaced. Amy got in here first thing after lunch yesterday and made sure the place was denuded of any sign that Kate Mackenzie ever worked here. Her files have been confiscated as well. My guess is, they've already met their fate with the office shredder. Amy is pretty thorough in her ruthless quest for total domination over the HR division of this company.

So unless Kate printed out a copy of her e-mail from Amy and took it home—which is exceedingly doubtful, knowing Kate, who likes to keep her work and home life separate—I'm sorry to say it's gone, never to be seen again.

Nice try, though, Romeo.

J

....

✉

To: Jen Sadler <jennifer.sadler@thenyjournal.com>
Fr: Mitchell Hertzog <mitchell.hertzog@hwd.com>
Re: Kate

I'm not giving up that easily. Give me the name and number of your IT guy, will you, Jen? Thanks.

Mitch

....

✉

To: Mitchell Hertzog <mitchell.hertzog@hwd.com>
Fr: Tim Grabowski <timothy.grabowski@thenyjournal.com>
Re: Kate

Got your message. Just tried calling but I got your voicemail.

Anyway, in answer to your question, the only way I could read Amy Jenkins's e-mail is through her computer. All of our e-mail is sent through a POP server. The mail program automatically down-loads mail from the server to the sender's hard disk, then it erases them from the server, so the only way to get to the sent e-mail is to go onto the hard drive of the computer from which it was sent.

Which, unless you've got a key to Amy's office, is going to be next to impossible.

Wish I could be more help. Kate's a cute kid, and we're all just crushed over what's happened. If you talk to her, tell her that the next *Farscape* marathon is at Raj's. She'll know what I mean.

Tim

....

✉

To: Kate Mackenzie <katydid@freemail.com>
Fr: Tim Grabowski <timothy.grabowski@thenyjournal.com>
Re: You

Hey, what's up with you and Dylan McDermott? You two an item yet, or what? I hope so. That guy is seriously easy on the eyes. But what's with the Superfriends ties? Hermès is so much classier.

Still, he seems to really like you. At least he really wants to help you get your job back, which is the same thing, practically. Got a message from him.

Invite me to the wedding?

Miss ya.

Tim

....

✉

To: Jen Sadler <jennifer.sadler@thenyjournal.com>
Fr: Kate Mackenzie <katydid@freemail.com>
Re: Mitch

What is going on with Mitch and IT? Tim just said Mitch had

been in touch with him. Come on. Spill. You know you can't keep a secret.

Kate

P.S. On my way to get a paper, I nearly got hit by a cab, and I didn't even care. Seriously. It was like, Oh, look, this cab is about to hit me. But I wasn't scared or anything. Because what would it matter if I died? Without my job, I have nothing to contribute to society anyway. I MIGHT AS WELL BE DEAD.

I was saved from the brink of death at the last minute by a Chinese food delivery man who pulled me back onto the curb. But still.

....

✉

To: Kate Mackenzie <katydid@freemail.com>
Fr: Jen Sadler <jennifer.sadler@thenyjournal.com>
Re: Mitch

That taxicab story is horrifying, but it is not going to induce me to tell you what Mitch wanted.

He made me promise not to tell.

But I swear to you, Kate, this guy's only got what's best for you in mind. He's the real deal.

You might want to rethink the suicide-by-cab thing. Just FYI.

J

✉

To: Jen Sadler <jennifer.sadler@thenyjournal.com>
Fr: Kate Mackenzie <katydid@freemail.com>
Re: He's the real deal

Sure, that's what they all say. Excuse me if I take this opportunity to barf some more. Oh, hold on, the doorman is buzzing. Flowers being delivered from Skiboy for Dolly, no doubt.

Hey, do you have to tip flower delivery guys?

Kate

✉

To: Kate Mackenzie <katydid@freemail.com>
Fr: Jen Sadler <jennifer.sadler@thenyjournal.com>
Re: Flower Delivery

Yes, you have to tip them. Two or three bucks, at least. Hasn't anyone ever sent you flowers before?

And how do you know they're from Skiboy? Maybe they're from the great Peter Hargrave himself. Call me and describe them, as Craig hasn't sent me flowers since we got married, and I've forgotten what they look like.

J

~*East Side Floral Company*~
"Say it with Flowers!"
1125 York Avenue • New York NY 10028

To: Kate Mackenzie
c/o Dolly Vargas
610 East End Avenue, Penthouse A

Forgive me?

Mitch

✉

To: Jen Sadler <jennifer.sadler@thenyjournal.com>
Fr: Kate Mackenzie <katydid@freemail.com>
Re: Flower Delivery

Roses. Two dozen of them. Pink ones.
From Mitch.
Like I'm just supposed to forget he got me fired.
Still. It's sweet of him. Considering I barfed on his shoes and all.

Kate

....

✉

To: Kate Mackenzie <katydid@freemail.com>
Fr: Jen Sadler <jennifer.sadler@thenyjournal.com>
Re: Flower Delivery

So are you going to have dinner with him, or not?

J

....

✉

To: Jen Sadler <jennifer.sadler@thenyjournal.com>
Fr: Kate Mackenzie <katydid@freemail.com>
Re: Dinner

Like a few flowers are going to make everything okay? I am so not
having dinner with him.

Please.
No way.

Kate

⊠

To: Mitchell Hertzog <mitchell.hertzog@hwd.com>
Fr: Kate Mackenzie <katydid@freemail.com>
Re: Hi

Hi, Mitch. I tried calling your office just now, but your assistant says you're out. Anyway, I just wanted to say thank you for the flowers. They're beautiful.

Thanks also for helping me last night . . . that is, Jen told me you helped. I don't actually remember it very well, except the part where I heaved on your shoes. Sorry about that. Every time you come near me you seem to get sprayed with something, don't you? Like I'm Mount St. Helens or something.

Anyway, if the offer for dinner still stands, I'll take you up on it.

Kate

⊠

To: Kate Mackenzie <katydid@freemail.com>
Fr: Mitchell Hertzog <mitchell.hertzog@hwd.com>
Re: Hi

Of course the offer for dinner still stands. Seven okay? Glad you liked the flowers. Don't worry about the shoes. I didn't like them much anyway.

Mitch

To: Jen Sadler <jennifer.sadler@thenyjournal.com>
Fr: Kate Mackenzie <katydid@freemail.com>
Re: Me

I'm going.

WHAT SHOULD I WEAR?????

Kate

To: Kate Mackenzie <katydid@freemail.com>
Fr: Jen Sadler <jennifer.sadler@thenyjournal.com>
Re: You

I so knew it.

Wear a skirt.

And remember, though he may be a cute wheelchair-basketball-playing lawyer with barf on his shoes, you still don't know where he's been. Don't forget to use a condom, Miss "I've Only Been with One Other Man My Whole Life."

J

To: Jen Sadler <jennifer.sadler@thenyjournal.com>
Fr: Kate Mackenzie <katydid@freemail.com>
Re: Me

EEEEEEEEEEEEEEWWWWWWW!!!!!!!!!

Kate

Journal of Kate Mackenzie

What am I doing? I mean, why am I obsessing over what to wear tonight to Mitch's? I shouldn't even be GOING to Mitch's. I have no job, no place to live, I'm on the rebound, relationship-wise. This guy has been nothing but trouble, and besides which, the two of us have nothing in common, except a mutual appreciation for Mrs. Lopez's brownies and the Travel Channel. I mean, he's a LAWYER.

Should I wear control-top panties, or not? You know they leave those lines . . . but if I don't wear them, my belly pooches out.

Oh my God, I can't even believe I'm obsessing over this.

Do I have time to whip up one of Mrs. Lopez's recipes? No . . . I can't make a bundt cake AND blow out my hair. . . . DAMN!!!!!!!!!!

```
D'Agostino Supermarkets #6
      1507 York Avenue
     New York, NY 10021


Reg 2        Time: 18:02
Cashier 411
Name: Dolores


1 lb. tiger prawn  $17.99
2 artichokes       $02.99
4 lemons           $02.00
1 Irish butter     $05.99
1 Fettucine        $03.99
1 French bread     $01.99
1 El Rey Cho Bar   $02.52
1 pd coffee        $06.99
1 garlic           $00.59
4 pears            $02.00
Subtotal           $47.05
Tax                $03.88
Total              $50.93


Charge
Mitchell Hertzog
xxxx-xxx-xxxx-xxxx
      Thank you for
   shopping at D'Agostino
```

```
Welcome to CVS


Reg 1          Time: 18:22



1 pk Lady Bic
Disp Razors          $2.99

1 L'eggs
Con. Top             $1.49

1 pk Trojan Ribbed   $7.99

1 Almay Pressed
Powder               $7.99


Subtotal            $19.49

Tax                  $1.61

Total               $20.09


Charge
Kathleen Mackenzie
xxxx-xxx-xxxx-xxxx


Thank you for shopping
        at CVS
```

✉

To: Stacy Trent <IH8BARNEY@freemail.com>
Fr: Margaret Hertzog <margaret.hertzog@hwd.com>
Re: Your brother

Stacy, I tried to phone, but no one picked up. Either you are all out, or your au pair is on the phone with her Swedish boyfriend again, and not picking up. I really suggest you get her a separate line. And I do hope you are deducting the cost of these calls she's constantly making to this boy from her weekly paycheck.

Anyway, I just received an extremely distressing phone call from your brother Stuart. He says you are being most uncooperative regarding the wedding plans. I understand that the week of June 21 is the only time in the foreseeable future the two of them can both be away from their jobs, and that—although Jason promised them use of your yard for an outdoor ceremony on Midsummer's Day—there seems to be some problem with—and I am finding this hard to believe, but Stuart swears he heard it directly from you—your coven?

Honestly, Stacy. Do you really expect me to believe that you have joined a coven? That you are some kind of practicing witch? You live in Greenwich, for God's sake. There are no covens in Greenwich.

Furthermore, I thought the Trents were episcopalian, not Wiccan.

If you are just SAYING you are holding a coven meeting or whatever it is on the summer solstice in order to make Stuart angry . . . well, you've succeeded.

What is wrong with you, Stacy? Why can't you play nicely with your brother? Stuart is, out of all of you, the only one who was born with any common sense. Why must you and Mitch antagonize him so? He's always been extremely sensitive, as I'm sure you're aware, particularly about the size of his head. Yet, that never stopped the two of you from calling him Tweety growing up, did it? Oh, you two were just hilarious.

Claiming you belong to a coven is hardly an amusing joke, Stacy. It's cruel, and it's insensitive, especially coming from a mother of three. What if the children should hear of it, Stacy? Besides, I want this Amy Jenkins to LIKE us. For God's sake, she's hardly had what I'd call a warm welcome into the family, with your father still not returning anyone's calls from Scottsdale, and Mitch causing this uproar in her office, and you saying you're a practicing witch, and Janice . . . well, just being Janice. Really, the poor girl is going to think you're all out to get her, and who could blame her? Finally we have a chance to get some NORMAL blood into the Hertzog family tree, and you're trying to ruin it for everyone.

Well, I won't have it. You're to let your brother have his wedding at your house, like your own husband promised him he could. Do you understand, Stacy?

And while you're at it, it would be polite if you'd host Amy's bridal shower. I'm not saying you have to have it at your place. We can have it here. But I think it would be a nice gesture if you and Janice hosted it.

Hopefully all the green will have grown out of her hair by then.

Well, that's all, call me.

Mother

....

✉

To: Kate Mackenzie <katydid@freemail.com>
Fr: Vivica <vivica@sophisticate.com>
Re: Dale

Hi. I know you probably haven't had a chance to look over the quiz I sent you. Dale says you're a human resources rep, and I know that is a very important and busy job. Not like being a model. I mean, when you are a model, you just, you know, try on clothes and smile and stuff. Although it is quite hard to smile when you feel as if your heart is breaking—which I felt like mine was. Until the other night, when I met Dale. I know he is your ex-boyfriend and all and you probably don't feel about him the way you did when you were first going out, but you guys are still friends, right? Dale says you are. So I was just hoping you could get back to me, because it's been a really, really long time since I met a guy as nice as Dale. Most guys, they don't even remember my name, they just want to hook up so they can go back to the office on Monday and tell everyone they scored with a supermodel.

Dale, he says he's gonna write a song about me. Just as soon as he can think of a word that rhymes with Vivica.

But no pressure about the quiz. Whenever you get to it. I know you're probably really busy with helping people and everything. Dale says you used to be a social worker. I think that is so admirable. I mean, people are our best resource. I once rescued a dog from the streets of Mexico City. But that isn't the same as rescuing a person. And the dog turned out to have heartworms and had to be put to sleep. You can't put people to sleep, which is too bad, because some of them deserve it, like my ex. But that's another story.

Well, anyway. Just get that quiz back to me when you get a chance. Thanks.

Bye.

V

Journal of Kate Mackenzie

Okay, breathe, Kate. You've got to breathe.

It's just, I never had a guy go to so much trouble for me. I mean, make a whole dinner for me, and all. Dale made me tea once when I was sick in bed, but that's about it. Plus he left the tea bag in it when he went to warm it up in the microwave and the staple ignited and the kitchen caught on fire and the fire department had to come put it out, and we had to get all new cabinets, so I'm not even sure that counts.

But Mitch. Mitch made me scampi. Shrimp scampi.

And it was good. The scampi, I mean. Really, really good. He says he went to cooking camp as a kid (Cooking camp! Apparently no one in his family was very thrilled with the idea . . . they wanted him to go to soccer camp with his brother Stuart. But Mitch says he was more interested in scoring pies than goals).

Anyway, he's in the kitchen now, making dessert. He won't tell me what it is. I sincerely hope it involves chocolate.

But that's not why I'm freaking out. The dessert thing, I mean. And the-having-a-guy-cook-for-me thing.

No, it's the fact that he just told me that he USED TO BE A PUBLIC DEFENDER.

It's true. He only came to work for his father's company because his dad had a heart attack, and then bypass surgery, and he begged Mitch to keep an eye on things at the firm while he was recovering.

Apparently, a large part of the recovery process for Mr. Hertzog is playing golf with his buddies in Arizona.

But whatever. The point is, Mitch isn't really a soulless corporate drone. He has never embraced big business and is in fact looking forward to getting back to work down at the criminal courts.

Where he apparently defends those who can't afford to pay for their own lawyer.

And the thing is, Mitch could get a job anywhere. He doesn't HAVE to be a public defender. He does it—well, probably for the same reason I became a social worker . . .

To make a difference.

HOW AM I SUPPOSED TO KEEP FROM LIKING HIM???? More than liking him, even.

He got me fired. He got me fired because he doesn't like his brother's girlfriend.

And I *still* totally want to jump his bones. I KNOW! There is something severely wrong with me.

Seriously. Because—oh my God—he's so perfect. I mean, he COOKS, and he VOLUNTEERS, and he WANTS TO HELP PEOPLE. . . . God, even his *apartment* is perfect. I mean, it's clearly a GUY's apartment, and it's a little messy—baseball caps stuffed in amongst the paperback mystery novels on the bookshelves; University of Michigan basketball season schedules lying around on the coffee table; a copy of Playboy peeking out from beneath the couch where he obviously recently shoved it.

But it's a beautiful apartment, one he inherited from his dead grandfather, two bedrooms (he uses one as an office and a guest room for when his nieces and nephew come to stay, he says) and two bathrooms—1800 square feet with a balcony overlooking the East River. He owns, which is good, because the rent on a place like this would be five grand a month at least. Maybe even more, because there's a health club in the building. The maintenance alone has to be at least fifteen hundred a month.

And he's got *three* TVs, one of them at least a 42-incher (for watching the games, he says).

And okay, all the furniture is brown: brown couch, brown armchair, brown place mats on the dining-room table, even brown sheets (I peeked on the way to the bathroom) on his bed.

But I could fix that. I mean, I watch *Trading Spaces*, I know how a few well-placed slipcovers can brighten up a space. . . .

OH MY GOD, WHAT AM I THINKING?

Professor Wingblade would be appalled. I mean, he always told us we have to develop a relationship based on trust and mutual harmony before we can—

OH MY GOD, HE'S GOT TIVO!!!!!! I just found the remote, wedged in between the sofa cushions. TiVo. I've never had a boyfriend who had TiVo. I've never had a boyfriend who owned his own TV. I mean, I bought the one Dale and I—

Wait. I need to get a grip. Yes, Mitch seems like he might—in spite of the whole getting me fired thing—be a great guy. And yes, he has a great apartment.

But, even though he used to be a public defender, right now he's making five hundred dollars an hour defending corporate giants from the likes of little Mrs. Lopez, who has never hurt anyone (who didn't deserve it, anyway).

And he's so cavalier about the whole thing, he got me fired. FIRED!!!!

Besides which, I have a lot of problems right now. I can't be jumping into a romantic relationship with someone I've only just met. I need to find a job, and an apartment, and a sense of purpose to my life. Professor Wingblade said that you can never truly love anyone until you learn to love yourself, and the truth is, I am finding it very hard to love myself since I got fired. Not that I define myself through my work. It's just that . . . without my work, who AM I? What is my purpose here on earth? I want to make a difference and help people, but no one will seem to LET ME. So if I can't do what I was put on this earth to do, WHY AM I EVEN HERE????

And seriously, supposing something DOES develop between Mitch and me. How am I going to introduce him to people? "Oh, this is my boyfriend, funny story: He's the one who got me fired?"

Um, that will not exactly endear him to my social set, if you know what I mean.

But, oh my God, he has such really nice lips! Mitch, does, I mean. What's a public defender doing with lips like that? It's not FAIR!!! I was looking at Mitch's mouth all through dinner, when he was telling me about the year he took off to travel around the world. And his lips really are very beautifully shaped. They look like they'd be really . . . strong. If there's one thing I can't stand, it's weak lips. But no need to worry about Mitch's. I have a feeling those lips of his could make a girl forget all about being destitute and homeless . . . and quite a few other things, as well—

Damn. The Praying Mantis. I forgot about the Praying Mantis! Are they dating? Are they just friends? What is up between the two of them? Why didn't I remember to ask over dinner? God, if he's seeing her, I will just have to KILL MYSELF. How can I compete with an Ingres-like praying mantis in designer duds, especially when I can barely afford control-top pantyhose?

What the hell. I don't want to have a relationship with a lawyer. Do I?

Oh my God, I just peeked into the kitchen, and he made braised pears in chocolate sauce for dessert. Braised pears in chocolate sauce with VANILLA HÄAGEN-DAZS for dessert—

HOW IS ANY WOMAN SUPPOSED TO RESIST THIS MAN?

Journal of Kate Mackenzie

Oh my God! This is HORRIBLE!!!! I was right! I was right! About his lips, I mean! They are VERY strong!

This is AWFUL. His lips are so strong, I am practically melting into the couch. Oh, WHY did I kiss him? WHY WHY WHY???? I do NOT need to be falling in love right now—particularly not with a lawyer!

It's all my fault, though. We were just enjoying our braised pears in chocolate sauce when suddenly something, I don't know what, came over me. I think it was when he was talking about his nieces and how he was teaching them to speak Japanese (for instance, that *bacca* means "stupid") and one of them asked how Japanese people could understand each other when they were all speaking this foreign language, and then one said to the other, "Because they were BORN speaking it, ya bacca!"

And something inside of me just snapped, and I HAD to jump on him and start kissing him, I just had to, Praying Mantis be damned!

And oh my God, he looked so surprised. But kind of happy, too.

And I was right. I was SO right. He has really, really strong lips, and he kisses like he means it, and we must have been kissing for like half an hour, because all the ice cream melted. But that's not all that melted, because I swear to God I think I am now one with my control-top panty hose, which I had to wear because the dress I borrowed from Dolly is so tight my stomach was pooching out in front, and now I think got so hot from all the kissing that my skin has become grafted to the Lycra, and thank God Mitch excused himself when he did, or there might possibly have been a small thermal nuclear reaction in the vicinity of my crotch, and now if I can just peel these stupid things off without him coming back while I'm doing it, maybe he won't ever know I was wearing control-top hose in the first place.

Where did he go, anyway? Oh my God, what if he left because he knows it's wrong to be getting involved like this with an unemployed homeless person? Even though he does keep insisting that he's going to get me my job back. Only I don't know how, it's not like I'm in a union like Mrs. Lopez and can sue the company for not giving me written warning or anything.

But excuse me, he makes a living—or used to, anyway, defending society's rejects. Who is HE to look down on a person just because she happens to be unemployed—thanks entirely to HIM, by the way?

Wait—what if that's not why he excused himself at all? What if he excused himself because of the Praying Mantis? What if I jumped on him before he got a chance to explain that he and the Praying Mantis are engaged?

Well, screw her. I don't condone boyfriend-stealing, but goddammit, you can't make braised pears for a girl and expect her to—

NO! God! What is WRONG with me? I do NOT want to be in a relationship right now.

WAIT! What if he went to go get a condom? Is that what guys do? I mean Dale never did because we were each other's first and onlies—well, until tonight, maybe—and who knows what is going on with him and that Vivica girl—

And besides, I'm on the Pill.

But this is different, this is two adults in the big city, not high-school kids fooling around in the back of the boy's mom's Chevette. Should I have said something, like, "Don't worry, I have protection," since I do, in my purse?

But maybe the girl isn't supposed to say that. Maybe that's, like, slutty. Maybe I should have just reached casually down and brought out the pack—

MAYBE I SHOULD JUST LEAVE!!!!!!!!!! Because, seriously, where is this going to go? I moved to New York to HELP people, how can I possibly have a relationship with someone who—

But public defenders help people, don't they?

Except he's not a public defender anymore, he's—oh, God—

What is the sound of one hand clapping? What is the weight of a single grain of sand? Equal to my interest in the message you are about to leave. Speak at the tone.

(Tone)

Mitchell. This is your mother. Mitchell, if you're there, pick up. Mitchell, this is serious. Your little sister is missing. Janice has run away. I came home from the American Doll Society meeting and she was gone. I have no idea where she is and I'm worried sick, because . . . well, we had a little tiff earlier. Is she with you, Mitchell? I can't think where else she'd go. If you hear from her, Mitchell, let me know. I know we aren't exactly speaking right now, you and I, but . . . well, I would think you could let your own mother know that her child is all right. I mean, it would be common courtesy to do so. Whatever your personal feelings about me might be. So . . . call me. Please.

(Click)

To: Stacy Trent <IH8BARNEY@freemail.com>
Fr: Mitchell Hertzog <mitchell.hertzog@hwd.com>
Re: We need to talk

Get whichever one of your children who is on the phone and not picking up the Call Waiting OFF the phone and call me.

This is serious.

Mitch

⊠

To: Mitchell Hertzog <mitchell.hertzog@hwd.com>
Fr: Stacy Trent <IH8BARNEY@freemail.com>
Re: We need to talk

It isn't one of the kids, it's Jason, he's on the phone with his grandmother. It's their semi-annual "what shall we invest our fortune in" discussion. What seems to be the problem?

Stacy

P.S. How was your big dinner last night? Did it work? The aphrodisiac shrimp scampi, I mean.

I'll tell you, it would take a lot more than shrimp to get ME to forgive a guy who'd gotten me fired. Hope she wasn't THAT easy, or you'll lose interest, I just know it. You always did love a challenge. Especially if it had breasts.

✉

To: Stacy Trent <IH8BARNEY@freemail.com>
Fr: Mitchell Hertzog <mitchell.hertzog@hwd.com>
Re: We need to talk

It's Sean. She showed up at my apartment last night. At a very in-opportune moment. I don't want to talk about it over the office e-mail system. I don't want Stuart to know about this. Can you come into the city and meet me for lunch today? It's important.

Mitch

⋯⋯⋯⋯⋯⋯⋯⋯⋯⋯⋯⋯⋯⋯⋯⋯⋯⋯⋯⋯⋯⋯⋯⋯⋯⋯⋯⋯⋯⋯⋯⋯⋯

✉

To: Mitchell Hertzog <mitchell.hertzog@hwd.com>
Fr: Stacy Trent <IH8BARNEY@freemail.com>
Re: We need to talk

I'll be there with bells on. Such a mystery! See you at noon.

Stacy

P.S. I'll call you from the building lobby. I don't want to run the risk of bumping into Stuie.

⋯⋯⋯⋯⋯⋯⋯⋯⋯⋯⋯⋯⋯⋯⋯⋯⋯⋯⋯⋯⋯⋯⋯⋯⋯⋯⋯⋯⋯⋯⋯⋯⋯

✉

To: Kate Mackenzie <katydid@freemail.com>
Fr: Jen Sadler <jennifer.sadler@thenyjournal.com>
Re: SO?????

HOW DID IT GO???? I can't believe you didn't call me last night. Did you even come HOME last night? Because I talked to Dolly already and she said by the time she and Skiboy retired to the boudoir—her exact words, by the way—you were still in absentia.

Oh my God, are you STILL with him? Where ARE you? CALL ME AND TELL ME ALL ABOUT IT!!!!!

J

P.S. I'm glad SOMEBODY is getting some. I mean, not that I'm not. But with this whole baby thing, it's kind of a drag only doing it when a little stick tells you to, and not just when you feel like it. Anyway. DISH!

....

✉

To: Jen Sadler <jennifer.sadler@thenyjournal.com>
Fr: Kate Mackenzie <katydid@freemail.com>
Re: SO?????

Sorry, I got back here really late and then overslept. I am turning into SUCH a slacker. I mean, just because I'm unemployed doesn't mean I have to ACT like it. But here I am already sleeping past ten. It's HORRIBLE!

Plus I missed *Charmed*.

Anyway, sorry to disappoint you, but nothing happened. Well, not NOTHING, but not what you think. I mean, we kissed. On his couch. For a long time.

And Jen: he has VERY strong lips.

I'm so confused.
Want to have lunch? Somewhere cheap 'cause I'm broke.

Kate

To: Kate Mackenzie <katydid@freemail.com>
Fr: Jen Sadler <jennifer.sadler@thenyjournal.com>
Re: SO?????

No offense, honey, but I ate lunch at noon, like a normal person. You're on your own with that one.

And as far as 'fessing up goes, Kate, that was pathetic. You KISSED? That's IT???

You MUST be confused, if a hot, wheelchair-basketball-playing lawyer makes you dinner, and all you do is KISS. I know it's been awhile, Katie, but please. You couldn't come up with anything better than THAT?

J

✉

To: Jen Sadler <jennifer.sadler@thenyjournal.com>
Fr: Kate Mackenzie <katydid@freemail.com>
Re: SO????

Please. That's not what I'm confused about. We'd have screwed like rabbits if his doorman hadn't buzzed. Mitch wasn't going to answer it, but I was like, "What if the building is on fire?" and he swore (!!!!!!!!!!) and went and answered the buzzer, and the doorman was like, "Sean is here to see you," and Mitch swore even more (!!!!!!!!) and said "Let me talk to her," and this woman's voice came on, and she was crying and going, "Mitch, you'll never believe what she did to me."

I swear to God for a minute I thought it was that praying mantis lady, the one I told you about, from the museum?

But then Mitch looked at me and said, "It's my little sister."

So of course I was all, "She sounds upset, you should let her up."

Which he did, but you could tell he didn't want to. Next thing I knew there was this girl with green hair crying on the sofa where we'd been making out (I can't believe I just wrote that. But it's true. We'd been making out! On his couch! AND IT WAS GREAT!!!!!!!!!!!! Oh, God, I am so going to hell).

Anyway, poor Sean—that's his sister. Or really, her name is Janice, but she wants everyone to call her Sean, and who can blame her, really? Janice is a bit of an old-fashioned name for a girl like her. I mean, she's only nineteen—was clearly in crisis and was just busting to tell Mitch all about it. I offered to leave, since I figured she didn't want a complete stranger to hear whatever it was.

But before I could go she just spilled it all out—about how their mother had made her leave college because she was concerned about a "friendship" Sean had developed with one of her roommates, and how Sean had tried to be reasonable about it, but how Mrs. Hertzog had forbidden her to communicate with this girl—Sarah—and how she'd taken away her (Sean's) computer so she and Sarah could not even exchange e-mails. Because of course Mrs. Hertzog had secretly been reading Sean's e-mails to Sarah, and had figured out that the girls' relationship wasn't exactly of the platonic variety, if you know what I mean.

Poor Mitch! I mean, it was clear he loves his little sister very much, and he was very good and gentle with her, offering to make her some hot chocolate—"the kind with the mini-marshmallows"—and let her stay the night if she wanted to.

But when he heard the part about Sean and Sarah's "forbidden love"—her words, not mine—I thought he might run out of there and never come back. I mean, he deals—or dealt, rather—with murderers every day, but the thought of dealing with his little sister's sexual identity crisis clearly threw him into panic. He sent me a look of such total and complete helplessness, well, I knew I couldn't possibly leave. I mean, he NEEDED me, Jen. He genuinely needed help coping with his tiny little lesbian sister.

So I sat right down and, just like Professor Wingblade told us to, I held Sean's hand and I listened to everything she had to say, which was most of the usual stuff for a kid who was coming out to her family for the first time. And I explained to Sean that her mother still loved her, but that Mrs. Hertzog was just frightened and confused, and that she hadn't meant any of the things she said, and that Sean should give her a few days to process the information, and she'd probably calm down and be able to discuss the situation rationally again.

Only Mitch didn't look as if he believed this. In fact, he even snorted . . . which, I let him know, wasn't helping. You know, when Sean wasn't listening. But Mitch just said I didn't know his mother, and that rational thinking was not one of her strong points.

But I find that so hard to believe. I mean, she gave birth to Mitch, didn't she? And—aside from the whole getting-me-fired thing—he seems like one of the most rational people I have ever met. I mean, after his initial shock, he took the whole thing with Sean in stride. In fact, when we said good night—after Sean had calmed down and stopped crying, and even cracked a joke or two about how sorry she was to have spoiled our "date"—he told me not to worry, that getting my job back was his biggest priority, especially now that he'd seen me "in action," as he put it.

In fact, he said I seem wasted on human resources, and should go into a private therapy practice.

But of course, it'll never happen. The private-therapy thing. Unless

I get an MSW, I mean. And how would I ever be able to afford to go back to school when I don't even have a job?

But it felt good to be of use to somebody for a change, instead of, you know, just mooching off everybody, like I've been doing since—oh, I don't know, it seems like forever. Sean seemed almost perky by the time I left.

I can't really say the same for Mitch. I mean, he didn't exactly look like he was going to slit his wrists or anything, but he didn't look too pleased.

I'm almost positive he thought he was going to score last night.

Um . . . so did I, actually. Thank God Sean showed up when she did, or I might have done something really, really stupid.

I miss you. I miss the office. What's happening? Has anybody jammed the copier accidentally on purpose so that the hot copier repairman has to come?

....

✉

To: Kate Mackenzie <katydid@freemail.com>
Fr: Jen Sadler <jennifer.sadler@thenyjournal.com>
Re: SO??????

Whoa. Ask and ye shall receive. That was some story.

But excuse me, Miss "Is The Hot Copy Repairman There." It sounds to me like you've got a hottie of your own eating right out of your little hand. I mean, counseling his little sister through her sexual identity crisis? Way to score! The guy must think you're freaking Dr. Phil. Only, you know, not bald, and with boobs.

Anyway, enough with the little sister. What are you talking about, "Thank God Sean showed up when she did, or I might have done something really, really stupid"? He's a nice guy, Kate. Why *shouldn't* you have jumped his bones? Because you don't like his choice of profession? Or because he's seen you with your head in Dolly Vargas's toilet?

J

P.S. Did he get into your bra? Please say yes.

J

....

✉

To: Jen Sadler <jennifer.sadler@thenyjournal.com>
Fr: Kate Mackenzie <katydid@freemail.com>
Re: SO??????

BECAUSE I HAVE NO JOB (THANKS TO HIM, REMEMBER)????

Not to mention, NO PERMANENT ADDRESS.

Also, I AM ON THE REBOUND.

God.

Kate

P.S. The answer is yes.

To: Amy Jenkins <amy.jenkins@theynyjournal.com>
Fr: Stuart Hertzog <stuart.hertzog@hwd.com>
Re: Bad news

I don't know quite how to tell you this, darling. In fact, I hesitate even to do so. You know I don't want anything to intrude on the dream that is our love for each other.

But the truth is, you're marrying a man who comes . . . not from a fractured home, per se, since my parents have enjoyed a married life of almost forty years. But definitely a home that—thanks to my siblings, who didn't have the same advantages as me, being younger and therefore not as important to my parents as I was, being the only child for three years—has known its share of controversy.

You've met Stacy, I know, and commented on how normal she seems, despite my descriptions of her as the heartless shrew who once locked me inside a car trunk.

And you've met Mitch, who—well, what can I say about Mitch that you don't already know? I mean, he's the man who claims you called him a foul name. That is the kind of low to which he's willing to stoop.

But you've never met my youngest sister, Janice. I was hoping, I will admit, that you never would—until her hair grew out, anyway. But now it appears that Janice's hair is the least of her problems. I'm afraid I have some hard news, Amy, and as it might actually have bearing on the outcome of our genetic testing—as they say these things can be inherited—I feel I have no choice but to tell you.

My sister Janice has been seduced by another woman.

I know it's shocking. My mother, rightfully, has forbidden Janice from ever communicating with the woman—her college roommate—

again. But this girl has my sister so thoroughly under her spell that poor Janice apparently fancies herself a lesbian.

Which is the most ridiculous thing I've ever heard, because of COURSE Janice isn't a lesbian. I mean, yes, she's always liked to keep her hair short, but she was never into sports as a child. True, she never played with Barbies like my sister Stacy, but she never expressed an interest in hiking, or even cargo pants.

I can only assume that this whole thing is a result of brainwashing on the part of the roommate. I don't actually know what my parents expected, allowing Janice to go to Berkeley, of all the colleges in the world. But . . . well, I just wanted to let you know, Amy, so you would be fully aware of what, exactly, you're getting yourself into, marrying into the Hertzog clan.

I hope you'll call me when you get this e-mail. I tried phoning a little while ago, but they said you were attending a staff meeting. Just remember the most important thing: Darling . . . I love you.

Stuart

Stuart Hertzog, Senior Partner
Hertzog Webber and Doyle, Attorneys at Law
444 Madison Avenue, Suite 1505
New York, NY 10022
212-555-7900

....

✉

To: Stuart Hertzog <stuart.hertzog@hwd.com>
Fr: Amy Jenkins <amy.jenkins@theynyjournal.com>
Re: Bad news

Darling! I can't believe you're worried about how *I* might be feeling at a time like this. You really are just the sweetest thing on earth. Please don't bother your head about me. Your poor mother is the one you should be worrying about. What that woman has suffered because of your siblings! I don't know how she bears it. Please send her my deepest sympathies.

And tell her not to worry. One of the girls in the Pi Delt house—a legacy, can you believe it?—went lesbian in grad school, but she snapped out of it two years ago. Some of the most happily married women in Manhattan are "hasbians," and you'd never know it to look at them. I'm sure Janice will be fine.

Kisses,

Amy

Amy Denise Jenkins
Director
Human Resources
The New York Journal
216 W. 57th Street
New York, NY 10019
212-555-6890
amy.jenkins@thenyjournal.com

This e-mail is intended only for the use of the individual to which it is addressed and may contain information that is privileged and confidential. If you are not the intended recipient, you are hereby notified that you have received this transmission in error; any review, dissemination, distribution, or copying of this transmission is prohibited. If you have received this communication in error, please notify us immediately by reply e-mail and delete this message and all of its attachments.

To: Courtney Allington <courtney.allington@allingtoninvestments.com>
Fr: Amy Jenkins <amy.jenkins@thenyjournal.com>
Re: Stuart's sister

Get this: the youngest one? Not the older one who claims to be a witch and is married to one of the Park Avenue Trents (though what he sees in her, God knows), but the younger one? Yeah. Turns out she's a full-on dyke.

What the hell am I going to do? I don't want a carpet-muncher in my bridal party.

Drinks after work? I need anesthetizing.

Ames

Amy Denise Jenkins
Director
Human Resources
The New York Journal
216 W. 57th Street
New York, NY 10019
212-555-6890
amy.jenkins@thenyjournal.com

To: Mitchell Hertzog <mitchell.hertzog@hwd.com>
Fr: Stacy Trent <IH8BARNEY@freemail.com>
Re: Janice aka Sean

Okay, look: It's not like it's the world's biggest surprise.

And the thing is, she's better off realizing it now than later, after she's married some dope and squeezed out a couple of kids.

Anyway. The thing is, what are we going to do with her? I know you don't want her staying with you, because she's screwing up your chances with Miss Girl of Your Dreams. But I don't want her staying with me, because Jason can't stand Bikini Kill. And that's going to screw up MY chances of getting laid.

And God knows we could never get Stuart to take her. Not that I'd let her go, if he offered.

So what's left? I mean, Mom. That's it, basically. Maybe if we could get to Dad before she does and explain the whole thing, he might be able to talk Mom into leaving the poor kid alone. What do you think?

Stace

P.S. Doesn't Mom ever watch TV? Doesn't she know by now that telling a kid you don't approve of them liking someone is almost like daring them to sleep with the person? Jesus. It's like she doesn't even live on this PLANET.

To: Stacy Trent <IH8BARNEY@freemail.com>
Fr: Stuart Hertzog <stuart.hertzog@hwd.com>
Re: Janice

I know you and Mitchell met today to discuss Janice. Don't bother denying it, I saw you hiding behind that potted palm in the lobby.

Well, while you two were yukking it up at Gramercy Tavern or wherever, I actually did a little research, and found the solution to our problem.

There are several well-established and respectable organizations that will, for a fee, transport (forcibly, if necessary) a child to a sexual-orientation rehabilitation center. The most successful results have been achieved at one called Right Way, in Utah, where, during the course of six weeks of intensive therapy, she'll be deprogrammed and ultimately made to see the error of her ways.

I've already given Right Way a call, and they do have an empty room at the moment. If we can get Janice there by this weekend, she'll graduate well in advance of my wedding. I think it's something we need to seriously consider. I've already discussed it with Mom, and she agrees: It's clearly the appropriate way to handle the situation.

I know, of course, that Mitch—given the lowlifes with whom he used to associate—will get into his ultra-liberal "it's genetics and not a choice" mode. But in Janice's case, this whole lesbian thing is clearly just her acting out because she's the youngest, and Mom and Dad never set appropriate boundaries for her. They were so worn out by Mitch that by the time Janice came along, they were just like, "Whatever you want to do, dear."

Well, I for one won't stand silently by while one of my siblings becomes a victim of left-wing politics and, eventually, a marginalized member of society. I'm hoping you, as one of the more rational members of this family, will back me up on this. Let me know.

Stuart

Stuart Hertzog, Senior Partner
Hertzog Webber and Doyle, Attorneys at Law
444 Madison Avenue, Suite 1505
New York, NY 10022
212-555-7900

....

✉

To: Stuart Hertzog <stuart.hertzog@hwd.com>
Fr: Stacy Trent <IH8BARNEY@freemail.com>
Re: Janice

Have you been sniffing glue or something? I'm not going to hire some company to kidnap Janice and ship her off to Utah to get made not-gay. Christ, Stuart, how would you like it if we hired a company to kidnap you and make you not marry a bitch with a stick up her ass?

Not so much, huh?

Leave Janice to Mitch and me. I think we can handle her.

Stacy

To: Stacy Trent <IH8BARNEY@freemail.com>
Fr: Margaret Hertzog <margaret.hertzog@hwd.com>
Re: Janice

Stacy, Stuart forwarded your last, exceptionally rude, e-mail to him. I couldn't believe—until I read it with my own eyes—that you would ever say something so cruel about your own brother's fiancée. Amy is a lovely girl. I can only think this "stick" business is due to the influence of Mitch. Stuart told me that Mitch is apparently besotted with a young woman whom, I understand, Amy was forced to fire for lying—under oath, no less. While it doesn't surprise me in the least that Mitch is associating with such a person, what DOES astonish me is that you would condone—even encourage—such a relationship.

I have to be honest with you, Stacy. I think Janice's choosing to stay with Mitch at this crucial time in her psychosexual development is a *very* bad idea. Mitch will only ENCOURAGE the unnatural feelings Janice has for this horrible Sarah person. I happen to know for a fact that he once made a donation to the Rainbow Coalition. If that is not condoning perverse sexual practices, I don't know what is.

Anyway, I would just like to suggest, young lady, that you apologize to your brother for saying such a nasty thing about his fiancée. And you had better do it soon, because I heard from your father a little while ago. He's coming home.

At last.

Never mind that it took finding out that his youngest daughter is having a *lesbian affair* to do it. He's on his way. Think about THAT.

Mom

✉

To: Mitchell Hertzog <Mitchell.hertzog@hwd.com>
Fr: Stacy Trent <IH8BARNEY@freemail.com>
Re: Mom

Dad's coming home. Because of the whole Janice thing. Just thought you should know.

Oh, also, I really hope you aren't thinking about marrying this Kate girl. Because I don't think Mom's gonna be real receptive to having her in the family.

Not, of course, that something like that would ever stop you. But it might bother your girlfriend a little.

S

....

✉

To: Stacy Trent <IH8BARNEY@freemail.com>
Fr: Mitchell Hertzog <Mitchell.hertzog@hwd.com>
Re: Mom

Marry her? I can't even seem to get five minutes alone with her without her ex or one of my family members bursting in on us.

But I'll tell you something . . . I've got a feeling about this one. Kate, I mean.

Okay, yeah, so far I've managed to get her fired, and set her up in a living situation I wouldn't exactly call ideal, given that there's a six-foot-five German ski instructor residing there as well.

But I plan on making it up to her. Getting her a job. And then maybe the living situation thing will take care of itself.

Although I'll have to get my little sister out of the guest room for that to happen.

One step at a time. . . .

Mitch   .

You've reached Ready Lock. Locked out? Don't call a friend! Call Ready Lock. Locks changed, keys made while you wait. Just leave a message, and Ed will get back to you in five minutes— guaranteed.

(Tone)

Eddie, it's me, Mitch Hertzog. You remember. Your lawyer for that little imbroglio you got into in Kip's Bay. You told me if there was ever anything you could do for me, just name it. Well, I think I've finally got something you can do for me. Give me a call.

(Click)

✉

To: Jen Sadler <jennifer.sadler@thenyjournal.com>
Fr: Mitchell Hertzog <mitchell.hertzog@freemail.com>
Re: Kate

Hi, Jen. Thanks for putting me in touch with your division's IT guy. Unfortunately, Tim wasn't able to give me the kind of help I was hoping for. I did, however, just speak to someone who happens to be an expert in the area of data retrieval. And I was thinking that if you and I put our heads together, we might be able to do something to help rectify the situation.

With Kate, I mean. And her current state of unemployment.

Of course, what I'm suggesting will involve—well, nothing illegal, exactly. But something that might, if it's found out, get you into trouble. Possibly even fired. I wouldn't even ask you to get involved if it wasn't for the fact that there is absolutely no other way, that I can tell, around it.

Anyway, if you're up for it, give me a call. You have my card.

And it'd be really great if you wouldn't mention any of this to Kate just yet. It might not pan out, and I'd hate to get her hopes up for nothing. Thanks.

Mitch

✉

To: Mitchell Hertzog <mitchell.hertzog@freemail.com>
Fr: Jen Sadler <jennifer.sadler@thenyjournal.com>
Re: Kate

Are you kidding? You can count me in.
Just name the date and time, and I'm your girl.

J

✉

To: Kate Mackenzie <katydid@freemail.com>
Fr: Dale Carter <imnotmakinganymoresandwiches@freemail.com>
Re: Vivica

Look, Viv told me how you won't answer her e-mails and shit. And I can understand why you might be mad, Kate. I mean, it might seem like one minute I was, you know, confessing my undying love for you in the lobby of your office building, and the next minute, I was, um, making out with a supermodel.

But the truth is if I thought there was even a CHANCE you might come back to me, I'd drop Vivica in a New York minute. Whatever that is.

But hell, Kate, you made it pretty clear last time I saw you that it was over between us. So I thought I'd take your advice, you know, and move on.

If you've changed your mind and want to get back together, though, just say the word. We're leaving for tour in a few days, but you could still fully sign on as like, costume mistress or something, and travel with us in the RV.

That's right, Kate. We get to go across country in our own RV. Just like your mom.

Don't get me wrong, Vivica's hot and all, and she's nice, too. But nobody could ever hold up a candle to you Kate. Just say the word, and I'm yours again.

Dale

....

✉

To: Dale Carter <imnotmakinganymoresandwiches@freemail.com>
Fr: Kate Mackenzie <katydid@freemail.com>
Re: Vivica

Hold a candle. Not hold UP a candle.

And the reason I haven't answered Vivica is because I've been busy, Dale. But really, I think it's great about the two of you, I hope you'll be really happy together. I mean it. I'm glad you're moving on, because I am, too.

At least, I'm trying to.

Take care, Dale. And good luck coming up with a rhyme for *Vivica*.

Kate

To: Kate Mackenzie <katydid@freemail.com>
Fr: Sean <psychodramabeautyqueen@freemail.com>
Re: Last night

Hi. I found your e-mail address in my brother's address book. I just wanted to say thanks for being so understanding and everything last night. You're a really cool person. You made me feel like I'm not this enormous freak which, frankly, I've kind of suspected lately that I really am.

So. Thanks.

And I'm sorry I messed up your evening with my brother. But if it's any consolation, I think he really likes you, because you're all he can talk about. Like he practically killed me after you left for crashing your dinner. And he's never been that way about any girl before.

So . . . talk to you later.

Sean

✉

To: Vivica <vivica@sophisticate.com>
Fr: Kate Mackenzie <katydid@freemail.com>
Re: Dale

Dear Vivica,

Sorry I didn't write sooner, but things have been kind of . . . hectic. I mean, I lost my job, and I sort of don't have a real place to live—Dale can tell you more about that, though.

Anyway, in answer to your questions about Dale, to the best of my knowledge, he's never tried to kill anybody. Once this guy threw a bottle at him while he was on stage in Jersey City, and Dale and he got into a fight, but that was totally provoked. And they were able to reattach the guy's finger just fine.

I don't really know Dale's opinion on driftwood sculpture—I don't think either of us has ever seen any of that. Kentucky is a land-locked state, you know.

But I'm sure Dale doesn't DISLIKE driftwood sculpture. And yes, he is good with pets. He even had a dog for most of the time we were going out, until it got kicked in the head by a cow (long story).

My only complaint about Dale—as he seems to have told you—is about the commitment thing. I think if you'd been going out with someone as long as I ended up going out with Dale, and then had him turn around and say he had to take it one day at a time and wasn't sure whether or not he could commit, you'd have moved out, too.

But maybe that's just me.

And maybe things will be different for you and Dale. You sound like a very nice person—I saw you on the cover of this month's *Vogue,* and you LOOK like a nice person, too. I sincerely hope things click with you and Dale.

In the meantime, could you please tell him that if he's planning on giving up the apartment early in order to leave for his tour, that I still expect my half of the security deposit back? I'm currently un-employed, as I think I mentioned, and could really use the money.

Good luck,

Kate

To: Kate Mackenzie <katydid@freemail.com>
Fr: Vivica <vivica@sophisticate.com>
Re: Dale

Oh my God, thanks SO MUCH for your e-mail. You totally made my day. I'm SO glad Dale never tried to kill anyone (although what's with the finger thing? Well, I'm sure he'll tell me when he's ready)!

You sound like a really nice person, too. I'm sorry you have no job, boyfriend, or place to live. You may not believe this, but when I first came to New York, I was just like you. I mean, homeless and poor. Until I signed with my agency, and all.

Hey, have you ever thought of being a model, like me? Dale showed me that picture of you two in front of the bagel shop, and you looked so cute! You're too short to do runway work, of course, but you could totally do print work. Why don't we get together for lunch sometime this week to talk about it? I found a new restaurant, and it is SO good. I don't know how you feel about foreign food, though. It's called the Olive Garden. It's Italian . . . like Pizza Hut. Only no pizza.

Anyway, let me know!!!! I would love to meet you!!!!!

Love,
Vivica

✉

To: Sean <psychodramabeautyqueen@freemail.com>
Fr: Kate Mackenzie <katydid@freemail.com>
Re: You

Thanks so much for your e-mail, but really, Sean, I didn't do any-thing. You are the one who took the brave step of admitting your true feelings to your family and, more important, to yourself. While it's unfortunate that certain members of your family weren't thrilled by the news, at least you can be satisfied that you were as honest with them as you could be. I hope you'll understand that their con-cern for you stems from their deep love, and maybe from a little bit of fear over something that might be foreign to them. It's up to you to try to educate them, and let them know that the choices you're making aren't self-destructive at all, but choices based entirely on your love for them, yourself, and for Sarah.

One thing Mitch mentioned that I almost forgot: Isn't it true that your grandfather left each of his grandchildren two hundred thou-sand dollars, to be held in trust until they turn eighteen?

Well, aren't you nineteen?

If your parents continue to refuse to pay for your schooling, couldn't you use the money your grandfather left you to pay for it yourself?

Just a thought.
Hope to see you again soon.

Kate

✉

To: Jason Trent <jason.trent@trentcapitcal.com>
Fr: Stacy Trent <IH8BARNEY@freemail.com>
Re: Janice

Look, it would only be a couple of weeks. You know the kids love her. So what's the big deal? I'll ask her to wear headphones if she's going to put on any Tori Amos. Don't be so unreasonable. I put up with YOUR relatives all the time.

Stacy

P.S. We're out of Honey Nut Cheerios.

✉

To: Stacy Trent <IH8BARNEY@freemail.com>
Fr: Jason Trent <jason.trent@trentcapitcal.com>
Re: Janice

Excuse me, but none of MY relatives are likely to quote Ani Di Franco at the dinner table. All of MY relatives are in jail, where they belong.

You're asking too much, Stace. I mean, what are you going to do when Haley and Brittany want to start dyeing THEIR hair green, too?

Jason

P.S. We employ an au pair, a gardener, a housekeeper, a pool boy, and a cook. None of THEM can run out to the store to get Honey Nut Cheerios? *I* have to stop and get them on my way home? What do we pay THEM for?

✉

To: Jason Trent <jason.trent@trentcapitcal.com>
Fr: Stacy Trent <IH8BARNEY@freemail.com>
Re: Janice

Excuse me, we entertain your brother and his wife and child nearly once a week. HE is not in jail.

And if Haley or Brittany end up wanting to dye their hair green, we'll tell them they can, when they are Janice's age.

Come on, Jason, this is important. Not just because I think Mom is going to pay somebody to kidnap Janice and have her sent to Utah for deprogramming, but because I think Mitch finally met a girl he really likes. He just needs some time alone with her to . . . you know.

S

P.S. God, it's just a box of cereal, what is your problem?

✉

To: Stacy Trent <IH8BARNEY@freemail.com>
Fr: Jason Trent <jason.trent@trentcapitcal.com>
Re: Janice

Oh, so now I'm supposed to let your sister live with us so your brother can get laid? I'll tell you what, Janice can come to stay if you promise SHE'LL get the Cheerios. But she's not driving the Range Rover!

Jason

✉

To: Katydid <katydid@freemail.com>
Fr: Jen Sadler <jennifer.sadler@thenyjournal.com>
Re: You

Haven't heard from you in a while. What are you doing? Has he called yet?

The T.O.D. is on a full-scale rampage today. She's already made the receptionists cry. She told them they couldn't do the filing anymore for overtime, they have to file during office hours. They want to know how they are supposed to be in the file room AND answer the phones at the desk, and the T.O.D. just said, "Work it out," and slammed her office door.

If she doesn't watch it, people are going to start burning her in effigy.

Where are you, anyway? I called and got no answer.

J

⸻

✉

To: Jen Sadler <jennifer.sadler@thenyjournal.com>
Fr: Katydid <katydid@freemail.com>
Re: Me

I just went out to grab the paper. You know. That whole job thing?

Is Steph

Oh, crap, the doorman's buzzing, hold on.

~*East Side Floral Company*~
"*Say it with Flowers!*"
1125 York Avenue • New York NY 10028

To: Kate Mackenzie
c/o Dolly Vargas
610 East End Avenue, Penthouse A

Thanks for everything the other night. You were great with Janice. Can we try dinner again sometime? Soon?

Mitch

Sleaterkinneyfan:	Whadja get?
Katydid:	Are you crazy? Don't IM me. You're at work, you're going to get fired, just like me.
Sleaterkinneyfan:	Are you kidding? With you gone, Amy's having to take on the L–Zs until we find a replacement. She's got so many PAFs to get through, she can't even find a spare moment to plan her reception. It's killing her. I've never been more assured of my job security. Now spill. Whadja get????
Katydid:	Oh. Flowers.
Sleaterkinneyfan:	FROM HIM??????
Katydid:	Yes.
Sleaterkinneyfan:	Describe.
Katydid:	Yellow roses this time. Two dozen.
Sleaterkinneyfan:	Um, if you don't want him, I'll take him.
Katydid:	Back off! You're married.
Sleaterkinneyfan:	Trade?
Katydid:	Um, no, thank you.
Sleaterkinneyfan:	Bitch. So now what are you going to do?
Katydid:	I don't know. Look for a job?
Sleaterkinneyfan:	I MEAN ABOUT THE BOY!!!!!!!!
Katydid:	Remember Professor Wingblade?
Sleaterkinneyfan:	How could I forget? You only quote him every five minutes.
Katydid:	Well, remember how he said before you can learn to love someone else, you have to learn to love yourself?
Sleaterkinneyfan:	No. I never went to his stupid class. You didn't have to. All the test questions were multiple choice and were straight out of the back of the book.
Katydid:	Well, he used to say that. And the thing is . . . I think he's right.
Sleaterkinneyfan:	God, eat some chocolate and get over it.

Katydid:	I'm serious! I know it's wrong to define yourself by your job, but, Jen, I kind of did, and now, without it . . . I just don't know why I'm even here. On this planet, I mean.
Sleaterkinneyfan:	Oh my God. You SO need chocolate.
Katydid:	I'm serious. I don't want to make another mistake about a guy. Not after what happened with Dale. I mean, I really thought the two of us were going to get married.
Sleaterkinneyfan:	Okay, okay. I'm not saying you should move in with the guy. But you could call him, at least. And thank him for the flowers.
Katydid:	I guess.
Sleaterkinneyfan:	And ask him over. And take a bubble bath with him in Dolly's Jacuzzi.
Katydid:	JEN!!!!!!!! I'm SERIOUS!!!!!!!!! Meet me at Lupe's after work so we can talk about it?
Sleaterkinneyfan:	Uh. Can't.
Katydid:	Why?
Sleaterkinneyfan:	Previous engagement. Sorry. Take a rain check?
Katydid:	Oh my God. You've found a new best friend. I'm out of the office for a few days, and you've gone and found a new best friend!
Sleaterkinneyfan:	Yeah, that's it, all right. I'm going out with my new best friend. God, get a grip. Look, I have to go, my 4:30's here. Talk to you later.
Sleaterkinneyfan:	logged off

✉

To: Orin Wingblade <orin.wingblade@universityofkentucky.edu>
Fr: Kate Mackenzie <kathleen.mackenzie@thenyjournal.com>
Re: Life

Dear Professor Wingblade,

You probably don't remember me. My name is Kate Mackenzie. I was in your Soc 101 and 102 class several years ago.

I just wanted you to know that I did graduate and went on to a career in social work. I wanted to "make a difference," the way you urged us all to. I was employed by the city (of New York) social work department for a year before I realized that it wasn't working out.

Professor Wingblade, it pains me to say this, but I really don't think that one person CAN make a difference. I've tried and tried. Back when I worked for Child Protective Services, I tried, and more recently, when I worked for the HR department of a major New York newspaper, I tried.

But both times, Professor, it was as if I were beating my head against a brick wall. Little kids still went to bed hungry while their parents watched DVDs on their wide-screen TVs, and good people—people I really, really liked—got fired for no good reason. In addition, the people I worked for LIED about firing someone—and then *I* got fired.

The reason I'm writing to you is . . . Professor Wingblade, what am I supposed to do now?

I went out into the world and tried to make a difference, but nobody's life is improved because of me, and my own life is, frankly, in shambles. I broke off a relationship because the man I was involved with made me feel like I wasn't worth much to him.

So now I have no boyfriend, no job, and no permanent place to live.

I don't want to burden my friends with my problems anymore—they have their own problems. My best friend wants a baby more than anything, so she's on fertility drugs, and I don't want to stay at her place—not while she and her husband are trying to make a new life.

Meanwhile, you know, high-school girls are getting pregnant right and left, and don't even WANT the responsibilities of parenting.

I want kids someday, too, but I can't seem to find a guy who will commit to tomorrow, let alone stay around long enough to fertilize an egg or see the egg become a baby and the baby become a college grad. I did meet a new guy, but—well, he's somewhat responsible for getting me fired in the first place, and may be interested in me out of sympathy. We're certainly attracted to each other sexually and he seems to really like me . . . only how can he, really, when I don't even like myself?

I should tell you that he's a lawyer. I know you said all people have worth and dignity. But are you sure that includes lawyers?

How can I open myself up to a new relationship—I'm already completely incapable of getting this guy out of my head and it's driving me CRAZY—with someone who not only got me fired, but is also a public defender turned high-powered corporate lawyer?

The other thing: I've met two members of his immediate family. One was very nice, but the other— Oh my God! What an ass! And things have gotten complicated. And not just because I let him put his hand up my shirt.

Oh my God. I can't send this to you now.

Well, yes, I probably can, because I feel you'll understand, on account of how your sharing with us about your wife grabbing the car keys and leaving without telling you where she was going. I sincerely hope that everything has worked out well for you and your wife.

Well, Professor, I have to go, Dolly's housekeeper is here to change the sheets of the bed I'm lying on.

Please, though, if you get a chance, I'd really appreciate it if you'd drop me a line. I have no one else to turn to.

Thank you,
Kate Mackenzie

....

✉

To: Jen Sadler <jennifer.sadler@thenyjournal.com>
    Tim Grabowksi <timothy.grabowski@thenyjournal.com>
Fr: Mitchell Hertzog <mitchell.hertzog@hwd.com>
Re: Tonight

You guys ready?

Mitch

....

✉

To: Mitchell Hertzog <mitchell.hertzog@hwd.com>
Fr: Tim Grabowksi <timothy.grabowski@thenyjournal.com>
Re: Tonight

Thunderbirds are go.

Tim

✉

To: Mitchell Hertzog <mitchell.hertzog@hwd.com>
Fr: Jen Sadler <jennifer.sadler@thenyjournal.com>
Re: Tonight

Are you kidding? I can hardly wait.

J

Delivery for
Kate Mackenzie
c/o Dolly Vargas
610 East End Avenue, Penthouse A

Dear Katie,

I hear from my lawyer that you are fired, too!
And because of me! I am very sorry to hear
this. And so I brought you some of the cookies
you like so much. I hope they will make you feel
better. Also I am taking some to the lawyer
man who made you fired. The ugly one's brother.
He is a good man, this brother, in spite of getting you fired. I think he'd be nice to you . . . not
like that no-good other boyfriend I see you with.

Here is the recipe for my cookies, so you can make them for this man, and he will love you.

Ida

Ida Lopez's Gingersnaps

1 1/2 sticks unsalted butter (softened)
1 1/3 cups sugar
1 egg
1/4 cup molasses
2 cups flour
2 tsp ground ginger
1 tsp baking soda
1 tsp cinnamon
1/4 tsp ground cloves
1/4 tsp salt

Preheat oven to 350°F. Beat butter and 1 cup sugar on medium until well blended. Beat in egg and molasses until fluffy.

Whisk ginger, baking soda, cinnamon, cloves, and salt into flour. Add flour mixture into butter/sugar mixture with mixer on low.

Using $1/2$ teaspoon, form dough into balls. Roll balls into remaining $1/3$ cup sugar. Place two inches apart on greased cookie sheets. Using fingertip, place a drop of water on top of each cookie. Do not press down on dough.

Bake 12–15 minutes or until cookies are flattened or crinkled. Cool for two minutes on sheets, then place on racks.

Note: 12 minutes for chewy cookies, 15 for crispy.

Hi, you've reached Jen—and Craig! We can't come to the phone right now, but if you leave a message, we'll get right back to you! Promise.

(Tone)

Hey, it's me. Kate. Where are you guys? Oh, right, it's Uno night. Well, that explains where Craig is. But where are you, Jen? Anyway, you're totally missing out. Mrs. Lopez dropped off a basket of cookies for me, on account of she heard I was fired. I must have five dozen cookies here. Ida Lopez's famous gingersnap cookies. But I guess you're not going to get any. Well, too bad, so sad. I'm going to eat them ALL.

(Click)

THE NEW YORK JOURNAL
New York City's Leading Photo-Newspaper

Security Sign-In Log

Name:	Visiting:	Time In:	Time Out:
Mitchell Hertzog	Jen Sadler/HR 3rd Flr	9:30	10:17
Eddie Barofsky	Jen Sadler, HR/3rd fl	9:30	10:17

✉

To: Sean <psychodramabeautyqueen@freemail.com>
Fr: Stacy Trent <IH8BARNEY@freemail.com>
Re: You

Hey. Look, I know you're hurting. And I want you to know, I'm on your side. As far as I'm concerned, you can love whoever your little heart desires (oh, God, except a married man. That, I'm afraid, I could not support).

But, you know, Mom's not exactly Ms. Open Minded. You can't blame her, really. I mean, she just wants what's best for us.

Oh, sorry, that was BS. I don't know what I was thinking. Mom could care less what's best for us. She just wants whatever makes her look good in front of the Antique Coalition.

Anyway, Jason and I were talking, and we thought it might be fun if you moved in with us for a little while. I know Mitch has got you covered, but, you know, our place is bigger, and we could let you have the guesthouse. Your own kitchen, so you can make those macrobiotic messes you like so much . . . the works. And Jason says you can use the Audi while you're here.

I know there's not tons to do in Greenwich, but we could still have a good time. The girls are dying to see their aunt Sean, and Mitch taught Little John some new words he's just dying to try out on someone.

Think about it, okay? It's just that I know Mitch works a lot, and I worry about you all alone in that apartment for hours on end. Come to Greenwich. You won't be sorry. We have puppies. . . . Well, one. Jason finally caved, and it shouldn't be too hard on Haley's allergies, if we don't let her sleep with it. The dog, I mean.

Call me.

Love,
Big Sis

....

✉

To: Stacy Trent <IH8BARNEY@freemail.com>
Fr: Sean <psychodramabeautyqueen@freemail.com>
Re: Me

Hey, thanks for the invite. I'd love to come out and see you guys, but I kind of have other plans. Don't worry about me, I'm good. I know Mitch wants me out of here so he can boff his new girlfriend (she's really nice, by the way). But it's all good . . . I've got a plan.

And no, it isn't a suicide plan, God, would everyone just chill (though I'm sure Stuart would prefer a dead sister to a lesbian sister).

I'll talk to you soon.

Love,
Sean

....

✉

To: Mitchell Hertzog <mitchell.hertzog@hwd.com>
Fr: Stacy Trent <IH8BARNEY@freemail.com>
Re: Sean

Where are you? I've tried your office, home, your cell . . . I am resorting to Blackberry again.

Anyway, just wanted to let you know, I invited Sean out to our place, and she said she has "other plans." Not sure what this means. She tells me she isn't going to kill herself, however. Somehow, I don't find this as reassuring as she might have hoped.

Call me when you get this and give me an update, okay? I'm really worried about her.

Stacy

P.S. I had to promise Jason all sorts of sexual favors to get him to let her move in. If she doesn't, am I still obligated to perform? I need a lawyer's perspective on this.

....

✉

To: Amy Jenkins <amy.jenkins@thenyjournal.com>
Fr: Stuart Hertzog <stuart.hertzog@hwd.com>
Re: The Test

Forgive me for writing, instead of phoning, or even speaking to you in person—but it's late, and I know you're working out.

Besides, if I had to hear your little voice, or look into your eyes as I say what I have to say, I might not go through with it. And I have to. I have to. So let me take the coward's way out.

Darling, I honestly . . . I don't know what to say. I wish I could have been more lucid in the geneticist's office, but I was simply so stunned. You've got to try to see it from my perspective. I expected, as I think you know, for there to be some abnormalities. I mean, anyone who knows Mitch—not to mention Janice, and even Stacy, who at times can be incredibly difficult, if you remember the Mercedes trunk incident I told you about—would naturally assume that SOME sort of genetic disorder runs through the Hertzog family.

But I expected it to be manic-depression, or possibly even autism. But *this* . . . I never suspected *this*.

That's why I'm writing. I couldn't articulate my feelings back in the geneticist's office. I simply was too stunned. But now that I've had some time to digest it, I can only come to one conclusion, and it's one that I dread—oh, so very much.

I feel a moral obligation, Amy, to tell you that if you should choose to be released from our engagement, I would understand it. I would be devastated, of course. My life would lose all meaning. But I would understand, because I would never want to drag someone as young and lovely, with as much wit and talent as you have, down to my level. You have the right, Amy, to marry the kind of man you want—the kind I once thought I was . . . until today, when my hopes were brutally crushed.

But yours needn't be, my sweet darling. You can go on to have the wedding . . . and the life . . . of your dreams. Sadly, however, I fear it will have to be with someone else.

Yours forever,
Stuart

Stuart Hertzog, Senior Partner
Hertzog Webber and Doyle, Attorneys at Law
444 Madison Avenue, Suite 1505
New York, NY 10022
212-555-7900

P.S. Pursuant to New York State law, an engagement ring is considered payment for fulfilment of a contract (marriage contract) and should the engagement be broken for any reason, the ring must be returned to the giver. I can have the firm's messenger service retrieve it in the morning, if you choose to break the engagement.

To: Stuart Hertzog <stuart.hertzog@hwd.com>
Fr: Amy Jenkins <amy.jenkins@thenyjournal.com>
Re: The Test

Stuart, MUST you be so silly? Of COURSE I'm not going to break up with you. Over something like THAT? You must have been nipping at that thirty-year-old scotch you like so much.

Darling, the geneticist said our kids would be fine, remember? It would be different if I were a carrier, too, but I'm not. How can you be so silly as to think I would ever break up with you over something so ridiculous? That's all in the past, darling. It has nothing to do with our future. Your ring is staying right on my finger, where it belongs.

Now if you don't mind, I have a half hour more on the treadie before bed. Kisses and sweet dreams, Stuart. In less than two months, I will be your blushing bride.

Amy

Amy Denise Jenkins
Director
Human Resources
The New York Journal
216 W. 57th Street
New York, NY 10019
212-555-6890
amy.jenkins@thenyjournal.com

view, dissemination, distribution, or copying of this transmission is prohibited. If you have received this communication in error, please notify us immediately by reply e-mail and delete this message and all of its attachments.

....

✉

To: Amy Jenkins <amy.jenkins@thenyjournal.com>
Fr: Stuart Hertzog <stuart.hertzog@hwd.com>
Re: The Test

Darling! I can't tell you how my heart swelled as I read your last e-mail. You really are the angel I've always suspected you were. An angel who fell down from heaven to live amongst us.

You've lifted me from the depths of despair to the height of giddy ecstasy. I'm the luckiest man in the world.

I love you, more than words could ever say. Good night, my sweet.

Stuart

Stuart Hertzog, Senior Partner
Hertzog Webber and Doyle, Attorneys at Law
444 Madison Avenue, Suite 1505
New York, NY 10022
212-555-7900

✉

To: Courtney Allington <courtney.allington@allingtonenterprises.com>
Fr: Amy Jenkins <amy.jenkins@thenyjournal.com>
Re: Stuart

Get this: we went in for genetic testing, you know, to find out if whatever the FUCK is wrong with his FUCKED-UP family is genetic, and guess what? He's a carrier for Tay Sach's disease. Ever heard of it? No, you haven't. Because only people of Eastern European—aka the Ashkenazis, aka JEWS—get it.

That's right. Stuart's a JEW. Somewhere along the line, somebody converted to Protestantism. But that doesn't change the fact that once upon a time in some Russian village somewhere, the Hertzogs were running from the Cossacks.

I mean, with a name like Hertzog, I certainly had my suspicions.

So NOW what do I do? I mean, it was bad enough when the sister turned out to be a dyke. Now I find out they're all Yids as well?

Really, how can this be happening? To ME??? I was the Pi Delt voted Most Likely to Marry Well.

He offered to let me out of it (the engagement), but I said no, because, hello, condos in Aspen and Scottsdale, not to mention the house in Ojai. And really, who is ever going to know? That he's Jewish, I mean? Except for you, but I know you'll never tell.

But now that I've had another workout, I'm wondering if I made the right decision. I mean, I know a lot of our friends would DIE if they found out I was marrying a Jew. Oh, sure, Miriam and Ruth would be all right with it. But they ARE Jewish. And of course we never see them anymore, now that we don't have to live with them.

338   *Meg Cabot*

What do you think I should do, Court? I mean, do you think I shouldn't settle? That I could do better? I think so, too, but the truth is, I'm not getting any younger—I had to switch from Dramatically Different moisturizer to Anti-Aging over at Clinique—and the truth is, I'm sick of the dating scene. It really eats away at a girl's work-out schedule.

Let me know what you think. Any thoughts—pro or con—would be greatly appreciated.

Ames

Amy Denise Jenkins
Director
Human Resources
The New York Journal
216 W. 57th Street
New York, NY 10019
212-555-6890
amy.jenkins@thenyjournal.com

Journal of Kate Mackenzie

So I'm innocently sitting here watching MTV *Cribs* when Dolly and Ski-boy came bursting drunkenly in, and start making out right in front of me. I have no objections to people, you know, making out. I myself enjoy a good make-out session as much as the next girl.

But is it entirely necessary for them to loll around on the couch RIGHT NEXT TO ME, with their TONGUES DOWN EACH OTHER'S THROATS?

Because that's what they're doing at this moment, and it is really kind of gross. I mean, Dolly could easily go into her bedroom to stick her tongue down her boyfriend's throat. I have a feeling they'd both be a lot more comfortable.

But NOOOOO, she has to do it here, right in front of me, and practically blocking my view of Mariah Carey's palatial—

Journal of Kate Mackenzie

Sorry about that. As I was writing that last bit, the front door burst open, and Peter Hargrave came in. That's right, Peter Hargrave, the owner and CEO of the *New York Journal*, and Dolly's boyfriend, the guy who set her up in this fabulous pad in the first place?

And did his face go all shades of purple when he saw Dolly on top of Skiboy!

But the thing is, even though I don't approve of cheating—even if you aren't married to the person—I owe Dolly a lot. I mean, she's let me live in her place rent-free, and eat all the Rye-Krisps and drink all the Tab I want. Which is pretty generous, you know.

So when I saw Peter's face, and how the veins were sticking out all over it and everything, I went, "Okay, okay, you made your point. You're a better kisser than I am, Dolly. Now give me my boyfriend back. Oh, hi, PETER!"

When Dolly heard Peter's name, she dropped Skiboy like he was a piping-hot thermal massage rock. She stood up and went, "Dahling!" and threw her arms around Peter like he had been away at the war or something.

Then I pulled Skiboy down next to me and put my arms around him, you know, to make it seem like we were a couple.

Peter just kept looking at Skiboy like he was Osama bin Laden, live in the flesh in his very living room.

"Playing a little game, are we, ladies?" he asked, in this kind of choked-up voice.

"Yes," I said. "Dolly was just showing me that I don't kiss right. Weren't you, Dolly?"

"Absolutely," Dolly said. Then she looked up at Peter, with her dewy, Botox-injected face, and went, "Katie doesn't use enough tongue."

Well, I guess there's nothing that gets CEOs of major publishing corporations hotter than the use of the word *tongue*, since Peter wrapped his arms around Dolly and said, "I've missed you so much," and stuck his own big fat one right in her ear.

Which, you know, ew, but whatever floats your boat.

Then Skiboy—I swear, he has a real feel for the theatrical—stuck his own tongue right in my ear.

So now we're all sitting here—me and Skiboy, Dolly and Peter—drinking Campari and watching B2K (what is with the all-white living rooms) on *Cribs*. I'm waiting for just the right moment to bring up the whole How I Got Fired thing. Dolly said she'd work on it for me, but it's clear Peter doesn't know a thing. He's too busy sniffing Dolly's hair. Geez, it's just Aveda.

Ew, Skiboy is still nuzzling me. He is taking this whole thing way too far. If he doesn't watch it, I may have to break up with him right in front of Dolly and Peter. Get off—why is the doorman buzzing at freaking midnight?

Katydid:	So? What's happening?
Sleaterkinney:	Oh my God. Where are you?
Katydid:	I'm upstairs, in Peter's office. His assistant Penny is letting me use the intern's computer. So WHAT'S HAPPENING?????
Sleaterkinneyfan:	No. Uh-uh. No way. You go first. What happened after Tim and Eddie and I left? Come on. SPILL.
Katydid:	You mean, after we made Skiboy put a steak on his eye?
Sleaterkinneyfan:	Poor Skiboy. He never saw it coming, did he?
Katydid:	I know! I never had a guy hit another guy over me. I mean, once at a New Year's party Scroggs felt me up, but Dale just thought it was funny.
Sleaterkinneyfan:	When we walked in and Mitch saw that big dope with his arms all draped around you, I really thought he was going to have a coronary. Mitch, I mean. He hit him HARD. Does Dolly mind?
Katydid:	About Skiboy's black eye? Or her grand piano?
Sleaterkinneyfan:	Both. Either.
Katydid:	I think she was more worried about the piano than Skiboy. But that thing needed tuning anyway.
Sleaterkinneyfan:	Okay. So what happened after the steak?
Katydid:	Well, Mitch suggested we go out for a drink. To celebrate.
Sleaterkinneyfan:	At MIDNIGHT? Where the hell did you go???
Katydid:	His place.
Sleaterkinneyfan:	You spill it all right NOW.
Katydid:	Not on IM! What if the T.O.D. is lurking?

Sleaterkinneyfan:	She's lurked her last. But you're right. E-mail me. I want DETAILS.
Sleaterkinneyfan:	logged off
Katydid:	logged off

To: Jen Sadler <jennifer.sadler@thenyjournal.com>
Fr: Kate Mackenzie <katydid@freemail.com>
Re: Last night

First of all, can I just say, because I don't think I was really all that intelligible last night, I was so stunned, what an incredible, cool, giving, generous, cool, smart, incredible friend you are? NO ONE has ever done anything like this for me before. I mean, you and Tim risked your JOBS for me. That is just the sweetest thing anyone has ever, ever, ever done for me.

I mean it. I just wish there was something I could do for you.

Kate

✉

To: Kate Mackenzie <katydid@freemail.com>
Fr: Jen Sadler <jennifer.sadler@thenyjournal.com>
Re: Last night

Those weren't the kinds of details I was looking for.

And duh. You are my best friend, Kate. Of course I'm going to help you any way I can.

Besides, I didn't really do anything. It was all Mitch's idea. He talked to Tim. He hired Eddie. All I did was come back to the office last night after everybody had gone home and signed them both in. They did the rest . . . well, with Tim's help.

You would, I know, have done the same for me.

Now. Details please. And remember that I am an old married lady and on massive amounts of hormones. So make it good.

J

....

✉

To: Jen Sadler <jennifer.sadler@thenyjournal.com>
Fr: Kate Mackenzie <katydid@freemail.com>
Re: Last night

Okay. Well.

You know, after you guys came in with the good news—at least, I hope it will turn out to be good news. If Peter really does what he said he was going to do, anyway—and Mitch hit Skiboy and I pretended to break up with him (SB, I mean) and we got the whole thing straightened out and everything, Mitch was like, "Let's get out of here," and I was like, "Why?" and he was like, "Because of that," and there was Skiboy, you know, all dejected on the couch.

And it WAS kind of depressing, what with Dolly and Peter making out right in front of him.

So, Jen, I went with him. You know he doesn't live that far away, it was just a few blocks' walk, and it really WAS just supposed to be to have drinks until things back at Dolly's cooled off a little. . . . I didn't imagine it would be anything more than a drink or two, and all, because you know I thought his little sister was still there.

But then we got to his place and I asked where Sean was and he said she'd left a note saying she was going to his sister's in Greenwich. . . .

. . . and that's when I realized I was in big trouble.

And oh! Jen, I know I shouldn't have, but he has such really nice lips, and he'd just committed a burglary for me, and hit Skiboy, and his knuckles were all raw so I was running them under the tap in the kitchen, when I happened to look up, and there were those lips, and . . .

Well, is it really my fault, what happened next?

Jen, he was so gentle and nice and STRONG (he CARRIED me from the kitchen to the bedroom) and underneath his clothes he is as much of a superhero as the ones on his ties, that wheelchair-basketball thing must be some workout, let me tell you.

And I know I've only been with one other guy before, and don't have a wide and varied experience to draw upon, but, Jen, I have to say . . . lawyers really DO do it better.

Or maybe it's just Mitch.

In any case, I didn't get much sleep, but I don't care, I don't feel tired or anything, just . . . HAPPY! Happier than I've felt in weeks. Maybe even years. Jen! He loves me! He told me! He loved me from the moment he first saw me, in the conference room, when I was dribbling on about chicken in garlic sauce! Remember how I told you about that?

Well, the whole time, he loved me, and was trying to figure out ways to get me to love him back, seeing as how he knew I hated lawyers, what with the whole Mrs. Lopez thing. He thought that if he could prove Amy lied about the letter that day I gave my second deposition, it would show me that he was really on my side—on Mrs. Lopez's side—and that then I might start to like him. But then the whole thing backfired, and instead of getting Amy in trouble, he got ME in trouble, and he just felt awful, and, JEN!!!!

HE LOVES ME!!!!

Boy Meets Girl   347

Oh, what did I ever do to deserve such a great guy?

He wants me to move in.

But you would be really proud of me, Jen. I said no. I said it was too soon. I said I needed to get my job back first—or some job, anyway—and then we could talk about it.

We made breakfast together, and shared a cab downtown. JUST LIKE HARRISON FORD AND MELANIE GRIFFITH IN *WORKING GIRL*!!!!!!

Oh my God, I'm so happy, I'm telling you, even if I don't get my job back, I wouldn't care. I have HIM!

Well, okay, I wouldn't care much.

Oh, all right, I'd care. Have you heard anything?

Kate

....

✉

To: Kate Mackenzie <katydid@freemail.com>
Fr: Jen Sadler <jennifer.sadler@thenyjournal.com>
Re: Last night

Sorry. Can't talk now. Must go into ladies' room to splash cold water on face.

J

✉

To: Mitchell Hertzog <mitchell.hertzog@hwd.com>
Fr: Stuart Hertzog<stuart.hertzog@hwd.com>
Re: Work

You remember work, don't you, Mitch? It's that place we all come to every day and sit at things called desks, and type on things called computers, and try things called LEGAL CASES.

It might behoove you to remember that you have a job, and that it starts at nine sharp. Not nine thirty, as you seem to think. You can't just come waltzing in here any time you damn please, just because you're the boss's son, you know.

Speaking of which, when Dad gets back, your ass is grass. When he hears that shit you pulled at the Lopez depo, you'll be back downtown, defending the Gomez brothers for assault and battery, or whatever the fuck it is you used to do all day.

Stuart

Stuart Hertzog, Senior Partner
Hertzog Webber and Doyle, Attorneys at Law
444 Madison Avenue, Suite 1505
New York, NY 10022
212-555-7900

✉

To: Stuart Hertzog<stuart.hertzog@hwd.com>
Fr: Mitchell Hertzog <mitchell.hertzog@hwd.com>
Re: Work

Promise?

Mitch

To: Amy Jenkins <amy.jenkins@thenyjournal.com>
Fr: Stuart Hertzog<stuart.hertzog@hwd.com>
Re: You

My angel. I can't tell you what your last missive meant to me. The fact that you will still have me, in spite of my deficiency, means more to me than all the money in the world. Can I take you some place nice for lunch, to celebrate? Daniel, perhaps? Please let me know.

Stuart

Stuart Hertzog, Senior Partner
Hertzog Webber and Doyle, Attorneys at Law
444 Madison Avenue, Suite 1505
New York, NY 10022
212-555-7900

To: Stuart Hertzog <stuart.hertzog@hwd.com>
Fr: Amy Jenkins <amy.jenkins@thenyjournal.com>
Re: You

Daniel sounds divine! One o'clock okay?

Amy

Amy Denise Jenkins
Director
Human Resources
The New York Journal
216 W. 57th Street
New York, NY 10019
212-555-6890
amy.jenkins@thenyjournal.com

✉

To: Courtney Allington <courtney.allington@alingtonenterpises.com>
Fr: Amy Jenkins <amy.jenkins@thenyjournal.com>
Re: Hey

I haven't heard back from you. Usually your replies are so prompt. Did you get my last, about Stuart being Jewish? I tried calling just now, but your assistant said you were in meetings all morning. Drinks after work? Let me know.

Ames

P.S. Courtney, the fact that my fiancé is Jewish—that doesn't bother you, does it? I mean, he's not a PRACTICING Jew. He's just of Jewish descent. I mean, it's not like he goes around in a yarmulke or anything. As if!

Ames

Amy Denise Jenkins
Director
Human Resources
The New York Journal
216 W. 57th Street
New York, NY 10019
212-555-6890
amy.jenkins@thenyjournal.com

✉

To: Amy Jenkins <amy.jenkins@thenyjournal.com>
Fr: Penny Croft <penelope.croft@thenyjournal.com>
Re: Meeting with Peter

Amy, Peter Hargrave would like to meet with you this morning at eleven. Please phone me to let me know whether or not you can make it. If not, can we reschedule? He really must meet with you at some point today.

Penny

Penny Croft
Assistant to Peter Hargrave
Founder and CEO of
The New York Journal

✉

To: Stuart Hertzog <stuart.hertzog@thenyjournal.com>
Fr: Amy Jenkins <amy.jenkins@thenyjournal.com>
Re: Promotion

Stuart, darling, remember that position I told you I applied for—vice president of Employee Development? Well, I just got an e-mail from Peter

Hargrave's assistant, wanting to schedule an appointment with the big man himself. Honey, I think it's happened! I'm going to be a VP!

Better call Daniel and tell them to chill the champagne. We're going to have a double celebration!

Amy

Amy Denise Jenkins
Director
Human Resources
The New York Journal
216 W. 57th Street
New York, NY 10019
212-555-6890
amy.jenkins@thenyjournal.com

....

✉

To: Mitchell Hertzog <mitchell.hertzog@hwd.com>
Fr: Stacy Trent <IH8BARNEY@freemail.com>
Re: Last night

So who was over last night when I called? That didn't sound like Sean. I'm sorry if I interrupted anything, I just wanted to know if you'd seen that comic dog on Conan. He was ripping on Eminem again, it was HILARIOUS. I know I'm not usually up that late, but Little John has a cold.

So. Who was she? Was it HER? What was she doing at your place after midnight? Naughty, naughty.

Besides, I thought she hated you, for getting her fired and all of that.

Stace

....

✉

To: Stacy Trent <IH8BARNEY@freemail.com>
Fr: Mitchell Hertzog <mitchell.hertzog@hwd.com>
Re: Last night

Yes, it was HER. Or Kate, as you had better get used to calling her, since I'm hoping she's going to become a permanent addition to— well, not the family, since I would never wish that on anyone, but at least to me.

Stacy, I have to say, when you married Jason, I thought you were completely insane. I mean, MARRY someone? Pledge to spend your entire life with one other person, until DEATH? For what? So you can end up like Mom and Dad, barely able to stand the sight of each other? Who in their right mind would ever wish such a thing on their worst enemy?

But I understand now. I get it. I want to be with her, and just her, forever. For the rest of my life. If she'll have me. Which I think she might, if I just play my cards right. . . .

I can't wait until you meet her. I think she'll almost balance out Amy.

Almost.

Last night was the most incredible night of my life. Is this how you felt, the first time you and Jason . . . you know?

No. Strike that. I don't want to know. The thought of the two of you. . . .

Gotta go.

Mitch

....

✉
To: Mitchell Hertzog <Mitchell.herstog@hwd.com>
Fr: Stacy Trent <IH8BARNEY@freemail.com>
Re: Last night

Oh, what, the thought of me doing my husband makes you want to barf?

Well, never mind. It does me, too.

Just kidding.

So, um, congrats on you and the girl. She must be something, if she's got YOU talking wedding bells. But I always knew you'd find the right girl eventually.

By the way, did you hear about Stuart's genetic test results? Turns out he's a carrier for Tay Sach's disease. Which means that somewhere back in our genealogical past, we were Jewish. No big surprise, is it, that we should have had a relative who, upon witnessing the pogroms, conveniently converted?

Mom is in fits over the whole thing. She thinks the country club is going to kick us out if they find out. Jason was like, "Why would she even want to belong to an organization that discriminates against ethnicity—or anything else for that matter?"

Poor Jason. You think he'd have learned by now, wouldn't you?

Hey, so, what was Sean up to while you and Little Miss Dreamgirl were reaching the heights of ecstasy on those brown sheets of yours (we so need to take a little trip to Bloomies)?

Stace

....

✉

To: Stacy Trent <IH8BARNEY@freemail.com>
Fr: Mitchell Hertzog <mitchell.hertzog@hwd.com>
Re: Sean

What are you talking about? Sean left me a note saying she was staying with you this weekend. Isn't she there?

Mitch

THE NEW YORK JOURNAL
New York City's Leading Photo-Newspaper

Peter Hargrave
Chief Executive Officer
The New York Journal
216 W. 57th Street
New York, NY 10019
212-555-6000

Amy Jenkins
Director
Human Resources
The New York Journal
216 W. 57th Street
New York, NY 10019

Dear Ms. Jenkins:

This letter serves to inform you that as of today's date, your employment at the *New York Journal* has been terminated. Your belongings from your workstation have been inventoried and packed. You are to be escorted from the premises by Security, and have been listed as Persona Non Grata at this location. Should you need to speak to anyone regarding the termination of your position at the *New York Journal*, you will need to do so by telephone. Your initials below indicate receipt of this letter.

Peter Hargrave

pc/PH

THE NEW YORK JOURNAL

New York City's Leading Photo-Newspaper

Security Division
The New York Journal
216 W. 57th Street
New York, NY 10019
212-555-6890

MEMO

To: All Personnel
Fr: Security Administration
Re: Persona Non Grata

<u>Persona Non Grata Notification</u>

Please note that the below named individual has been classified Persona Non Grata in 216 W. 57th Street as of the date of this notification, and will continue to remain so indefinitely. This individual is not to be allowed on or near the premises of 216 W. 57th Street at any time during the term of above sanction.

Name: Amy D. Jenkins
ID#: 3164-000-5001
Description: (photo attached)
White female, 30 years of age
5 feet, 6 inches, 120–130 lbs.
Blonde hair, blue eyes

Contact Security immediately upon sighting of above individual.

THE NEW YORK JOURNAL
New York City's Leading Photo-Newspaper

Peter Hargrave
Chief Executive Officer
The New York Journal
216 W. 57th Street
New York, NY 10019
212-555-6000

MEMO

To: All Departments
Fr: Peter Hargrave, CEO
Re: Human Resources Director

Please be aware that Amy Jenkins is no longer with the company. The newly appointed acting Human Resources Director is Jennifer Sadler. Please welcome Ms. Sadler to her new position. We are very pleased and fortunate that she agreed to take on a position of so much responsibility with so little advance notice. Thank you, Jennifer!

pc/PH

THE NEW YORK JOURNAL
New York City's Leading Photo-Newspaper

Jennifer Sadler
Director
Human Resources
The New York Journal
216 W. 57th Street
New York, NY 10019
212-555-6870

MEMO
To: All Departments
Fr: Jennifer Sadler, Director, Human Resources
Re: Kate Mackenzie

As my first act as director of Human Resources, I'd like to reinstate Kate Mackenzie to the division. I'm sure you all agree that Kate was sorely missed. Kate will be taking over my former position. Thank you, and welcome back, Kate!

THE NEW YORK JOURNAL
New York City's Leading Photo-Newspaper

Security Division
The New York Journal
216 W. 57th Street
New York, NY 10019
212-555-6890

MEMO
To: All Personnel
Fr: Security Administration
Re: Persona Non Grata

<u>Persona Non Grata Lift Notification</u>

Please note that the below-named individual has been declassified as Persona Non Grata in 216 W. 57th Street as of the date of this notification.

Name: Kathleen Mackenzie
ID#: 3164-000-6794
Description: (photo attached)
White female, 25 years of age
5 feet, 4 inches, 120–130 lbs.
Blonde hair, blue eyes

The above individual may enter the building freely.

THE NEW YORK JOURNAL
New York City's Leading Photo-Newspaper

Features Division
The New York Journal
216 W. 57th Street
New York, NY 10019

MEMO
To: All Departments
Fr: Features Division
Re: Promotion of Jen Sadler
        Reinstatement of Kate Mackenzie

We, the undersigned, staff members in the Features Department of the *New York Journal*, applaud the promotion of Jen Sadler to the position of Human Resources Director, and the reinstatement of Kate Mackenzie. We hope these brilliant hiring decisions will be followed by yet another: the reinstatement of Ida Lopez as dessert cart operator in the senior-staff dining room.

In the meantime: NO MORE TRUST GAMES!!!! WHEEEEEEEEE!!!!!!!!!!!!

George Sanchez
Melissa Fuller-Trent
Nadine Wilcock-Salerno
Dolly Vargas

Sleaterkinneyfan:	Can you believe this??
Katydid:	I'm freaking out. I really am. Jen—I have my job back. And you . . . you have the T.O.D.'s job! You are a DIRECTOR! A DI-RECTOR!!! You so, so deserve it.
Sleaterkinneyfan:	I think you're going to have to pinch me. I feel like I'm in a dream.
Sleaterkinneyfan:	Ow, bitch, that really hurt.
Katydid:	Did you see how she was crying? I felt a little sorry for her.
Sleaterkinneyfan:	Sorry for her? After what she did to you? Kate, you are way, way too nice. So where do you want to go to lunch to celebrate? My treat.
Katydid:	Can't. I have plans already.
Sleaterkinneyfan:	With Loverboy?
Katydid:	No, Dale's model, actually. I promised I'd go to the Olive Garden with her so we can talk about Dale.
Sleaterkinneyfan:	Oh my God. You really ARE too nice.
Katydid:	After work? Drinks at Lupe's?
Sleaterkinneyfan:	You're on. No drinks for me, though.
Katydid:	Why? Directors can't drink?
Sleaterkinneyfan:	No. Pregnant women can't.

To: Kate Mackenzie <kathleen.mackenzie@thenyjournal.com>
Fr: Jen Sadler <jennifer.sadler@theynyjournal.com>
Re: You

Oh my God, I'm sure they heard you all the way up in Peter's office. Would you calm down? I'm trying to keep it under wraps. How thrilled are they going to be when they find out they just promoted a lady who'll be on maternity leave in seven months? So keep the celebrating to a lower pitch, will you, please?

And yes, of course you can be the godmother.

Jen

⊠

To: Mitchell Hertzog <mitchell.hertzog@hwd.com>
Fr: Margaret Hertzog <margaret.hertzog@hwd.com>
Re: The News

By now you've heard the tragic news. I suppose YOU won't see what's so tragic about it. I suppose you're PROUD that you're descended from Those People. I suppose you just laughed when you heard, the way your father did.

But believe me, it's no laughing matter. And it's killing your brother. I know that you and I haven't seen eye to eye about much lately, but maybe we can at least agree on this: Your brother needs you, Mitchell. He's hurting, and quite badly. Can't you, just for once, do the decent thing, and offer to go with him after work to that cigar bar he likes so much, or maybe take him to play basketball with those friends of yours? You know it was never easy for Stuart to open up to new people—he's far too sensitive. What few friends he's had, he's never managed to keep for very long . . . except, of course, those friends he's made through work. But of course they can't afford to alienate him, or they'll lose their jobs.

But what Stuart needs right now isn't friends. It's family. Won't you, for once in your life, think about someone other than yourself, and help your brother?

I'd ask your sister Stacy, but she said something very rude to me about Stuart over the phone just now. It's clear she's in one of her moods.

If you won't do it for Stuart, Mitch, will you do it for me?

Mother

....

✉

To: Margaret Hertzog <margaret.hertzog@hwd.com>
Fr: Mitchell Hertzog <mitchell.hertzog@hwd.com>
Re: The News

If you'd stop feeling sorry for yourself for half a second, Mom, and take a look around, you might notice something. That's right. You're all alone. You're all alone, because you, like Stuart, have managed to alienate everyone you know, too. For instance, your daughter Janice. Where is Janice, Mom? Do you know? You don't, do you? That's because she's RUN AWAY. No one knows where she is right now. Your youngest child is missing, and all you can seem to think about is the fact that you married a Jew.

Get over it, Mom. For once in your life think about someone other than yourself. And then do us all a favor and GROW UP.

Mitch

✉

To: Stuart Hertzog <stuart.hertzog@hwd.com>
Fr: Amy Jenkins <amy.jenkins2000@freemail.com>
Re: WHERE ARE YOU???

I've been calling and calling. Your assistant says you're on a conference call. Well, get OUT OF IT. Stuart, I've been FIRED! FIRED! That bastard brother of yours—I don't know how he did it—but somehow he got his hands on an e-mail I sent to that bitch Kate— I really thought I'd deleted all the copies, but I guess I forgot the one in my *send* file—and he got it to Peter Hargrave who fired me for forgery and insubordination, and Stuart, I HAVE NO JOB!!!! I HAVE NO JOB NOW, and it's all that bastard Mitch's fault!

Call me. I'll be at the gym, trying to work out some of my frustration.

How could they do this to me? Jen, Kate, all of them—after everything I've done for them over the years? I'm the best boss any of them ever had! Oh, the ungrateful bitches.

✉

To: Mitchell Hertzog <mitchell.hertzog@hwd.com
Fr: Stuart Hertzog <stuart.hertzog@hwd.com>
Re: You

Amy told me everything.

How you can even show your face in this office today, I can't imagine. Oh, wait, yes I can, because those are the two things I like least about you: your face(s).

I suppose you thought you'd get away with it. How did you do it, anyway? Ask one of your former low-life clients to break into her office and print out that e-mail yourself? Don't try to deny it, Amy says she saw your name on last night's sign-on sheet.

Just what did you hope to prove, anyway? Amy doesn't remember writing that e-mail. If she did, well then, she simply MADE A MISTAKE. Should she be TERMINATED for that?

I'm sure you think so, because you think Amy was lying.

But I know my love, and I know that she hasn't a deceitful bone in her body.

There were all sorts of people at that sorry excuse for an office building who were out to get Amy, as well as her job. Any one of them could have forged that document, in order to make Amy look bad. Incompetent employees naturally despise those who call them on their inadequacies. And Amy has never been one to remain silent when she sees an error in need of adjustment. She is as fastidious about her work as she is about staying a perfect size six.

And I for one applaud her.

Oh, but then I happen to have something that you don't: a heart.

I hope you realize that this is the end of our relationship. Was it worth it? Severing your relations with your own brother, all to get your girlfriend's job back? So that some old lady can go back to refusing to serve pie to people she resents because they are more successful than she ever has a hope of being? Oh, yeah, you've really struck a blow for humanity with this one. Boy, I'll bet they'll give you the Nobel fucking prize. Mrs. Lopez got her job making pies back. Yippee! Kate whateverhernameis can go back to filing. Yay!

While one of the kindest, most brilliant, beautiful women in the world is at home right now, sobbing on her treadmill.

I hope that makes you happy.

Oh, but don't get too excited. Amy won't be unemployed for long. She's already been contacted by three headhunters. She'll be pulling in three times what she was getting at that rag in a matter of weeks.

And if you think this is going to stop me from marrying her, you can just think again. I still intend to marry her, but you—and anyone associated with the *Journal*—will NOT be welcome at the ceremony. And not just because of what you did last night, either. I've let Stacy know that she will not be invited to our nuptials, either. Not after the way the two of you have behaved concerning Janice. Apparently, "alternative lifestyles" are perfectly acceptable to the two of you (I shudder to think what kind of values Stacy is teaching those poor innocent children of hers). Well, same-sex partnerships aren't acceptable to me, or to my future wife. Janice is a spoiled brat and always has been, and this "Sarah" business is just to get attention from Mom and Dad. The sooner you two realize this, the better.

It pains me to have to say this, but I feel like you've left me no other choice: Mitch, I never want to see or speak to you again. Even the thought of working in the same office as you makes me sick. Kindly stay the hell out of my life.

Stuart Hertzog, Senior Partner
Hertzog Webber and Doyle, Attorneys at Law
444 Madison Avenue, Suite 1505
New York, NY 10022
212-555-7900

✉

To: Stuart Hertzog <stuart.hertzog@hwd.com>
Fr: Mitchell Hertzog <mitchell.hertzog@hwd.com
Re: You

Right back atcha, buddy.

Mitch

Dear Mom, Dad, Stuart, Stacy, and Mitch,

Sorry if any of you have been worried about me for the
past twenty-four hours. I'm actually fine. I just finally
came to a decision about my life, and, well, as soon as I
came to it, I decided to put it into action. I didn't want
to wait. But I thought I'd write and let you know that
I'm all right. I'm back at Berkeley, actually. I'm with
Sarah.

Mom, I know you pulled me out of school because you
don't like Sarah—or don't like that I love her, I guess,
would be more accurate. But a friend of Mitch's re-
minded me—Kate, Mitch. She's really cool. You should
try to hang onto her—that Gramps left me some money.
I know you always said I wasn't to touch it, Mom, and
that I should save it for a rainy day. But, well, here's
the thing: It's raining. I'm going to use the money
Gramps left me to pay for finishing up school, and then
Sarah and me, we're thinking about starting a kayaking
service up in Puget Sound. You know, where the orcas
are? Sarah and I just love orcas.

Mom, I know this has probably got you pretty mad,
but the fact is, Gramps left me that money for when I
turned eighteen, to do with whatever I want. Frankly, I
think paying for school where I want to go, and then
starting my own business, is exactly what Gramps would
have wanted—just like I doubt he minded that Mitch

spent his on a trip around the world, or Stacy spent hers
on those horses of hers, or that Stuart spent his on . . .
Stuart, did you ever even spend yours?

   Well, anyway, I just wanted to let you know that I'm
all right, and no hard feelings, and stuff.

   Stuart, I hope I'm still invited to your wedding and all,
but if I can't bring Sarah as my date, I'm not coming.

   Dad, call me sometime. You know the number.

   Mom. Whatever.

   Mitch and Stacy, thanks for everything.

Love to you all,
Sean

To: Mitchell Hertzog <mitchell.hertzog@hwd.com>
Fr: Stacy Trent <IH8BARNEY@freemail.com>
Re: Sean

She fax you a copy of her letter yet? I'm so proud I could burst. I hope she and Sarah DO come to Stuart's wedding, whether they're invited or not. You know they'll be the only couple there worth talking to.

S

To: Stacy Trent <IH8BARNEY@freemail.com>
Fr: Mitchell Hertzog <mitchell.hertzog@hwd.com>
Re: Sean
Fwd: ✉ Re: You

I wouldn't count on any of us getting invited. Get a load of the forwarded e-mail.

To: Mitchell Hertzog <mitchell.hertzog@hwd.com>
Fr: Stacy Trent <IH8BARNEY@freemail.com>
Re: Sean

No fair! I want Stuart to refuse to speak to me, too! You get all the luck.

FYI, thanks to Sean's letter, Mom's taken to her bed. She got somebody to refill her script for Valium.

My question is: Where the hell is Dad? I thought he was supposed to be home by now. Oh well.

Stace

....

✉

To: Kate Mackenzie <katydid@freemail.com>
Fr: Vivica <vivica@sophisticates.com>
Re: Lunch

Oh my God, it was so nice to meet you! You really are just as cute as your picture. I'm so sorry Dale wouldn't marry you like you wanted him to. You totally deserve to have a nice husband . . . especially after you traded plates with me (who knew bococino meant cheese?) It's no joke, being lactose intolerant. I can't even have sour cream on my potato skins anymore!

I'm sorry you won't consider being a model. Really, it is just loads of fun. And I'm almost positive Ricardo could get you a gig or two. I mean, maybe not *Vogue*, but like, catalog stuff, or something.

Anyway, it was really fun meeting you, and I hope we can get together again sometime soon. I don't know when, though, 'cause like I said, the band leaves tomorrow for its tour and I'm off to Milan. . . . but I'll call ya when I get back!!!!!

Love,
Viv

A Note from
Dale Carter of
I'm Not Making Any More Sandwiches
Liberation Records

Dear Kate,

Look, Kate, I know I'm not your favorite person in the world right now, but I just want to say thanks for not telling Vivica about how I bit off that guy's finger. I mean, biting off a guy's finger, that's like fighting dirty, and I don't want Vivica to think I'm a dirty fighter. I mean, the guy DID keep shoving his hand in my mouth, so it wasn't like I had a choice.

But Viv wouldn't know that. So thanks. Really. For not telling her.

I'm really sorry things didn't work out between us and all, but I think you're right about it being better this way. I mean, Vivica is a totally dope girl, and I never would've met her if you hadn't dumped me.

And don't worry about your security deposit. I feel real bad about all that, and about you losing your job and all of that. So I'm messengering over a check for your share of the deposit and some other stuff. Like, you know, to pay you back for all the shit you bought for the place, like the TV and all. Hope it'll be enough to help you find a new pad of your own.

Well, okay, I guess that's it. Peace out.

Dale

P.S. What do you think of this new song?

When the stars come out at night
I call them Vivica
And when the moon, it shines so bright
I call it Vivica
And when the sun comes up, and warms us
with its healing rays
I call it Vivica,
Vivica,
My Vivica.

Dale Carter		0002
207 E. 3rd St., Apt. 10J		
New York, NY 10003	DATE MARCH 23, 2004	
Kathleen Mackenzie		$ 10,000.00
PAY TO THE ORDER OF		
Ten thousand and 00 cents		DOLLARS
NY MetroBank		
Park Avenue, New York		
MEMO For the apt and shit	_Dale Carter_	
⑆000305849⑆: 859785399⑈⑆ 0002		

✉

To: Jen Sadler <jennifer.sadler@thenyjournal.com>
Fr: Kate Mackenzie <kathleen.mackenzie@thenyjournal.com>
Re: Dale

Oh my God. That freak Dale—you know what he did? Messengered me over a check for ten grand.

TEN GRAND.

What do I DO????

Kate

✉

To: Kate Mackenzie <kathleen.mackenzie@thenyjournal.com>
Fr: Jen Sadler <jennifer.sadler@thenyjournal.com>
Re: Dale

What do you mean, what do you do? You cash it!

And don't tell me you don't think you should. You EARNED that money. You cooked and cleaned like a slave for him for all those years, and for what? A big fat, "I have to take it one day at a time"? You take that check and you run, don't walk, to Chase and deposit it, before he sobers up.

✉

To: Jen Sadler <jennifer.sadler@thenyjournal.com>
Fr: Kate Mackenzie <kathleen.mackenzie@thenyjournal.com>
Re: Dale

You're right. I'll deposit it after work. There's something else I've got to do right now, though.

Kate

Hola! You have reached the line of Ida Lopez. Ida is not here to take your call. Leave a message and she will get back to you.

(Tone)

Hi, Mrs. Lopez? It's Kate. Kate Mackenzie. You know, from the *Journal?* I just wanted to say thank you so much for the cookies. They were really delicious. You shouldn't have gone to so much trouble. But thank you so much for thinking of me.

Also I was wondering if your lawyer had been in touch with you yet. Because—I don't know if you know this yet—but I got my job back, and I just now got the reinstatement papers for you on my desk. Which means the paper wants you back, Mrs. Lopez. With full benefits, and no lost pay from the time you were gone. Oh, I really hope you'll come back, Mrs. Lopez. We really miss you around here. And you know, Stuart Hertzog just tendered his firm's resignation as the *Journal's* attorneys, so it's not like you'll be seeing him around anymore, either. Both he and Amy—you know, my boss? They're gone. So please let me know, Mrs. Lopez, about whether you're coming back. I'm keeping my fingers crossed!

(Click)

✉

To: Kate Mackenzie <kathleen.mackenzie@thenyjournal.com
Fr: Tony Salerno <foodie@fresche.com>
Re: Ida Lopez

Hi, Kate. You don't know me, I'm married to Nadine Wilcock, you know, the food critic over there at the *Journal*?

Anyway, I own the restaurant Fresche—you might have heard of it. I'm also Ida Lopez's new boss. Yeah, that's right. Nadine told me all about Mrs. Lopez and her chocolate chip cookies and all, so I did a little investigating, and well . . . she's my new pastry chef. No offense, but I pay her a lot more than you guys did, so I can see why she might not want to leave. Have you ever tasted her blueberry blintzes? Mind-blowing.

So, anyway, looks like your loss is our gain . . . but it's Ida's gain, too.

And you can tell all those ravenous *New York Journal*-ists that if they miss Ida's home cooking, they can just come on over to Fresche anytime they want!

Best,

Tony Salerno
Owner/master chef
Fresche

To: Margaret Hertzog <margaret.hertzog@hwd.com>
    Stuart Hertzog <stuart.hertzog@hwd.com>
    Stacy Trent <IH8BARNEY@freemail.com>
    Mitchell Hertzog <mitchell.hertzog@hwd.com>
    Janice Hertzog <janice.hertzog@hwd.com>
Fr: Arthur Hertzog <arthur.hertzog@hwd.com>
Re: All of you

Just a quick note to say there seems to be some kind of misunderstanding concerning my whereabouts. I am not, as many of you seem to believe, on my way back to New York. The fellas and I are on our way to Pebble Beach, to try our hand at the most challenging course known to man.

I can see how this information might be upsetting to some of you. However, I had a near death experience a year ago, and it taught me one thing: Don't waste your time on stupid shit. And frankly, all I seem to hear from some of you people is stupid shit.

Stuart, you could have a lot worse things wrong with you than the fact that you're a carrier for a disease that you'll never actually have. I heard you're engaged to that girl you brought home for Thanksgiving dinner. Mazel tov. Tell her to eat more, she's too skinny.

As for your problems with your brother, I have a feeling that those will soon be alleviated: I just got off the phone with Mitch, who has informed me that he has had enough with corporate law. He's returning to his position as a public defender downtown where, he says, the clients are friendlier and less apt to commit perjury. I won't stand in his way. Stuart, I know that by now everyone at Hertzog Webber and Doyle will have gotten used to my absence, and Mitchell's leaving the firm shouldn't have a deleterious effect on anything.

Margaret, I understand that you're upset with Mitchell for something he did to Stuart's fiancée. I told you when they were kids, and I'll tell you now that they're adults: Keep out of it. It's your own fault, anyway. If you didn't keep on telling Stuart he was your favorite, he wouldn't have gotten such a swelled head to begin with.

And no, Stuart, I don't mean that literally.

As for Janice's becoming a lesbian and drawing against her capital: Again, Margaret, keep out of it. I don't know about this lesbian business, and frankly, I don't want to know. But that money is Janice's to do with as she pleases. I do have to draw the line at her spending it on school. I've never heard anything so ridiculous in my life. I will pay for Janice's tuition, as I did for all you kids. Janice, your orca business sounds like a damned stupid idea, but it's your money, and if it makes you happy, you kayak around Puget Sound as much as you want.

Now I would appreciate it if you would all quit calling me, e-mailing me, Fed-Exing me, faxing me, and leaving messages for me at the hotel desk. I am on VACATION. I will let you know when it's over. But I can tell you, it won't be anytime soon.

I think I can get nine more holes in before dark, so I'm off. Good-bye.

Dad

....

✉

To: Kate Mackenzie <kathleen.mackenzie@thenyjournal.com>
Fr: Helen Green <helen.green@universityofkentucky.edu
Re: Professor Wingblade

Dear Ms. Mackenzie,

I regret to inform you that Professor Wingblade is on sabbatical this year in Uganda. Due to the lack of electricity in the remote vil-

lage in which he is doing his research, he does not have access to
e-mail. If your message is of an urgent nature you can attempt to send
it via "snail mail." However, the postal system in the area in which
the professor is currently staying is unreliable at best. The professor
has asked that all mail of a non-urgent nature be held until his return.
Please let us know if we can be of any further assistance to you.

Sincerely,
Helen Green
Administrative Assistant
Department of Psychology
College of Arts and Sciences
University of Kentucky

....

✉

To: Helen Green <helen.green@universityofkentucky.edu
Fr: Kate Mackenzie <kathleen.mackenzie@thenyjournal.com>
Re: Professor Wingblade

Dear Helen,

You know what? It doesn't matter. I think it's going to be all right.
Tell Professor Wingblade hi from me when he gets back.

Kate

....

✉

To: Kate Mackenzie <kathleen.mackenzie@thenyjournal.com>
Fr: Mitchell Hertzog <mitchell.hertzog@hwd.com>
Re: You

So, now that you've gotten your job back, you'll probably want to
start thinking about finding a place to live.

And I just wanted to let you know, there's a vacancy in my building. In my apartment, actually. And I was kind of wondering how you felt about that.

Mitch

....

✉

To: Mitchell Hertzog <mitchell.hertzog@hwd.com>
Fr: Kate Mackenzie <kathleen.mackenzie@thenyjournal.com>
Re: You

Interesting proposition. Let's meet at your place to discuss after work today.

Kate

Be sure not to miss
Meg Cabot's *New York Times* bestselling

The Princess Diaries

Immortalized by the silver screen, Princess Amelia
Mignonette Grimaldi Thermopolis Renaldo
has a life most can only dream of.
Now in her own words the (fictional) story
of a real American princess.

....

Friday, October 10

Princess lessons.

I am not kidding. I have to go straight from my Algebra review session every day to princess lessons at the Plaza with my grandmother.

Okay, so if there's a God, how could this have happened?

I mean it. Like, people always talk about how God doesn't ever give you more than you can handle, but I'm telling you right now, I cannot handle this. This is just *too much!* I *cannot* go to princess lessons every day after school. Not with Grandmère. I am seriously considering running away from home.

Here is how my first "lesson" went, yesterday after school:

The concierge himself escorted me upstairs to the penthouse, which is where Grandmère is staying. Let me tell you about this penthouse: It is very fancy. I thought the ladies' room at the Plaza was fancy? The ladies' room is nothing compared to this penthouse.

First of all, everything is pink. Pink walls, pink carpet, pink curtains, pink furniture. There are pink roses everywhere, and these portraits hanging on the walls that all feature pink-cheeked shepherdesses and stuff.

And just when I thought I was going to drown in pinkness, out came Grandmère, dressed completely in purple, from her silk turban all the way down to her mules with the rhinestone clips on the toes.

At least, I think they're rhinestones.

Grandmère always wears purple. Lilly says people who wear purple a lot usually have borderline personality disorders, because they have delusions of grandeur. Traditionally, purple has always stood for the aristocracy, since for hundreds of years peasants weren't allowed to dye their clothes with indigo, and therefore couldn't make violet.

Of course, Lilly doesn't know my grandmother IS a member of the aristocracy. So while Grandmère is definitely delusional, it's not because she *thinks* she's an aristocrat; she really IS one.

So Grandmère comes in off the terrace, where she was standing, and the first thing she says to me is, "What's that writing on your shoe?"

But I didn't need to worry about getting caught cheating, because Grandmère started in right away about everything else that was wrong with me.

"Why are you wearing tennis shoes with a skirt? Are those tights supposed to be clean? Why can't you stand up straight? What's wrong with your hair? Have you been biting your nails again, Amelia? I thought we agreed you were going to give up that nasty habit. My God, can't you stop growing? Is it your goal to be as tall as your father?"

Only it sounded even worse, because it was all in French.

And then, as if that wasn't bad enough, she goes, in her creaky old cigaretty voice, "Haven't you a kiss for your grandmère, then?"

So I go up to her and bend down (my grandmother is like a foot shorter than me) and kiss her on the cheek (which is very soft because she rubs Vaseline on her face every night before she goes to bed), and then when I start to pull away she grabs me and goes, "*Pfui!* Have you forgotten *everything* I taught you?" and makes me kiss her on the other cheek, too, because in Europe (and SoHo), that's how you say hello to people. I bent down and kissed Grandmère on the other cheek.

"Now," Grandmère said when she felt we'd been affectionate enough, "let's see if I have this right: Your father tells you that you are the princess of Genovia and you burst into tears. Why is this?"

All of a sudden, I got very tired. I had to sit down on one of the pink foofy chairs before I fell down.

"Oh, Grandmère," I said in English. "I don't want to be a princess. I just want to be me, Mia."

Grandmère said, "Don't converse in English with me. It's vulgar. Speak French when you speak to me. Sit up straight in that chair. Do not drape your legs over the arm. And you are not Mia. You are Amelia. In fact, you are Amelia Mignonette Grimaldi Renaldo."

I said, "You forgot Thermopolis," and Grandmère gave me the evil eye. She is very good at this.

"No," she said. "I did not forget Thermopolis."

Then Grandmère sat down in the foofy chair next to mine and said, "Are you telling me you have no wish to assume your rightful place upon the throne?"

Boy, was I tired. "Grandmère, you know as well as I do that I'm not princess material, okay? So why are we even wasting our time?"

Grandmère looked at me out of her twin tattoos of eyeliner. I could tell she wanted to kill me but probably couldn't figure out how to do it without getting blood on the pink carpet.

"You are the heir to the crown of Genovia," she said in this totally serious voice. "And you will take my son's place on the throne when he dies. This is how it is. There is no other way."

Oh, boy.

So I kind of went, "Yeah, whatever, Grandmère. Look, I got a lot of homework. Is this princess thing going to take long?"

Grandmère just looked at me. "It will take," she said, "as long as it takes. I am not afraid to sacrifice my time—or even myself—for the good of my country."

Whoa. This was getting way patriotic. "Um," I said. "Okay."

So then I stared at Grandmère for a while, and she stared back at me, and Rommel laid down on the carpet between our chairs, only he did it really slow, like his legs were too delicate to support all two pounds of him, and then Grandmère broke the silence by saying, "We will begin tomorrow. You will come here directly after school."

"Um, Grandmère. I can't come here directly after school. I'm flunking Algebra. I have to go to a review session every day after school."

"Then after that. No dawdling. You will bring with you a list of the ten women you admire most in the world, and why. That is all."

My mouth fell open. *Homework?* There's going to be *homework?* Nobody said anything about homework!

"And close your mouth," she barked. "It is uncouth to let it hang open like that."

Have you ever dreamed of being a princess, but weren't sure where to begin? Then *Princess Lessons* is the book you've been waiting for! It's all here:

- Preventing your tiara from slipping off

- Keeping your pores squeaky clean

- Winning the heart of the man of your dreams (or, at the very least, the cute guy you see at Starbucks every morning)

- Avoiding a military incursion by a neighboring prinicpality

- And much, much more!

By following the invaluable advice of Mia, you will be well prepared for the day you finally ascend the throne . . . or at the very least, you'll know the difference between a fish fork and a salad fork. All without having to endure Grandmère's princess lessons.

With illustrations by Chesley McLaren

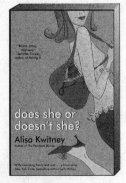